DARKGHOST
ASSIGNMENTS

DARKGHOST
ASSIGNMENTS

DANIEL E. MCLEAN IV

iUniverse

DARKGHOST ASSIGNMENTS

iUniverse books may be ordered through booksellers or by contacting:

iUniverse
1663 Liberty Drive
Bloomington, IN 47403
www.iuniverse.com
1-800-Authors (1-800-288-4677)

ISBN: 978-1-4917-6099-4 (sc)
ISBN: 978-1-4917-6100-7 (e)

Print information available on the last page.

iUniverse rev. date: 02/09/2016

Dedication

I dedicate this book to the memory of my big brother.
He taught me how to write for fun and boy did he love to write.
I miss his letters and flawless penmanship. Thanks big bro.
Darren Elihue McLean (Pee Wee)
1959-1987

To my mother Pearline McLean, I know she loved me unconditionally. She introduced me to Jehovah. Thank You. I miss u dearly...

To my father Daniel McLean Jr., your lessons of manhood will never be forgotten. You're the reason why I'm mechanically incline. Thank you. I miss u dearly...

To my siblings Demetrius, Denise, Calvin, Aneta, Xina, and Tamiko each of you have taught your baby bro (me) things that have been helpful in my life. Thank you.

To all my children, Ean, Taiwan, Raqwan, Tristan, and Brishae. Keep working hard to make your dreams come true. If it worked for me it can work for you. Thanks for being great people. Love you guys.

To Kerrie Waddy and Shelby Willis, your military insight helped me greatly. Thank you.

BOOK ONE: The Present

BOOK BROTHERS

In times of war and uncertainty there is a special breed of Warrior ready to answer our Nation's call. A common man with uncommon desires forged by adversity he stands alongside America's finest Special Operation Forces to serve his Country, the American people, and protect their way of Life. - Navy Seals Creed

PROLOGUE

Texas, 1991

To some people life is all about taking care of their family and being loyal to their friends. I too share in that enjoyment but my true enjoyment is being a Chief Petty Officer in the United States Navy. I moved up in the ratings with my leadership skills and a high rate in successful missions. When it's time for me to command my unit out in the field on a mission, a calm sensation comes over me and then I get psyched up for the mission at hand.

Yesterday we were briefed on our next mission: a Colombian drug lord. He happens to be crossing over from drugs to buying black market weapons to protect his main investment: cocaine.

Mr. Felipe Cartagena has purchased twenty stingers and launchers and fifteen Javelin surface to air missiles. Intel tells us that he has planned to purchase 100 more of each by the end of the month.

Now he's threatening to aim them at any armed forces or investigators the United States send to Colombia. Bad move. What he didn't know is a special ops team is being sent in to take him out. Deployment is at sunset.

The Home of Ms. Cruz

"Before we got together, I explained what I do and how serious I am about it."

"Yes I know that but today is our son's first birthday and…"

"He'll have more." The Chief Petty Officer said cutting his fiancé off.

"It's nothing like your first birthday and don't you ever cut me off like that again if you want to be my husband and be happy."

"I don't have time for this command has paged me and I must get to base ASAP." The Chief Petty Officer said and then stuck his head out for a kiss.

"You got to be kidding right…" Ms. Cruz said responding to the Chief Petty Officer's advancement and then continued "…what you need to do is go over there and give your son a hug and kiss and I'll see you when you get back from God knows where."

As the Chief Petty Officer walked by he kissed his fiancé on the side of her head and then walked over to his son's play area and did as he was told. When he placed his son back down, the Chief Petty Officer turned and said.

"I love you. Please try to understand this is something I must do."

After saying his peace he turned and walked out the two bedroom apartment and jumped into his car and headed for command at the Naval Air Station Corpus Christi.

Colombia, 1981

Deep within the Andes Mountains of Colombia a new business alliance is forming and the birth of corruption is born out of human flesh.

"Mr. Cartagena it's my pleasure to extend my other services to you as well."

"And what services is that, Mr. Andreev?"

"Human slaves."

"What can you offer me?" Mr. Cartagena said spreading his arms apart and then continued "…when I clearly have people doing what I want."

"Yes, I see but they are your own people and soon they will tire. You risk a chance of mutiny."

"Mutiny huh."

"Let me interject, what my partners and I offer is people of other races."

"What nationality is this?"

"Korean." Mr. Kim said.

"Let me think about it." Mr. Cartagena snapped back.

"Why don't we do this then, we'll put three female slaves in our first shipment to you this week. And if they don't work out, you owe us nothing for them, but if you have use for them just add $15,000 in your payment. Deal?" Peter said.

"That's a generous offer. I think I'm going to enjoy doing business with you Mr. Andreev."

"Please call me Valentin, and you will be doing business with us." Valentin said while pointing at his partners.

"Expect your first shipment by the end of the week. Have a good day, Mr. Cartagena." Mr. Kim added.

All the men exchanged handshakes and parted ways.

Texas, 1991

The Chief Petty Officer reached the base within ten minutes and ready to rock & roll within fifteen. The rest of the Navy Seals unit whom were called in for the Colombian mission dubbed "Crack the Whip" filed into the ready room one by one. As the unit sat quietly, the door to the Ready Room snatched open and Seaman Nebs appeared and said

"Attention on deck."

The whole unit snapped to attention.

"As you were..." Lieutenant Commander Cornelius Woodear II paused while scratching his beard and then said "...I have some bad news to tell you men. We have been put on standby."

"Until when sir?"

"Until orders from the brass come down."

"Politics at work sir?"

"At the finest."

"All I know is if that crap that our dear Mr. Cartagena is pushing, was being pushed hard in the suburbs we'll be over there now sir."

"Maybe so but for now our orders are to standby."

"I'm tired of standing by sir especially when the orders don't affect their kind sir." The Chief Petty Officer said sarcastically.

"Chief Petty Officer, watch what you say next." Lieutenant Commander said with sternness in his voice and his eyes locked onto the Chief Petty Officer.

"Yes sir. I'm just tired of standing by sir."

"I know and so am I."

CHAPTER ONE

HOME LIFE

Tuesday, is the third day of my work week, since my work calls for me to work seven days a week. There was a cool drizzle of rain coming down but it was still warm even though it was 3:27 in the morning. I have decided to wear blue jeans, a yellow polo shirt with gray pin-stripes and brown soft sole shoes to my meeting later today. Anyway, first I need to shit, shave, and shower and then grab some breakfast; toast and a cup of java. Before I can leave I just got to give the misses a kiss. She look so beautiful sleeping, wish I had enough time for a quickie but last night session will have to due until I return from my business trip. I truly believe that if I don't get that kiss my days won't end the right way and in my line of work I need all the extra help I can get.

Oh, pardon my manners, my name is Emad Elijah McWhorter, my family and friends call me Eli. I'm a retired Lieutenant Commander of the Navy Seals, my wife Veronica believes I'm still retired from the military and now works as a consultant to the Navy. I made a promise to her that I would get out of the killing game but the excitement is my life fuel. What I really do is strategically assassinate corporate head honchos whom seem to get in the way of America's way of life. Yes I work for the Central Intelligence Agency, for America's foreign affairs and the Federal Bureau of Investigation, for America's domestic affairs. Only a chosen few in both organizations know of what I do, even though the President of the United States know of me and my team and the covert missions we are involved in for America's wellbeing. He will never acknowledge my team. Like I said I love my country. I am a patriot still doing Sam's will. The only difference now is we get paid well for doing so.

On the other hand my wife Veronica loves the laid back life. So after I retired we moved closer to our family on the East Coast. To be exact we moved to the 1600 block on Hulseman Street, South Philadelphia. She really enjoys the quiet neighborhood we live in, no gun fire at night or anytime of the day unlike Camden, NJ her old 'hood where she grew up. Better known as crime central USA.

We have eight children and for the most part they're some really great kids. As if they had a choice, because Veronica didn't play and when it came to school, she was a beast. In fact she has to first get them out the house before she can get ready for school herself. Brooklan and Tre'shawn are the youngest, and then its Malcolm, Ashantia, and Taavetti all whom live at home. Evan our eldest decided to join the Navy and then go into Navy Seals training school and Askia and Shafiq the twins live in Rhode Island and New York respectively.

Veronica comes from a big family as well as myself. We vowed to have a big family of our own because of all the fun we had growing up with our siblings.

Veronica McWhorter my loving wife is a very meticulous person. Everything in our house has its own place. Even the way she gets ready for the day was routine. She would shower her 5'10" olive complexion skin with Dove and then lotion up with a baby oil and body lotion mixture she keep secret. Her voluptuous curvy body will make heads turn when she walked by even women have taken notice of her beauty. Her long wavy dark brown hair had to be groomed daily. No beauty salon could do her hair the way she did it and beside they wouldn't get the chance of ruining what she had created. Perfect hair. Pressed tailored pants suits were all she would spend extra money on and all she would wear when she went to class at Temple University. Veronica is in her sophomore year getting her bachelor's degree in forensic science. Social work at the community center on the weekends is her hobby she takes seriously.

Even though I was trying my best not to interrupt Veronica sleeping peacefully, she woke up anyway.

"What time is it?" Veronica asked rubbing her eyes.

"Go back to sleep its 3:30." Emad responded

"You know what?"

"What?"

"I'm still moist." Veronica said licking her lips.

"Come on honey you know I have a flight I need to catch."

"What's twenty minutes going to hurt; I won't see you for at least a week."

"Ok I can spare five."

"Fifteen."

"Ten."

"Deal, you know you wanted to anyway." Veronica said with a devilish smile.

"Have to play hard to get." Emad snap back.

After twenty minutes or so has past, I jumped up and got dress as fast as I could. I looked in on the kids, packed my breakfast to go, and grab my luggage. As usual when I leave my row house home I look both ways even though crime around here is at its all-time low but my old habits is hard to break from my past living in the PJs of Newark, NJ. I'm originally from a town called Neptune, NJ which is nothing like Newark and a little cleaner.

I started walking towards the corner news stand which supplied my favorite reading material. No matter how much of a rush I was in, I would always stop there and speak with Mr. Foreman to catch up on neighborhood news.

Before I can catch a flight to Virginia for briefing about my next job, I must first meet with my team at the office on the northeast side of town.

Ring.

Ring.

"Hello."

"Thanks baby for this morning jump start."

"It's my duty to please your booty." Emad laughed.

"Whatever, where are you at now?"

"Around the corner from my office."

"The kids are off to school and I just wanted to say I love you and have a great day and a safe flight."

"Love you too honey. Tell the kids I didn't want to wake them but I love them and will see them when I get back. Hugs and wet kisses."

CHAPTER TWO

This week we'll be working for the CIA in Greece and Russia. There's a man by the name of Valentin Andreev who thinks he can run his smack through the guise of his crude petroleum business and candy factory. Yrsa his sick and demented wife, 5'11", no ass and deep dark icy Blue eyes that could kill anyone or thing at will, loves the drug game and the money that supports her lavish lifestyle.

Valentin holds the majority stock while Ivan his cousin and business partner holds the least amount of stock. Ivan has no clue to what Valentin is doing. Valentin raises the prices of his crude petroleum at Yrsa whims; she also loves to mess with the USA. Ivan wishes to do good business with America but his hands are tied. Let see what we can do about that.

As per their contract, if one of them shall die due to natural cause or accident without any crime over tones, after a thorough investigation, the other can buy the remaining shares, even though the one who died has left a will. In that case the person in the will would be set up in a trust fund but will have no power in the business.

The CIA got a whiff of a plot to kill Valentin and Ivan by Yrsa. Remember she's sick and demented. This is where I come into the picture. Valentin and Yrsa are on holiday in Salamina, Greece and Ivan he's in al Basrah, Iraq running the crude petroleum business as usual. Ivan had plans of his own and felt Valentin didn't need to know he was going to Yaroslavl, Russia but he told his cousin in-law his plans. Bad move.

Valentin and Yrsa Andreev's home

Valentin Andreev a man of modern times. Six foot two but chubby with blonde hair, distinctive smoky gray eyes, and never smiles. A real brute.

Valentin walked out of his study to see what's all the noise and commotion out in the foyer.

"I'm not wearing that!" shouts Chrissy.

"I'm on a very important phone call and I wish not to be disturbed!" Valentin said angrily

"She won't put on her ear muffs." Yrsa explained.

"If I'm disturbed one more time Chrissy I won't buy you that pony you just got to have." Valentin said calmly.

"When will I get it poppa?" Chrissy asked.

"Just be quiet baby please." Valentin said.

"You spoil her too much and I have to put up with it, while you go about your business." Yrsa said looking upset.

"I'll buy you a freaking whatever you want too, just shut up while I'm on the phone. Or go somewhere else with the noise."

Back in the study where Valentin was discussing business with his partners in crime, Jeung Hyong-Kim and Peter Becker, South Korea and America respectively, via satellite phone and imaging on his big screen monitor about their heroin business.

How it works is this. Mr. Hyong-Kim has a factory that makes sugar. That's the front for their heroin business. Mr. Kim exports his heroin out of his factory, from a small village approximately 20 miles east of Suwon, South Korea dressed in sugar and then its ship from South Korea to Russia. Heroin is made to look like cotton candy at the Yaroslavl, Russia factory which Valentin cousin Gregori Tarasov supervise but managed by Valentin. After the smack is made into cotton candy, it will be shipped out to China. Why not just ship directly to China from South Korea you ask. Well in these days we live in, South Korea and China aren't getting along and even though they do business amongst each other, shipments from one to the other are highly investigated. Now where was I, oh yea? China. A 6' redhead who goes by the name of Samantha Becker runs a sweatshop in China for her father. Sammy as her father likes to call her, melts down the candy and then injects the dope into shirts. After the shirts are injected they are package and then delivered to Kansas. In Kansas Mr. Becker then distributes the shirts to three U.S. cities: Detroit, New York, and L.A. It's at these locations where the smack is extracted, package, and then sold to some nasty street bosses.

Man these guys have everything figured out; they even have US custom agents on all shifts so they can ship to the States anytime they want to. It seems like a lot and it is but we're not talking 20ki of dope. This business generates 1000ki a week. Do you know how much money that's on the streets? NO! Well I do and this crime has made all three men close to being billionaires.

The Book Brothers as they like to call themselves started thinking of this lucrative business back when they attended Columbia University. It's at Columbia where they form a bond of trust that is as strong as granite. Two exchanged students and one American citizen decided they can make more money selling dope than what they were going to college for and they were exactly right.

Back to the conference call

"Jay I need about 20% more sugar in this week shipment." Valentin said

"Are you crazy we already…"

"Watch your language Jay" Peter said cutting Jeung off.

"Watch your language, we already got this week shipment ready to go and now you want me to add 20%. Why."

"If you must know" Valentin said with a smirk.

"I must."

"Come on you two, why can't we just get to business." Peter reminded them

"My apologies check your emails I sent you the new client in Miami whom wishes to do business with us…" after a short pause "…his description and money proposal is in there too."

"Another city huh." Peter sighed.

"Something wrong Petey." Valentin said jokingly.

"Why do you act like that? We're suppose too be handling business and you trying to piss me off…" Peter said with a little bass in his voice. "…you know I don't like to be called that."

"Damn, all business no play huh." Valentin responded.

"Anyway I'm the one out here, you two only have one site to look after I already have three and now you want to add more sites."

"I was thinking after Yrsa and my vacation; I would come there and help with two of the cities."

"What about Yaroslavl?" Jay asked.

"Gregori is handling things there quite well don't you think."

"Do you think that is wise with him being in the dark about what we're really doing?" Peter reminded Valentin.

"Yrsa is going to stay here with Chrissy. And keep an eye on Gregori."

"How is she doing, I'm talking about Chrissy?" Peter asked.

"Very well thank you, she loves to give Yrsa a go for her money."

"Very good." Jay chimed in.

"Listen I already ran it by Yrsa and she's down with it. This way it won't be all on you in the States Peter and I'll stay for a couple of months until you can get acclimated. How does that sound?"

"Sounds good and every other month you come back here."

"Sure that's not a problem."

"Well then I guess that's settled. Val give us a call when you return from holiday."

"You got it."

"Enjoy yourself."

"You forgot Peter I'm going with Yrsa."

All three men busted out in laughter and then The Book Brothers said their goodbyes.

CHAPTER THREE

My team is made up of two Navy Seals, a Marine, and one ex-military member turned criminal. Derrick, Denise, and I are retired from the military. We are the best at what we do and that's kill people for our country. I formed the team and coined the name Darkghost because we all share two things in common. Being on Special Ops in our respective military branch and having one parent of the Black or African-American race depending on who you talk too.

Like I said before I'm retired from the Navy but not America. What you don't know is that I'm 6'4" all muscle with an athletic body shape. Mild tempered but get on my bad side and you'll wish for not being born.

I always felt a void in my life as a police detective at my hometown police department. So naturally I applied at the CIA. After that my life changed forever. Everyone thought I would join the Navy because my older sister taught me to swim at an early age. And I've been in water ever since. My mother Naomi keeps all my swimming trophies on her fireplace mantle. Before I became a government agent, my sister would call me over to our mother's house and tell me what I did wrong in each of the meets that I won or lost. She believes she can still out swim me and her Olympic gold medal says she can.

I excelled in hand to hand combat while I was in the military and became a leader of men with the stern help of my commanding officer.

One day I'll tell Veronica the truth about what I do for my country now, but today isn't a good day for that.

My right hand man on the team is Derrick if Denny don't mind me saying that. Former Navy Seals Petty Officer First Class Derrick Varnell's father was a Staff Sergeant in the Army and had met his mother while stationed in Spain. As a kid Derrick loved firecrackers so obviously when he went into Navy Seals training straight from boot camp he would specialize in demolition. His true passion was being a sniper marksman, who can hit a fly 300yrds away. He always keeps himself in the best physical shape. He prefers calisthenics over weight training to keep his tall frame looking good. When he's not on a mission, he runs five miles a day around his neighborhood. Within his neighborhood he's known for telling politically incorrect jokes and being a male chauvinist. No one is safe not even his grandmother who practically raised him since his mother passed away when he was nine. He's also known for getting slap by his grandmother Pearl for telling those kinds of jokes.

And then its Juka Tidesdale, computer analysis extraordinaire can fix anything with wiring. Honorably discharged from the Air Force and then became a criminal for hire. We'll get back to Juka later.

Lastly we have Denise Sato who speaks seven languages, shot expert with both handgun and long range weapon all of her career while she was a sergeant in the Marines. How she put up with this bunch one never knows. If you think because she's slim and beautiful you can handle her anyway you feel like. Her jiu-jitsu training will prove you wrong. Her smooth butterscotch complexion makes her a 5'10" walking goddess. A deadly weapon goddess. Denny as she prefers to be called was a foster child. Her mother kidnapped her from her father at the innocent age of five and then abandoned by her at the age of seven. Denny didn't meet her father again until she was nineteen. Akira Sato found her through the efforts of her foster parents. James and Josephine Stevens was once a military couple who found out early into their married that they couldn't have children. They decided to adopt instead of not having children at all. They figured it was in Denny's best interest if she knew her parents and their family to help give her a sense of where she comes from.

Denny's mother overdosed when she was nine years old so she never got a chance to try and build a relationship with her. Denny just so happened to follow her biological father's footsteps and join the Marines.

Emad was the last to get to the office. He made eye contact with Denise and gave her a head nod as he walked over to his desk. Denise like working for Emad, he wasn't a chauvinist pig like Derrick. Derrick believed outside of Denise all women should be seen and not heard.

"I need you guys to be ready to move out within 2hrs after I brief with the big cheese at Langley." Emad explained to his teammates.

"This mean we're going overseas whoop who!" Tidesdale said excitedly.

Now let's get back to Juka. You see Juka hack all the way to the top of an Iraqi organization named Jitow. When he wouldn't hack into an American company based in Iraq. The bosses of Jitow got angry at Juka for his insubordination and turned him over to the Iraqi government for the crimes he committed for them.

While Darkghost was gathering Intel on Jitow, assets to our country found out about what had happen to a certain hacker. A decision was made to help get him out of the situation.

Juka Tidesdale like I said use to be a criminal. With my help he changed his life around. It was either that or death by hanging.

Five Years Earlier

Darkghost was on assignment for the CIA in Iraq. An organization there was hiding secret documentation and maps to the whereabouts of weapons of mass destruction for the Iraqi government.

Jihad Its Our Weapon (JITOW) had a reception party for new buyers' of their new weapon Bushwack 90-LK5. This weapon had the capability of destroying all human sensory power and any electrical equipment functioning within its blast radius and only electrical equipment two miles outside of its radius.

An asset of the CIA has been buying weapons from Jitow for the past two years and was able to get an invitation to the party. Mark Cummings set up an introduction for Denise to meet some of Jitow high ranking officers. Denise known to Jitow as Kiata Fumiko, an Asian black market weapons buyer. Ms. Fumiko was able to sweet talk her way to getting an invitation to the same party.

Denise will have the assistance of three other CIA agents acting as her body guards when she goes to the new buyer's reception party.

The mission is for Darkghost to retrieve the documents and maps. Destroy any buildings holding munitions to help Jitow in their way of life: terrorism.

Emad and Derrick will set up outside of the compound and provide assistance in the way of cover fire and evacuation for Denise, the CIA agents, and one prisoner.

Jitow Compound night of the party

"Alpha I'm in position." Derrick said.

"Affirmative Charley. Let Sparrow do her thing. So sit tight Charley." Emad commanded.

"Have she signaled you yet?"

"No she hasn't said a word yet..." Emad paused for a second and then he continued "...once she grabs the documents she'll signal and then we can do our thing. Radio silence from here on out. Alpha out."

"Charley out."

Denise was escorted around the compound by a soldier of Jitow. Her body guards were not allowed into some of the most delicate areas because of security reason. Denise used the excuse to use the ladies room so she could get her chance and quietly killed the soldier escorting and hide his body in an empty room.

Now Denise can do what she came to the party for. Denise ease her way through sandy corridors planting infrared targets for Derrick to shoot and at the same time searching for the documents and maps of the secret location to weapons of mass destruction and the cell keeping this hacker the Iraqis want dead. The maps of the compound burned into her memory were spot on.

"Hey you!" A guard shouted.

"I thought the ladies room was this way." Denise replied keeping her cool.

"The boss wouldn't like it if I told him you are over here..." the Iraqi soldier said while walking towards Denise with a smile on his face "... so what are you going to do for me to keep me from telling him?" The Iraqi soldier was within 10 feet of Denise now. Denise plotted to herself as soon as he got close enough she would break his neck. The guard got within six feet of Denise.

With a jump off the wall Denise kicked the soldier in his stomach. His eyes open wide with a surprise look on his face. Denise stayed on him and swept his feet from underneath his body. When he got to his feet Denise quickly moved around and was standing behind the soldier. Before he could react, his neck was broken. Denise needed to get the soldier out the corridor before anyone else came around the corner. She opened the door to a large room and dragged the dead guard with her as she entered the threshold. "What's up with this? Is everyone on break?" Denise questioned and then she thought "did I say that out loud?" With quick movement Denise was over to the file cabinets thumbing through each folder. Nothing there. She walked over to the desk near a window. While ruffling through the desk drawers, a reflective light came from her right side. The safe was left open. Quickly she moved to the safe and bingo, yellow folder with documents and maps they wanted. 'My luck can't be this good' her inner voice spoke.

"Alpha I have all documents and maps. I'm on my way to the prisoner."

"Affirmative Sparrow. Keep your head low and we'll meet you on the roof as planned. Alpha out." Emad commanded.

"Sparrow out."

Denise exited the large room. Standing next to a window she tore off the bottom half of her dress and pulled out her Glock 9mm pistol from her left inner thigh. When Denise peeked out the window a loud noise resounded from somewhere.

Boom.

The force of the explosion from the west side of the compound tremble the east side where Denise held up. 'Derrick is doing his thing' Denise thought to herself. A raspy voice came over the speaker. "Code green all men to the west wing. I repeat code green we have intruders."

Denise leaped out the window as the last man turn the corner of the building she was in. Leaving two men to guard the prisoner across from the window she jumped out. As she hit the ground Denise fell to her knees and tuck rolled on the ground, back on her feet with dazzling speed, pistol in hand shot both men in the chest. Ran over to the door. Pulled C4 from her right inner thigh, place it on the lock; put the detonator in the C4.

Denise knocked on the door and then said

"Hey you in there get away from the door or else you'll get hurt."

"What are you talking about?" the prisoner responded.

"You want to play 20 questions or escape from this cell."

"I'm moving."

Denise step away from the door, aimed the trigger at the C4.

Bang.

The door flew off its hinges.

"We have to get to the roof. That's the extraction point." Denise said to the prisoner.

"Follow me I know the shortcut." The prisoner responded.

Once on top of the roof Emad lowered a ladder down from the stealth helicopter. Up they went. Safely inside the helicopter the prisoner said "...thanks for the help but who are you guys?"

"I'm Emad and this is Denise we're..." Emad put his hand over his right ear as if he was listening to someone speaking into his earphone. "...hold on we have one more to pick up."

Derrick had already broken down his sniper weapon and was ready for extraction from the other side of the compound. Soldiers of Jitow fired at the helicopter as it passed over the compound. The copter hovered over Derrick and Denise lowered a roped ladder. Derrick quickly scaled the ladder. Once inside Derrick said with excitement in his voice "...yea now that's what I'm talking about. Did anyone see those high flames from the massive explosions?"

"We all we're there Derrick." Denise scolded.

Derrick looked over towards the new guy and extended his hand and said "...I'm Derrick and you?"

"Juka, Juka Tidesdale."

CHAPTER FOUR

Kidnappers are thinkers to a certain extinct. Greed for money and selfish needs is their downfall. And the fact that criminals think they'd never get caught. On this day our kidnappers have devised a foul proof plan. At least that's what they think.

Samantha Becker runs her sweatshop with an iron fist. And her sweatshop is proximate to the center of the red light district and the red light district has all the hustle a Bostonian girl can hope for.

The women work at the sweatshop topless and just for spite the men work without pants, and if you're caught stealing, a nipple or groin might just get clip.

This week shipment arrived on Wednesday at 10:30am as usual. When the truck backed into the loading dock of the warehouse too unload its cargo from the Yaroslavl factory. Two dock workers hurried over to the trailer door and pulled it up to open it. Bullets rang out like hail storm. The fire power of the weapon nearly tore one worker in half. Four men came out dressed like commandos and armed to the teeth. Samantha heard the sounds of a gun fight and hid in her office closet. Her father told her to keep a Mossberg shotgun deep in her closet just in case something happens and she needs to hide. A loaded Mossberg in hand Samantha emptied the rest of the shells out of the box onto the floor between her legs. Remain calm she kept telling herself. Only a clear mind can think of a way to get out of this is what her father taught her. The gun fight stops abruptly. All remain is whispers and footsteps. Footsteps in her office, made her grasp the weapon firmly. The closet door jerks open. Samantha pulled the trigger and pumped the shotgun to chamber another shell and pulled the trigger again.

Boom.

Boom.

Both men went flying backwards with gaping holes in their chest. She was so fast with this weapon she didn't realize she pumped and pulled the trigger twice. She was surprise at what she had done. Close the door girl. Slide back. Reload. Get ready for more action. Samantha heart was racing. 'Calm your nerves girl' she keeps telling herself. Heart rate slows. "If you don't throw out your gun, we'll just blow the whole damn room up!" The leader of the gang said. "What do you want or why do you want me dead?" Samantha asked. "You and we would prefer alive if that's ok with you." the kidnapper replied. That's right keep talking fool. Samantha thought as she activated her recording machine.

In this region there are a lot of crooked cops who try to muscle money from the merchants and factory owners. If a merchant didn't give in, they would trump up some phony charges on them. When learning of these facts of the police, Samantha had a recording devise installed in a hidden place in her closet as per her father's previous advice. The hidden speakers planted throughout her office will compliment her hidden cameras throughout the warehouse and shop. She can activate it from her desk or from within her closet. If she made it out alive or when her father found the recording they could listen to the recordings and try and find her attackers.

"Ok I'm coming out please don't shoot." Samantha said.

"First throw out your gun or guns." the kidnapper replied.

The Mossberg slid across the floor and Samantha exited the closet. Without a word Samantha was snatched up, handcuffed, lips duct tape, and had a hood put over her head. Samantha plan to keep them talking didn't quite work as she wanted but she did get some footage. When they got outside one of them talked about a note they forgot to leave and suggested that the other one return and leave it on her desk.

This ordeal took about 5-7 minutes. These guys were efficient or had they been here before. Samantha believed the latter. She thought she recognized one of the voices, now all she has to do is put a face to the voice. Keep thinking. If they never take this hood off, it might be essential for me to remember his face if I survive this. Samantha felt a hard knock on her head, she started passing out. "Sorry miss, but we can't have you listening to our voices right now." The gang's leader said to Samantha as she lie motionless in the back of the van.

CHAPTER FIVE

Darkghost Office

"I need you guys to get the equipment and meet me at the motel on Jefferson Blvd." Emad instructed.

"The same motel we use for the Virginia Beach fiasco?" Derrick asked.

"Yes, I'll get the rooms and the keys will be at the front desk…" Emad paused, crossed his arm with a finger to his cheek and then he continued. "…Derrick I need my two Smith & Wesson with 17 in the clip, a black Remington semi 20 gauge shotgun, and all my tactical gear…"

"Gotcha, but on the Smitty's which one are you talking about, the 40 or the 45? " Derrick responded.

Emad continued. "…the 40 and if we need anything special I'll know after the briefing and I can get Steve in Norfolk to send it up to us…"

Steve is an eccentric weapons dealer, I like to deal with when we're crunch for time. Steve has always come through for us in the past. Like the Virginia Beach thing mentioned earlier. Well when we needed two stinger missiles within two hours, without a doubt Steve came through.

Emad continued "…I'm flying down to Newport News in about an hour the briefing is at fourteen hundred hours. See y'all around fifteen hundred thirty hours. You guys be safe."

"You do the same." Derrick replied.

Handshakes and hugs were distributed between Emad and his team.

Virginia

It was a quick flight from Philadelphia International to Newport News/ Williamsburg International but it still gave Emad enough time to reflect on his family. Evan his eldest son was heading towards Navy Seals training. Emad chest poked out with pride at the thought of Evan following his footsteps. How nice it would be to work with his son but Emad knew by time Evan was ready for his line of business he'd be a dinosaur. If Shafiq can stick to one thing in college he would've graduated by now. It shouldn't take six years to get a bachelor's degree in anything. If he doesn't graduate this year he'll have to pay the tuition for the following year or years. A buzzing noise woke me up out of my daydream. The captain started his descending instructions, followed by the stewardess taking of my comfortable pillow.

When I landed in Newport News a rental car was waiting for me so I could land and drive. I don't like waiting around because it feel as if time is wasted if I stand somewhere idled.

First things first get the rooms for my teammates. So I drove north on Jefferson Blvd toward my designation; the Days Inn. I had reserved two rooms previously while I was on the flight in; all I had to do is check-in.

Next I needed to check on the team progress. Good they're on the DC belt. Take a shower, change clothes, and then the hit the road to Langley.

Langley

Director of Operation (DO) Mitchel Hallden and two of his junior colleagues he used as assistants were waiting for Emad in a big rectangle shaped room with vaulted ceiling, wood grain desk and tables, and black metal file cabinets. Emad made his way through security and had taken the elevator to the basement. As he stepped through the doorway, a young lady said how nice it was to see him again. Emad gave a wink, a smile and said likewise. "Nice of you to join us Eli." Now if you're finished flirting with Ms. Steedmore we can get started." Very blunt and to the point the D.O scolded. Hallden is a burly, no neck, and 5'8" man with a disposition of an elephant. Quiet but when he gets going, it's only one direction he's concerned about and that's forward.

"Apologies Mitchel let's get to it." responded Emad.

"Have a seat. In front of you are all the particulars in the dossier. We're going to roughly state the facts." said Mitchel.

Mitchel's underling to his left started talking first. Stewart despised working for Hallden and Michael liked him no less. Stewart began by saying who and what, and the relationship who and what had with America's interest.

"There's a band of brothers if you will selling major drugs in America. They're names is Valentin Andreev, Jeung Hyong-Kim, and Peter Becker. They have a very intricate web of deceit going on with how they sell their dope." Michael the underling to his right interrupted. "This is what's going on. Valentin wife Yrsa has enlisted one of our field agents to murder her husband and his cousin Ivan Tarasov. We can't have the latter of the two murdered. Ivan could be a valuable asset to America interest into crude petroleum over in the Mid-East."

"Now this drug ring is secondary, our primary concern is keeping Ivan alive. How that happens I don't care." The D.O interjected.

Emad was thrown back. Whenever he has worked for the CIA in the past it has always been about some terrorist trying to take over the world or kill everyone except the people around them. Drug dealers. This could be interesting and maybe a cake walk. Emad usually almost never underestimated anyone. Drug dealers how smart can they be. Wait until you read the dossier. Most international drug dealer were lethal in protecting their interest but they lack the intellect of a navy seals and Emad wasn't an ordinary seal as if there are any. Emad snatch up the dossier motioned for the door when he felt a hand on his shoulder.

"There's more we want it to be messy…" Stewart whispered into Emad's ear. "…make it look like rivals if you know what I mean."

Emad usually is never surprise by people actions or what they do but this caught him off guard. The D.O never ordered how he wanted Emad to do his thing. For that matter he never ordered anything, just laid out the facts and Emad always took it from there.

Moscow

It was overly hot today, 40°C in Moscow. Trying to plan a vacation for your family while smoothing things over with your partners can be a task for feeble minded, one track, unintelligent have no clue what the real world is about type person. Money. The haves and have not. Survival of the fittest. Valentin have a lot of money and survived the horrors of Russia and his father. Since his IQ was above average he went to all top notch schools Russia had to offer. His wife Yrsa comes from a privilege family. Her father was a military man and her mother was a physic professor at the Moscow State University.

"Did you have your assistant make the arrangement for our holiday?" Yrsa asked with aggravation in her voice.

Valentin wanted to control this vacation because Yrsa seem to always want to be in South America. It was as if she was obsessed with the continent. Valentin had important business going on and if anything went wrong he wanted to be close to home. That's why he chose Salamina, Greece. It's beautiful and they have gorgeous beaches. The Miami prospect wanted to buy 100ki at a 30% discount. Valentin is willing to oblige and needed the approval of his partners to go ahead with the deal.

"Yes sweetheart Dasha confirmed our reservations yesterday…" replied Valentin he continued even though he was agitated by her asking. "…we'll be on the beach in Salamina."

"Greece!" Yrsa snapped furiously.

"Yes Greece, I need to stay close to home. After our holiday I'll be going to America like we discussed." Valentin detest repeating himself. "Is Peter and Jay on board with our program?" Our program Valentin thought but wouldn't dear say it out loud to her. "We leave tonight at 11pm."

China, Wednesday, June 18th, 11:17am

Insurgents belonging to a group against foreign business owners operating in China's Beijing area have captured Samantha and getting her ready for the phone call to her father, to inform him of their most valuable catch of the day. Cold water is refreshing when you drink it or maybe swimming in it but when ice cold water is thrown on you when you have been knocked out, well let say it's not as refreshing.

"What the fuck…" Samantha wide awake, shaking the water off her face."…you guys are going to pay for this." Samantha said still wearing her new headdress except now it's wet.

"You will behave or we'll knock your ass out again and start over understood…" the leader said.

He must be the leader you can hear the authority in his voice. He meant it too.

"…now all you have to do is keep your eyes closed while I remove the shroud and insert earplugs into your ears. Repeat what you hear and don't diverse from what you hear or a bullet will be nicely placed between your eyes and we go home. Are we on the same page Ms. Becker?"

"As long as it doesn't have me putting my family into any type of danger" responded Samantha.

"Your shroud is being taken off."

One of the leader minions removed the hood and put the earplugs into Samantha's ear and then the hood was replaced. A prerecorded message started playing directed to her father. The message had Samantha saying who she was and that she was taken into captivity. She will remain in captivity unharmed if he did exactly what she said. He was to drop 50 million dollars off with 20ki of dope at a location and time they would later tell. "Dope, why do they want the dope." Samantha ran through her head.

Newport News, Tuesday, June 17th, 4:05pm

On the way back to the Days Inn Emad check with his team to see if they made it to the motel yet. Denny answer the phone and reassured Emad that everything is well. Three fourths of Darkghost was just sitting around cleaning weapons, drinking tea, and waiting for Emad return. Next Emad called Steve to see if he had a contact over in Eastern Europe he could call on his behalf to purchase a .50 caliber sniper rifle. Steve said the guy they wanted to see is Ralph. Ralph Swartz lived in Vienna, Austria. Smooth.

Emad parked in front of his so called suite and went inside. Emad gather his team around and began briefing them.

"Listen up we're heading to Greece…"

"The Mediterranean I hear it's beautiful there." Denny cut in.

"…serious I need you guys to pay attention. We have one mark and one capture and release. First the mark. Yrsa Andreev, wife of an international drug dealer. It's just so happens Yrsa want her husband Valentin and his cousin Ivan Tarasov dead. We are to take out the wife. No capture as usual, but we must make it look like a rival drug dealer hit. Ivan Tarasov is our capture and release. First step, Austria to pick up the .50 cal. D.O wants it to be messy. If we can save Valentin fine, if not oh well. Just in case she met with someone else besides CIA field agent. I need Denny and Juka to go to Yaroslavl, Russia and protect Ivan. He's the asset the big cheese need alive. Here's your passports and tape recording of the proposition Yrsa made to the agent. The description and photos of all the key players is in this dossier…" Emad handed everyone a copy. "…ok guys let's get ready to go to the airport, Mitchel have a private jet taking us to Italy and then to Austria. If CIA Intel is correct the Andreev's are boarding in Moscow as we speak on their way to Salamina. So while we're in the air we can all go over our course of action."

There will be no drinking tonight, it was forbidden the night before an operation. Only tea and sleep.

*Moscow, Tuesday, June 17*th*, 11:05pm*

Valentin, Yrsa, and Chrissy boarded their airplane to paradise.

*China, Wednesday, June 18*th*, 4:05am*

The kidnappers are putting the last touches on their plans.

CHAPTER SIX

Peter Becker just finished his breakfast of eggs over hard, toast, a rationing of bacon, and OJ. Newspaper time with coffee was his breakfast dessert. Peter always liked to read the bad news first and then world news followed by the obit and then finished off with local and business news. Peter wanted out of the drug game. He had his heart set on going legit. He always thought how long they could do this without going to prison. The business of choice was an upscale man's clothing store, really nice inexpensive suits, ties, shirts, and shoes. Accessories included.

Ring. Ring.

Why whenever I'm relaxing someone feel the need to speak to me, Peter thought to himself. Peter answers the phone the way he usually do. "Peter Becker at your service."

A raspy electronic voice started speaking. "Don't talk just listen." The voice instructed Peter.

"Dad…"

"Samantha what the…" Peter replied.

"I said listen don't talk!" The voice shouted aggressively.

"…dad, this is Samantha I've been taken hostage. The ransom is 50 million dollars and 20ki of heroin. Since I know you don't want to go to jail the police or FBI won't be called. You have 1hr to confirm your partner in Korea will send up the dope and you have a flight to Beijing. Once the confirmation is confirm on our side, you will have 24hrs to get to Beijing with the money and dope or they will mail you my body parts over the next 12 months. Starting with my little toes. The location in Beijing will be given once you have landed in China. Time is of the essence so get your ass off the fucking phone." Dial tone.

Peter sat for 3mins in shock. He shook his head like his head was maracas. Peter snapped to it, he picked up his phone hit speed dial three. Peter's assistant Peggy answer the phone on the fourth ring and Peter wasted no time. He told her he needed a flight out of Wichita Mid-Continental Airport to Beijing, China within the next 6hrs but needed the confirmation info within 30mins.

Next, Peter called Valentin and Jay in Salamina and Korea respectively. He explained the situation and told them he had 24hrs. Peter told Jeung of the tape recorder he ask Samantha to install and ask if he could retrieve the tape before he got to China. No questions ask was his type of attitude, this is his baby. Of course his partners were on board but Valentin wanted the abductors dead. He cared about Samantha but why take from all three of them. Meaning, why do they want the dope too. Greed infuriated him, at least when someone else is greedier. Jay reassured Peter that 20ki would be nothing to get together and he'll bring it to China personally. He'll also be able to get the tape without anyone noticing if he was there. They all agreed Valentin should stay on holiday and stick with their plans on the Miami connect.

One hour later

Ring. Ring. Ring.

"Hello Peter Becker." answered Peter.

"Do you have the confirmation?" The same raspy voice.

"Yes I do but the flight is 28hrs long I need more than 24hrs and I can't leave here until 4:10pm central time zone." Peter begged.

"Give me the flight plans and I'll work with you from there."

"I'm flying Delta flight 726 departing @ 4:10pm and arriving in Beijing @ 8:25pm tomorrow. My confirmation numbers is 625 T as in Thomas D as in David 368, do you need me to repeat them."

"No that's quite ok..." the voice paused. After a moment went by he continued. "...we have confirmation and what of the dope?"

"That's a go too, but what insurance do I have you haven't or you won't kill my daughter?"

28

"Do you have faith Mr. Becker?" asked the voice.

"Yes sir." replied Peter.

"Only this time before you get here and when you arrive here you will be allowed to speak to your daughter but if you or she tries anything funny I'll start mailing her to your address in Kansas." The voice started talking to Samantha. "If you try to tell him anything except hello, I'll slit your throat and he can keep his money and drugs."

"Hello daddy." Samantha said sternly. Samantha was a real trooper how else could she survive in China all these years.

"Is that good enough…"

"No I want her at the money and drug drop." Peter cut the voice off.

"Well it's going to have to be for now. When you arrive she'll say hello and read the headline of the morning newspaper. Next you have until midnight our time to be at Li Chan meat market. There's a phone on the right side of the wall outside of the market. After the phone rings two times pick up and receive your next instructions. Good luck." Dial tone.

Vienna, Wednesday, June 18th, 5:45pm

Darkghost were on their way to meet with their contact in Austria. The air was sticky; humidity made it hard for a breeze to blow in fact there was no breeze at all. Denny cell phone rang. She didn't recognize the number but she answered it nonetheless.

"Hello." Denny answered suspiciously.

"May I please speak to Denise Spain?" Asked the caller politely.

"This is she." Denny knew this caller was one of two: either business or an old friend.

"My name is Peter Becker…" Denny perked up. Becker, where do I know that name? "…you don't know me but you went to school with my daughter Samantha…" Oh yeah, Denny remembered now. Peter continued. "…she told me if I ever needed someone internationally to get things done you were the person to call…"

Thrown back by this Denny specifically remember telling Samantha if she needed her 'don't hesitate to call'. "I don't know what you're talking about sir. I believe Sammy is mistaken and…"

"Ms. Spain she's been kidnapped in China. I can't go to the police because of my business." Peter said cutting Denny off.

"What business is that, sir?" Denny snapped.

"Over the phone I can't say but if you can meet me in Kansas at the Wichita Mid-Continental Airport I'll pay for your ticket and tell you everything you need to know." Peter said.

"I'm sorry sir but I'm on my way to St. Croix as we speak and I won't return to the States until two or three days."

Peter started thinking how this information could work in his favor. "May I please call you again, once Samantha has returned and will you be interested in helping me find these men who have taken her?"

"Sir, have Sammy call me once she's safe. Let's say Saturday the 21st and I'll see what I can do."

Peter appreciated her candor, said thanks and goodbye.

Emad looked quizzically at Denny and she told him she will explain when they were done with the task at hand. Darkghost is seconds away from meeting Ralph.

"Now listen up, Derrick park right here. The location is three doors on the right around the corner. Steve said Ralph is a bit jumpy so I can't wear a wire but I'll have this transmitter under my skin of my right forearm…"

Emad inserted the tiny bug and Juka checked to make sure it worked. Emad continued "…if there's any trouble I'll tap it twice and y'all come in guns blazing ok."

The team simultaneously gestured ok with thumbs up.

Ralph's Warehouse

Ralph Swartz is tall, muscular, and had blonde hair pulled in a ponytail. Two behemoth men guarding the door greeted Emad. Patted him down, checked the briefcase, and ushered him through the threshold. He was directed to walk down the hall on the left second door Ralph will be waiting. Emad knock twice and was told to enter. The large room smelled of cheap cigar and it was smoky to boot. Emad choked. Ralph stood up motioned Emad over to his desk and extended his hand. Just as Steve described him, Ralph eyes were jumpy but he seemed calm. "Let make this quick, leave the money, go back down the hall the way you came in and the next door on the right is where you will find the M107 .50 cal rifle and ammunition. Nice doing business with you, goodbye."

Ralph quickly dismissed Emad. Emad liked how fast this went down. He opened the briefcase, pushed it to Ralph and said thanks. Emad exited the room and proceeded to walk back down the hall to the other room and sure enough the rifle and ammunition was there. One of the behemoth men escorted Emad out back to the alley, told him to go get his vehicle and they will load it up. Without incident 3mins later Emad returned with the van and the big men loaded the weapon and Darkghost was on their way to Greece and Russia.

Emad chartered two Cessna's from a private company through the help of a CIA asset in Vienna. A no ask no tell establishment, which made him quite happy. Denny and Juka flight headed to Yaroslavl. Derrick and Emad flight to Athens. Derrick held onto the .50 cal, he loved new toys.

Salamina

Yrsa found a way to leave Valentin and Chrissy for 'some alone time' as she so eloquently put it. What neither Valentin nor the CIA Intel knew was she was meeting with a hit man in Athens. Dressed in a blouse, silk pants, and 2"heels, braided her hair in two cornrows going back. Yrsa grab her purse and was out the door. To pay attention to details was the type of woman Yrsa has become. She knew exactly how she wanted Valentin and Ivan murdered. An extra $20,000 to the man that dots all I's and cross all the T's. Valentin throat was to be cut and his groin cut off because she felt he didn't have balls to take over the drug business from his partners. The hit man dispatch members of his team to Yaroslavl, to take care of Ivan. As for Ivan, his head will be chopped off completely with an ax and glued to his back. In Yrsa mind this represented, watch your back and you should've saw this coming. Sick and demented. She was a connoisseur of death if you will. Yrsa embraced gory horror movies, the more blood the better. After her meet and greet, Yrsa smiled intensely until she reach the hotel suite and at times while riding in the cab giggled. She would be done with Valentin and his cousin. Peter and Jay will have to do business with her she thought. This thought pleased Yrsa to her core. If they didn't she will have them murdered as well and find someone else to run their side of the drug empire. Yrsa had gotten far ahead of herself. The Book Brothers drug empire ran so smoothly because they were all college graduates, loved and trusted each other, and it was three not one. There is no way Peter and Jeung will do business with Yrsa, not after she had one of their brethren murdered. They would know she had something to do with it too. She had failed before she got started.

Athens, Wednesday, June 18ᵗʰ, 9:21pm

Emad double checked the equipment, while Derrick went to get the truck parked in the rear of the hangar by a field agent. Derrick leap out of the truck and help Eli load the equipment and into the truck. It's a ½ hour drive plus a ½ hour boat ride until they reach their mark. Derrick put the truck in gear and proceeded west. Along the way Emad called Denny to see where they were at in terms of the mission. Denny gave her coordinates and ETA to Yaroslavl.

Yaroslavl, Thursday, June 19ᵗʰ, 2:40am

Juka was the only team member without any out in the field military background. He grew up on the hard streets of Jersey City, NJ. What he lack in military training, he made up with his quick thinking ability and his black belt in Wado-Ryu karate he learned at the BKG school. Beikoku Karate-Do Goyukai (BKG) teaches a deadly hand to hand combat style of karate. If Juka grabs a hold of you, whichever bones in your body he wants to break will be broken.

Denny and Juka got a room diagonally from where Ivan's apartment stood. Even though Ivan yearly income was seven figures he lived a frugal lifestyle. He refused to spend money unwisely. Half of Darkghost took post ready to protect an asset of America on foreign petroleum, waiting for further Intel that will let them know when and where the attempt on Ivan's life will happen. If Denny get any of the murderers in her M200 Intervention Sniper Rifle cross hair, they wouldn't know it until they were at their cross roads. Denny worried about not hearing from Emad, she checked her phone.

Salamina, Wednesday, June 18th, 10:10pm

A private villa on the beach was much better than a hotel suite so Yrsa demanded Valentin to get them one immediately. As Emad and Derrick were setting up shop inland, Intel came through on how the hit will happen.

"Check this Derrick stop what you're doing, we have to go to the beach..." Emad said disgusted. "Eli you got to be joking." Derrick said smirking.

Emad continued "...and Denny need to be at Ivan's residence around 2125hrs tomorrow see if you can reach her while I get us a villa on the beach. We need to be in position by 2025hrs tomorrow." Emad instructed Derrick.

Derrick pulled out his phone and then paused as if a light bulb turned on in his head. "I like how this bitch works she's going to have them murdered at the same time. Talk about intense..." Derrick chuckles and then continued. "...I'm on the job boss." Derrick said excited about the near action he was going to be engage in.

Derrick tried calling Denny with this new Intel but all he kept getting was her answering machine. Which mean one of three things; a dead battery, she turned her phone off which she wouldn't do or she's in a dead spot. The former was better in the sense that if she was in a dead spot, there's no telling how big it was and depending on where Denny's located, this could be bad. Emad and Derrick will still take care of the three men plotting to kill Valentin and then kill Yrsa and if Valentin get in the way he can get some too. Emad despised drug dealers.

"I can't reach Denny, knowing her she will tail Ivan anyway..." Derrick said looking a bit worried.

"She's a big girl as you know." Emad added

"...but she don't know what time it's going down and knowing that will give her a heads up." Derrick pointed out.

"We can't worry about that we have our job to do let's get going." Emad commanded.

<u>*China, Thursday, June 19th, 8:20pm*</u>

Peter's flight to Beijing arrived a little early. He wasted no time finding Jay waiting with the dope. Jay had been waiting patiently in a rented Bentley since 8 o'clock. Peter went to the trunk put his luggage next to Jay's. Peter hurried to the front passenger door and jumped into the car.

"Li Chan's meat market, did you get the GPS like I ask?" Without any pleasantries Peter ordered and asked. Jay understood Peter need not to say hello. If he had children, he'd be the same way.

"No problem, I took care of everything. Look in the glove box…" Jay responded.

Peter reached in the glove box and retrieved the GPS. Jay continued. "…just put in…"

"I know how to work it." Peter rudely snapped cutting Jay off.

Jay understood but now Peter is going too far. Jay looked over at Peter and got his attention. "Hey Peter I know your baby girl has been taken but there's no need to be rude bro. I'm not the one who took her ok." Jay said sympathetically.

"Sorry man it won't happen again. I know you got my back." Slap. The sound of hands colliding filled the air in the car. Peter leaned over and hugged Jay and told him thanks for being there for him. "Now can we go get my baby?" Peter said.

"Certainly." Jay said.

<u>*Salamina*</u>

The villa majestic white columns bring to mind of a coliseum in ancient Greece. Amethyst and gold shear silk fabric enclosed the back patio of the villa. A 4' high brick wall covered in stucco surrounded the property. If any privacy out back was wanted you will have be inside to entertain that thought.

Yrsa thought jackpot as they walked up to the villa. The hit-man she hired described the villa to a tee.

No matter where they took holiday, Valentin at sunset had to sit outside and think for an hour. He said 'it's when the day is at its quietest moment', Yrsa thought of this as bullshit.

Finally Derrick got through to Denny and fed her the Intel they had received earlier in the day. Now everyone was on the same page. After both teams had finished their job, Denny and Juka would secure Ivan and transport him to a safe house, where there will be a field agent waiting to give Ivan the low down. Juka and Denny will hop back on their jet and rendezvous with Emad and Derrick back at Vienna. No one knew what time the rendezvous would take place. Just get there in one piece but no team will leave East Europe without the other or confirmation that someone can't make it.

Derrick took position on the roof of his villa. Its flat surface made it easy to lie down and get a good look at the Andreev's villa. Emad lied next to him with binoculars in hand scanning the terrain for would-be murderers. The ocean to his left gave reassurance that the team of hit men wouldn't come that way. Three sides he need worry about the far side of the villa, front, and near side. Sure enough here comes Valentin getting comfy on a chartreuse cushioned stone chair with ottoman outside on the patio. Soft music playing in the background gave off a serene atmosphere. This man knew how to relax. Not long after Valentin started relaxing, Yrsa came out to bother him. They talked for about 10mins and then she headed towards the beach. As Yrsa was walking down the beach, Emad got off the roof and started walking up the beach as if he was meeting her. One of the hit men popped up right into Derrick scope vision. Derrick calmed his breathing and pulled the trigger. As the man head exploded, Derrick was reloading and ready for another shot. He radioed into Emad "one down make your move". Emad was 5yds from Yrsa when Derrick informed him of the situation. When Emad approached Yrsa, Emad pulled out a cigarette and ask her for a light. The oldest trick in the book and it works every time. When Yrsa motioned to her purse two bullets hit her in the head, blood gushed out the backside of her head and painted the sand as if an artist had splashed his canvass violently with paint. Then the earth opened up and pulled her down with force. At once Emad started running top speed towards her villa. The hit-man Yrsa hired was sneaking around the far end of the villa. Derrick had no shot. Another was creeping through the house. Derrick saw him in his sights. Derrick moved his sights two windows ahead. When this would-be killer enters his cross hair this time its RIP for him. The hired hit-man was leaping at Valentin just as Emad got there.

Valentin eyes were as big as silver dollars. Terror had taken over his face and the blade of the hit-man had sliced his throat. With a jumping round house kick Emad had knocked back the hit-man. Surprised at what just took place the hit-man reached for his pistol but Emad landed in the ready. His Smith & Wesson pointed out shoulder level at the hit-man, gave a wink and four shots rapidly hit the killer two to the head and twice to the torso center mass. Holstered his gun and reached around his back for the Remington shotgun. Walked up to the stack of dead meat and pumped two rounds into him. Now Emad was searching for the other killer. Meanwhile no one heard the .50 caliber round shot Derrick had pumped into the killer inside the villa. Chrissy was sleeping not far from where all this took place. Emad took out a prepaid cell phone he'd purchased before they got the .50 cal rifle. He called the police and asks for an EMT unit as well and disappeared. Valentin wounds were superficial he will survive this evenings ordeal. Valentin rushed over to Chrissy and checked her to see if she was hurt. Then he shook her, she awakened immediately. Good. Valentin started calling out for Yrsa. No answer. He called out again and again and still no answer. The police cars screeched around the corner as Valentin was exiting the villa holding Chrissy in his arms. Police jumped out their cars with guns drawn and aimed at Valentin. He was ordered to put down his daughter and lie down on the ground. Chrissy started crying and asking for her mommy. Police approached slowly. The EMT unit came to a screeching halt with sirens blaring. The police approached Valentin frisked and handcuffed him with his hands behind his back. One of the cops walked over to Chrissy and picked her up and gave her to an EMT tech. Valentin began telling the officers what had happened and he didn't know where his wife was. All he knew is that she went for a walk down on the beach. Valentin was pointing with his head to the right of the villa. Two of the officers went running slowly in that direction. About 50yrds down the beach they discovered Yrsa body.

Salamina Police Department

After a long and intense interrogation by the local police, Valentin was allowed to take Chrissy back to Mother Russia as he so intimately called his home country. Valentin sister Sasha received Chrissy with open arms and Chrissy will spend the next two weeks with her until Valentin figure what to do next.

Darkghost's Villa

Derrick had nearly finished packing the truck when Emad returned. They wiped down the villa for fingerprints and were on their way to the dock so they can return to Athens and then rendezvous with the other team members.

CHAPTER SEVEN

Juka crept up through the backyard of Ivan's apartment building. Denise played lookout for the hit squad. She was feeling rather bored and would rather be out there with Juka doing surveillance. Juka placed little motion detectors on the out skirts of the yard perimeter. If anyone tried to sneak up on him Denise will be warned of their presence if she didn't spot them in her scope. Juka told Denise he was putting down the last of the detectors and was ready to return. Denise gave the ok for him to do so by saying "the coast is clear". Juka wasted no time and had leaped over the 6' brick wall without making any noise. When Juka walked through the door of their makeshift watch tower, Denise greeted him with a smile. Juka checked his watch impatiently to see if they were near the time the hit will be going down.

The apartment complex to where Ivan lived was shape like a horseshoe. The yard has a water fountain in the middle with wrought iron benches surrounding it. Ivan's apartment was located on the right corner coming in from the back. Setting the detectors worked to Darkghost favor because it's Thursday and the grass is cut every two Fridays. The hit squad will stumble on the detectors and not even know it. This will allow Darkghost to damn near be on top of the hit squad before they could respond.

In this part of the city people are quiet and mind their own business. Window blinds are always drawn closed. Police hated when crime happened in downtown Yaroslavl because solving them was next to impossible. No one talks. Denise scanned the yard through her scope on the M200. Juka sprang to his feet as the detectors transmitter light started blinking.

"I don't see anyone moving." Denise said.

"Look closely it may be rodents." Juka responded.

True it was a mouse scurrying about through the yard and then something flashed quickly. Denise said to Juka "Let's get going..." she paused to wipe her eyes and then continued. "...they're here."

Juka snatched his K-bar knife, holstered his Glock 40 handgun, and plastic twist ties. Denise had her pistol holstered on her waist already and was walking out the door. Denise came from the front. There's an alley on the side of the complex covered by a six foot pressure treated oak wood fence. The alley is about three feet wide and as long as the length of the complex.

Denise secured the alley. Coming in from the rear Juka spotted two men scaling the outside of the far wall. He radioed Denise and said "Two going up the wall I'm following. See you inside. Do you copy Denny?"

"Copy." Denise replied.

Juka got a running start and jumped on the wall and scaled the rope that the two men had left behind. Denise double back and went through the front. Followed the signs to the stairs and started climbing. Just as she hit the first stairwell landing a slap came down on the left side of her face. Denise stepped back and forces herself to the floor and rolled back as he attacker was closing the gap between them. When he got close she swept his feet from underneath him. As he fell to the ground, Denise sprang up and jumped on his chest. The muscular man let out a sigh. Denise then grabbed his left wrist and maneuvered her legs as to crisscross them around his arm and pulled back and down at the same time. Snap. Attacker arm broke. The attacker let out another scream. Denise shut him up with a 9mm slug to the face.

Juka was hot on the heels of the two men whom have scaled the outside wall to the roof. Both men were through the door exiting the roof. Juka knew he had to pick up the pace if he wanted to save Ivan's life.

Denise was taking stairs two sometimes three at a time not knowing the status of Juka with the other men. At each floor Denise would stick her head in the door to make sure no one was hiding or trying to out flank her. Fifth floor. Denise peeked into the hallway as she was entering the floor. Now with her 9mm Glock drawn and raised ear level as she ventured down the corridor. The two men coming down the stairwell from the roof made it to the fifth floor but they were on the East side of the building. And they didn't know Juka was right behind them. The taller of the two stayed behind just in case someone tried to flank from the back side. He didn't know that this stairwell will be his final resting place. The other hit-man moved forward through the door slowly but with a steady pace trying not to look suspicious.

As Denise started moving to her left she read the apartment number and realizes she was going in the wrong direction.

Juka peered over the railing and saw a man standing in front of the 5th floor doorway. Steadily moving down the stairwell he decided that when he gets to the seventh floor he would take steps five at a time which meant he'll be at his destination in two minutes.

Denise saw a man kneeling at a door and said "hey you"! The would-be killer spun around pistol up and pulled the trigger. Two shots rang out and he received one to the mouth in return.

The other hit-man in the stairway looked up the stairwell as if he heard something. Juka swung around the railing and was flying through the air towards the would-be killer with his feet in front of himself. The killer pulled up his pistol but Juka was on him.

POW.

The gun fired as it went flying out his hands. That was ok for him and Juka knew this by what the hit-man said next.

"I've been wanting to kill someone with my hands for some time now. Thanks for giving me this opportunity."

Juka looked at him and replied "I aim to please."

Juka then leaped forward but was caught with a spinning back fist to the face which surprised him. The man charged forward what a mistake that was. Juka lowered his center of gravity so he could get leverage and upper cut his attacker to the gut. The attacker eyes open wide. Juka sprang up using his head as a battering ram to the attacker chin. Sidekick to the kneecap Juka knew he broke it by the way it snap back and the big man scream of pain. Juka pulled out his K-bar and cut his jugular vein. The big man fell like gravity ask for his presence on the floor. Juka kneeled down over him and whispered in his ear. "I told you I aim to please..." Juka stepped back and continued "...now you're a good guy".

Juka opened the door to the 5th floor and peep through to see if there was anyone waiting for him on the other side. What he saw was Denny kneeled down over a man bleeding from his mouth. Denny waved him over and Juka crouched over and quickly walked over to Denny.

Denny said "This is Ivan's apartment let's get him and get out of here."

"No problem I'll enter first ok." Juka replied.

Juka knocked on the door and there was no answer. He knocked again and then a deep baritone voice answer from inside.

"Who is it?"

"Police!" Juka shouted out.

Ivan opened the door without looking through the peep hole. Juka rushed in and grab Ivan by his shirt and swung him against the wall behind the door. Denny was right on his heels. Juka covered Ivan's mouth and asked "Is there anyone here with you?" Ivan shook his head no.

Denny came around to Ivan's right side and started explaining who they are and why they were there. She also told him they will check the rest of the house and if he wanted to run he was free to do so but he must understand that they don't know if they got all the men who were sent to kill him.

Denny and Juka secured the apartment and told Ivan he had 5 minutes to get some things together and then they had to leave and get him to a safe house.

The safe house was approximately twenty minutes away southwest from Yaroslavl. A beat down ranch shape log cabin house with white shutters that hang slantingly against the window sat in the middle of the woods about five minutes off the main road. As they drove up the dirt road to the safe house Juka began getting a weird feeling. When they approached the cabin that appeared out in a clearing.

Juka put the car into park and then said "Is it a safe or haunted house. I'm not going inside either way. So Denny you have to go up there and talk to them."

"No problem scary cat."

Ivan sat quietly he didn't know what to think. His life was turn upside down and for once in his life he didn't have a plan.

Valentin parents raised Ivan as their own child. They shared everything like brothers. With Valentin being two years Ivan senior, when his parents died they left him the majority of the business. Ivan was glad they left him something. You see Ivan has a passive personality. Even though he's taller, bigger, and stronger than Valentin, he would let Valentin boss him around.

Denise exited the car and walked up to the house, as she reached the steps a field agent exited the cabin and greeted Denise with his hand extended. Denise accepted his hand and asked to see his credentials. Agent Poskov reached into his blazers inside pocket and retrieved his wallet which had his picture identification and shield and handed it over to Denise. After Denise checked his creds she motioned for Juka to bring Ivan over. Agent Poskov asked Denise if she and her colleague would like some coffee for the road but scary cat said they were in a rush and had to be going.

The mark was turned over to the feds and half of Darkghost returned to the car and on their way to rendezvous with the other half of Darkghost.

While in the air Denise called Emad on his cell phone and gave him their ETA to the rendezvous point.

"Hello."

"Eli we should be there in 5hrs. The drop-off was a success. Give better details at the debriefing."

"Good Job. See you guys soon and have a safe flight."

Click.

Dial tone.

CHAPTER EIGHT

Peter Becker and Jeung Hyong-Kim were on their way to the meat market where Peter could get his phone call from 'the voice'. Peter's eyes were blood shot red with exhaustion and jumping from side to side looking for Li Chan's meat market. Jeung sat still and felt uncomfortable with the dead silence and had decided to break the silence by saying.

"Peter have you heard from Sammy's mother?"

Peter ex-wife Margaret Simmons was a piece of work. All 5'9" of her was as mean as a rattlesnake. By the end of their marriage if you could call it that she loathed Peter. Peter believed she married him for his money not for love because she never took his name. And by the way she got nothing when they divorced because the selfish and stupid woman counted her eggs before they had hatched. She never thought Peter was smart enough to hire a PI and discover she was having an affair in Minnesota with an old acquaintance.

Peter responded "Hell no why would I call that bitch and she hasn't talked to Sammy in about a year..."

Silence filled the car again and then Peter continued "...why would you ask me about her in the first place?"

Jeung looked at Peter and saw how angry he had become and offered an apology. "...sorry Peter didn't mean to get you upset. I was just trying to break up the silence."

Peter didn't respond so Jeung paused for a moment and looked out his window and started speaking again "...you need your head in this man..." Jeung paused again and pointed out the front windshield up ahead to the right and then said "...look its Li Chan's..." Jeung started hitting Peter on his arm like he was squatting a fly and then continued "...stop here bro lets park. I'll drive from here."

Peter walked over to the phone outside of the market.

Ring.

Ring.

"Hello." Peter answered.

"Are you ready?" the voice asked.

"Yes."

"Do you have all I asked for?"

"Yes"

"The money and the drugs?"

"Yes, now if you're finished with asking 20 question. I would like to talk to my daughter now." Peter said aggravated.

"Ok next to the phone is a newspaper vending machine. Buy today's paper and your daughter will read today's headline and then you can ask her one question. Don't be stupid Mr. Becker."

Peter dropped the phone and let it hang while he brought the day's newspaper and then returned to the phone.

"Ok I'm ready you can put my daughter on the phone." Peter said.

There was dead air on the phone and then a familiar voice spoke slowly.

"Hello dad are you coming to get me?" Samantha asked.

"Yes baby just hold on. I'm on my way."

"Just read the damn headline." the voice ordered.

"Foo Ling pleaded guilty and received 12 years in prison." Samantha read out loud.

"What's my mother maiden name?" Peter asked.

"Stein." Samantha answered.

"That's enough give me the damn phone." The raspy voice said.

The kidnapper snatched the phone from Samantha and said to Peter "Ok, you need to go inside LI Chan's and then walk over to counter helper and say "swing kid". He'll give you an envelope with your next instructions. Oh yea Mr. Becker leave your friend behind this time. Good luck."

Peter did exactly what the voice instructed him to do.

Li Chan's meat market was established in 1978. Still had the same decor it had from the time it was established. Wooden meat racks with metallic hooks hang from the ceiling and various animals hanged upside down attached to the hooks. Some workers skinned the animals while others cleaned them and then handed them off to the butchers. Who then with cleavers chopped and cut; duck, rabbit, pheasant, and chicken.

The wooden floor splashed with blood made it difficult for Peter to find his footing. Even at this hour the market buzzed with patrons. The counter helper was speaking Cantonese to a customer with a horseshoe bald haircut and Mandarin to a short petit lady. The Mandarin speaking customer order was wrong and she screamed at the helper to get it right. Peter felt dizzy and shook his head to focus on the task at hand. Peter stepped up and said "swing kid". The counter helper looked quickly towards Peter and bowed and explained how sorry he was for making him wait. He reached under the counter and pulled out a large manila envelope and handed it to Peter. Peter spoke Mandarin and said "Toe chie" and grabbed the envelope and turned around and walked out of the market.

As he was walking towards the car Peter opened the envelope and read his next instructions:

INSTRUCTIONS

1. GO TO WUSHAN FISHERY ON WUSHAN ROAD DOCK 14b.
2. COME BY YOURSELF AND LEAVE YOUR FRIEND BEHIND.
3. YOU HAVE 25 MINUTES TO GET THERE. STARTING NOW.

Peter ran over to the driver side of the Bentley and motioned for Jeung to get out. Jeung opened the car door and with his hands in the air said "What?"

"I have to go at it alone from here Jay." Peter said while getting into the driver seat.

"Are you sure about that bro?"

"They're watching me and instructed me to leave you behind..." Peter said pointing at Jeung and then continued "...I need your car ok?"

"No problem and return with my goddaughter."

"Thank you Jay and I will return with her."

Peter and Jeung shook hands and then Peter turned towards the dashboard to program the GPS with his next destination, pushed the ignition, and pressed the gas pedal. Peter sped off and didn't look back.

The GPS beeped and a lady voice started speaking. "Fifteen miles to destination." A short paused and then she spoke again "Two miles to Pi Pan Boulevard and make left onto Zhan Xi Street." Peter pressed the gas pedal hard and the Bentley engine hummed and accelerated to 65mph in 3.5 seconds.

Peter thoughts were becoming more clear as he traveled to his next destination; Samantha abductors. Peter thought about Samantha when she was a little girl.

When Samantha was a young lady she was considered a 'tom boy'. She played tackled football, basketball, and ice hockey with the boys from her neighborhood. She never backed down from a challenge or dare and thought the girls in the neighborhood were too sensitive. Once a neighborhood boy named Tommy dared her to jump off her second floor roof backwards doing a flip onto a mattress. She did it without second thought and sprang her ankle. She didn't even cry and wouldn't tell her father because she thought he would be mad and wouldn't let her play with the boys anymore. When her father found out he determined he would never hold her back from anything she wanted to do and made her promised to tell him anything and everything. From that day forth they have had a strong father and daughter bond.

The lady from the GPS chimed "Zhan Xi Street 0.2 miles ahead and turn left onto Zhan Xi Street." the lady paused and then continued "turn left onto Zhan Xi Street and then go eight miles on Zhan Xi Street and then turn right onto Wushan Road."

Peter reached into the back seat and grabbed his duffel bag. Once he retrieved his duffel bag he reached into the bag and retrieved a .45 Smith & Wesson handgun and then put it on the passenger seat next to him. He also pulled out a hunting knife he used when he fished back home. He felt there will be dead bodies if Samantha was hurt or worse: DEAD.

"Wushan Road 0.2 miles ahead turn right onto Wushan Road and then go five miles on Wushan Road your destination on the right."

Peter slowed down and pulled over. Went into his duffel bag again and grab his shoulder holster and put it on. After which he grabbed his Smith & Wesson and holstered it. Put the hunting knife into his boots and stepped on the accelerator to the car and began moving again towards his destination: Samantha.

"Destination…" Peter pressed the off button on the GPS and said to himself "enough of that lady." Peter pulled over slowly and put the car into park. While sitting in the car Peter pushed in the trunk release button. As he stepped out of the Bentley, Peter looked side to side. No one was in sight. The trunk popped open and rose slowly. Peter walked around to the rear of the car. Inside the trunk were two extra-large luggage bags which sat side by side. Peter reached in and grab both of them one after the other. Pulled up the handles and started walking towards the docks with the bags rolling behind.

As he got close to the docks a flashlight shined in his face and a voice said "don't come any farther…" Peter stopped in his tracks. The voice continued "…drop the bags and open them and take ten steps back."

"No way man. Where's my daughter?" Peter snapped back.

"She's here…" the voice said "…now open the bags and step back as I said." This time the voice seem agitated

"Again I need to see my daughter and then I'll do whatever you ask." Peter said with authority.

The voice told one of his cohorts to get Samantha and then said "if you don't do what I say after she gets here I'll put two in her head."

Samantha came into the light and said "daddy I'm ok give them what they want."

Peter dropped the bags, zipped them open, and walked backwards fast while saying "I'm going to take you home baby."

Two men walked forward with Samantha in the middle of them. When they got a couple of paces away from the bags they release her and she ran to her father. One of the two men kneeled down and examined the contents in the bag and zipped the bags closed. The flashlight beam went dark and the kidnappers disappeared.

As Peter and Samantha got close to the car the voice said "here's some compliments from your friend." Bullets started ricocheting off the Bentley. Peter grabbed Samantha down to the ground and returned fire, shooting over the car hood blindly. Samantha opened the driver side door slid into the seat lying down and told her father to get into the back. Samantha searched the ignition for the key and gave it a turn. Nothing happened.

"Why the car won't start?" Samantha asked.

"You have to push in the button." Peter answered.

Samantha pushed in the ignition button and the Bentley started with ease and hummed. With her feet pressed the brake and shifted the car into reverse and then pressed the gas pedal until it hit the floor.

While driving in reverse a bullet grazed Samantha neck and planted into Peter shoulder. Samantha grabbed her neck and then hit the brake and turned the wheel hard right. The car spun 180 degrees and now they were pointing away from the docks. Samantha quickly put the car into drive and sped off.

"Are you ok daddy?"

"I'm fine baby. You're bleeding from your neck."

"It's a flesh wound I'll be ok."

"I took one in the shoulder and it's still there. Get us out of here." Peter said with pain in his voice.

"Which way?"

"The GPS is preprogrammed with the hotel where Jay is staying. Press the on button and when the GPS comes on press the button that reads home."

Bullets still ricocheting as the kidnappers give chase. Peter reached out the window and returned fire. When they got to the end of the road, just as fast as the kidnappers started shooting, the shooting stopped abruptly.

Peter and Samantha Becker had escape with their lives intact and were now on their way to meet up with Jeung.

CHAPTER NINE

Peter and Samantha Becker made it to the hotel where Jeung was waiting. Samantha knocked on the door while her father leaned on her for support. Peter had lost a lot of blood and needed to get the bullet out of his left shoulder. Jeung hurried over to the door and looked out the peep hole and saw that it was the Becker's. He swung the door open with great force and help Peter over to the bed.

"Go in the trunk of the car and get the first-aid kit." Jeung commanded Samantha.

Jeung ran over into the bathroom and got some towels and a pail with hot water. On the way back from the bathroom he grabs a bowl from the room service tray. Samantha rushed through the door with the kit in hand.

"I need the tweezers and alcohol and put them into the bowl to sterilize before I can abstract the bullet from his shoulder." Jeung instructed Samantha.

Jeung looked over to the table and chairs and sized up the chair.

"That will have to do." Jeung said.

He ran over to the chair and snapped one of its legs off and ran back over to the bed.

"Peter you need to bite down on this while I'm taking the bullet out of your shoulder." Jeung said.

Jeung took the tweezers and swooshed them around in the bowl with the alcohol and started digging into Peter's shoulder. Peter started squirming and his moans were muffled by the piece of wood but he screamed nonetheless.

"Sammy hold him down I almost got it."

Samantha put all her weight on her father's right side.

"Ok there got it." Jeung said enthusiastically.

Jeung drop the bullet and tweezers into the bowl and grab some dry towels dip them into the pail with the hot water and cleaned out Peter's wound.

"Hand me the sutures so I can stitch up his shoulder..." Jeung instructed Samantha and then said to Peter while stitching "...listen Peter we need to get out of here fast. We don't know if you two were followed."

"Let's get going then. I got my daughter back..." Peter paused with tears in his eyes and rubbing Samantha's back, he continued "...I'm ready to get out of this country..." looking up at Samantha he said "... what about you?"

"I think you should rest before we get on the airplane back to America." Samantha said now standing up over her father.

"An hour no more. Like I said we don't know if you were followed and we must assume you were." Jeung explained.

"Thanks..." Samantha said looking at Jeung and then kneeled down and kissed and whispered to Peter "...you need some rest try and sleep."

The 28 hour airplane ride back to Wichita Mid-Continent Airport was rough on Peter's shoulder but he'll survive. When the Becker's got home, the first thing Peter did was call his partners on a conference call.

"Jay is you there...? Peter asked.

"Yeah." Jeung responded.

"...and Valentin?"

"I'm here too..." Valentin replied and then Valentin continued "... there was an attempt on my life a couple of days ago..."

"What happened?" Jeung and Peter said in unison.

"Come to find out my wife hired some hit men to kill me."

"I knew that bitch was fucked up." Peter chimed in.

"That's not all Ivan has disappeared and the way it looks as if someone tried to kill him too. That's the info I received..."

"Are you saying?" Jeung cut off Valentin.

"...wait there's more. The American feds have him. I also believe they saved our lives..." Valentin interrupted Jeung and then paused thinking of what to say next and then continued "...they may also know about our business or they may be questioning Ivan at this very moment."

"Do you think Valentin..." Peter said sarcastically and then he continued "...my daughter is kidnapped and there's an attempt to have you and Ivan murdered..." Peter paused to let what he just said sink in. As if to pick up where he left off he said "...do any of you think it's a coincidence?"

"The only way this is not a coincidence is if the Feds, Yrsa, and whoever kidnapped Sammy are all working together." Jeung responded.

"Yeah that's a stretch." Valentin said.

"A far stretch." Peter said.

"Peter did you call Sammy's friend back?" Jeung asked.

"No, Sammy gonna do that tomorrow."

"Ok this is what we have. Ivan is in the United States government custody or protection and we need to find out which one first. Next, shut down all business, especially in the States and I mean right now. And then find out who kidnapped Sammy using her friend if we can. The men who tried to kill Ivan and myself were hired hit men and I don't need to worry about that..."

"And why is that?" Peter asked cutting off Valentin.

"...because if anyone of them are left they know that the U.S. government is involved some kind of way and I bet they don't want to end up like Yrsa and their buddies." Valentin explained.

"You're probably right on that one. Ok I agree we should shut down shop and Valentin, you have to get rid of that new buyer." Peter said.

"I already did."

Let's conference call tomorrow morning around 9am your time Peter." Jeung ordered.

"Until then be safe my brothers. Goodnight." Valentin said.

"Goodnight." Jeung and Peter said together.

CHAPTER TEN

Darkghost mission was a success and both teams made it to the rendezvous spot without a hitch. They all felt a bit sluggish because of the different time zones they went through and the zones they're about to go through going back home. Juka wanted to debrief and see what happened with the other half of the team's mission. Denny objected to doing it now while on the jet and suggested they wait until they got a day's rest so that they could give an accurate account. Eli agreed and made a statement to the fact that he had to be in Langley, CIA Headquarters on Monday for his debriefing.

The flight was long and I couldn't wait to get home to my family. After the jet landed, the team gathered their belongings and exited the Cessna.

Derrick exited first and hurried over to the waiting Suburban on the tarmac. Denny and I walked together pulling up the rear. I looked at Denny as one of my daughters and with my arm over her shoulder I said "I'm glad you're ok girl" and squeezed her tightly.

Denny smiled and said "Eli you know I'm a bad mamma jamma".

"Denny you know I love you as one of my own. And your father would kill me if anything happened to you." Eli chuckled and they walked on in silence.

As Denny and Eli approached the SUV Juka had half his body out of the front passenger window sitting on the door and yelled out "Come on you two I'm ready for a stiff drink and y'all slowing down my unwind process."

"Hold your horses' man..." Denny replied and then Eli said "There's enough liquor and beer at Rubin's."

"I know but life is short and I'm trying to spend it having some fun." Juka replied now sitting inside the SUV.

Eli and Denny both hopped into the truck and Darkghost was on their way to their separate homes. Derrick was driving and Eli house in South Philly was the first they got to and then Juka and Denny in North Philly. The plan was that Derrick would park the Suburban at his house until the next day but first he must store all the weapons and equipment in the storage unit they used for the mission.

Hulseman Street in South Philly was well lighted by street lamps and people littered the streets walking and jogging at odd hours. Eli smiled widely as they approached his house and then he said as he exited the truck "Ok guys see y'all tomorrow at the office. 1pm sharp so sleep in and lunch on me at Reading Terminal Market..."

Eli started to close the right rear passengers side door but a thought popped into his head and reopened the door and continued "...by the time you guys get to the office your payment will be deposited into your accounts. Goodnight and thanks again for a job well done."

Simultaneously the rest of Darkghost said "Goodnight."

Emad had a separate entrance to his home office. Just in case he needed privacy before he saw his family. Emad walked into his home office and surveyed it and opened his arms to stretch and yawned

All red mahogany oak wood furniture decorated his office. Black metallic cabinets occupied the left wall, his majestic dark stained desk littered with two rows of family photos and each row had three photos sat near the middle of the office, a celadon chaise lounge decorated the wall opposite the desk, mini blinds drape with jade and burgundy curtains highlighted the window, track lights gave Emad the power to dim or make the room as bright as he wanted, wood flooring covered with a 19th century Persian rug, and shelving with all his military decorations and medals encase in glass to the right of the room. The wall painted white outlined with hints of mauve paisley boarders surround the perimeter. Emad pride and joy of his office is two things: his plush chinchilla cushioned Louis the Fifth armchair and the LG 50" plasma 3D and HD TV accompanied by a Blue-ray laser disc DVD player that filled his wall across from his desk. As you can see Emad spent all of his extra money on this office. Some men have man caves Emad has his office.

The computer sitting on his desk was glowing with an apple bouncing from side to side like an old Atari table tennis video game.

Emad let his luggage drop to the floor and he sunk into his armchair and kicked off his socks and shoes. The thick Berber rug was comforting to his toes. After Emad deposited the team payment into their accounts, he dozed off for some time before he was awakened by a kiss from Veronica. He didn't realize how long he'd been sleeping and didn't even open his eyes while Veronica was kissing him; he just enjoyed the warmth of her lips on his.

"What time is it?" Emad asked his wife now looking into her eyes.

"It's time for you to come to bed honey." Veronica said sashaying

"In a minute baby I have to finish up some things."

"No now!" Veronica insisted because she had something planned.

"Ok I need 5min to send my assessment of this week conference."

Veronica standing in the doorway punching her fists said "Alright not a minute longer..." before she walked away she added "...and honey go say hi to Elaine she misses you." "And then I'm coming to see you." Emad said licking his lips.

In North Philadelphia, Pennsylvania early morning people with employment hurried about trying to get to work on time. And people with nothing better to do stood on corners holding it up. The block Denise lived on like most ghettos had litter, a bodega, and a liquor store. Denise liked living with 'the people in the struggle' as she called them. Her father James and Emad have tried over and over again to get her to move to a more suitable neighborhood but Denise will have none of that.

After returning from the mission Denise noticed she was without eatable food and needed to go shopping. No one in her neighborhood knew exactly what she did for a living. Some had their suspicion but had no proof. All they knew was that she was once in the Marines and now did some kind of consultant work for the military.

While at the grocery store Denise spotted the 83 years old nosy neighbor Mrs. Johns and decided this will be a good time to tell the neighborhood where she been. On a business trip in NYC. Telling Mrs. Johns anything is like getting on a megaphone in the middle of the street and broadcasting your business.

Denise finished running errands and food shopping. She had some time to go home and relax before her debriefing at the office. Denise made herself some tea and toast and was sitting in her recliner watching ESPN Sportcenter report about the Philadelphia Phillies when her cell phone rang. Denise was hesitant to answer it but it kept ringing. She thought to herself 'why every time I'm relaxing the damn phone rings' but this time it was someone she hadn't spoken to in a very long time.

"Hello?" Denise answered the phone on the sixth ring.

"Hello Denny is it you?" the voice seem familiar but Denise couldn't quite grasp it yet.

"Yes this is she. May I ask to whom I speaking to?"

"It's me girl, Sammy..." Samantha said giggling "...my father said he spoke to you a couple of days ago and said you would only talk to me. So how you been?"

"I'm well thank you. I see your home safely I assume, that's good. Tell me what happened and don't leave anything out."

"Wow girl straight to the point huh."

"My time is very valuable so please tell me what you need to say. I have business to handle in a few minutes."

"Well my father runs..." Samantha paused thinking of what to say next and then continued "...wait, if we could meet in person this evening in Old City down at the Market, I can tell you everything you need to know..." she paused again "...is 8pm good for you?"

"That's fine. See you then but no one else but you Sammy is to be there ok."

"No that's fine. See you then." Samantha hung up and Denise went back to relaxing.

Darkghost assembled once more for debriefing at the office near Old City. Emad rented a small office near the capitol building. A desk, file cabinets, and four chairs occupied the space. He didn't even have pictures on the wall which Denise thought was ugly. She been trying to get him to at least put Phillies poster up but Emad said 'if any posters go up it'll be ones of the Yankees'.

Emad waited for everyone to settle down and then started with Juka and Denise, next Derrick and lastly himself. They all spoke about what they did and how they could do things better to improve on the next job. One thing they all agreed upon is that they shouldn't split up anymore to accomplish a mission.

Emad informed the team, after he debrief with D.O. Mitchel Hallden in Langley on Monday morning. He also has a meeting with both Hallden and Director of Domestic Affairs Charles Conover in DC about joining forces that will include teaming up with agents from both agencies.

"Are you crazy Eli?" Derrick was the first to speak out.

Now this question was rhetorical and Emad knew this but he answered nonetheless.

"Listen guys I know we always work alone but this one is huge and both agencies want a piece of the pie..." Emad looked everyone in the eyes and then continued "...I'm not happy working with others I've never worked with in the past but the pay on this one is double."

"As long as we aren't splitting up, I pretty much can work with anyone." Juka said.

"I'll bring your concerns up in the briefing and if their talking about splitting us up who's willing to still do this?"

No one answer.

"I'll tell them how we feel."

The team exited the office and made their way to Reading Terminal Market for lunch. Inside the market there are different types of eateries to choose from. Today the team voted all in favor of cheese steak. While in line waiting for their food Denise whispered to Emad if they could speak alone once they got their food.

When walking to their table Denise eyed Emad to remind him to follow her before they sat down. Emad and Denise excused themselves and walked out to the street.

Emad looked at Denise and said "What's on your mind Denny?"

"Remember when we were on our way to the airport and I got a Phone call?"

"Yes go on."

"Well that was my old friend Samantha Becker's father Peter Becker. He told me Samantha was kidnapped in China..." Denise paused and looked at Emad and saw he had one eyebrow raised which meant 'what the hell' Denise continued "...she had been recovered since then and I'm meeting her tonight right here. I believe she may want revenge and I don't know how I should handle this situation."

They walked for a while in silence and then Emad said "We're not in that type of business Denny. You do need to think about this one but first hear what she has to say since she is an old friend..." Emad paused and then said "...would you like for me to accompany you on the meet?"

"I was hoping you wouldn't mind but you have to stay out of sight sort of speak. I don't think she know you so you can sit in the next table from us."

By now Denise was holding on to Emad biceps and leaning her head on his shoulder.

Emad stopped walking and spun Denise around and then said 'What time is the meet?"

"Tonight at 8pm."

"Ok let's get back and finish our lunch and tell Derrick and Juka what's going on. They probably would want to help if you decide to help your friend..." Denise smiled and Emad continued "...don't be smiling all hard you know we got your back."

"I know but I couldn't ask you to help because I or we may have to go to China and I don't know if she can afford all of us." Denise responded.

"No problem let's get back now." Emad suggested.

When they returned Derrick and Juka had already finished their cheese steak Emad brought for them and had went back and purchased one more each. Derrick looked up from his plate with a mouthful of food and said "Are you guys finished holding each other hands?"

"Yes and stop talking with your mouth full..." Denise said and then hit Juka on his arm to motion him over so she could sit down and then continued "...the reason I pulled Eli to the side..." Juka interrupted and said "...we don't need to know."

Denise continued "...will you shut up and listen. As I was saying a friend of mine by the name of Samantha Becker needs my help to what extent I don't know yet. It may involve me going to China and looking for a person or persons. Once I find out the details I'll share them with you guys."

"What do you know now?" Derrick asked

"Ok as of now I know she was kidnapped in China this past Wednesday. She has been recovered when or how I don't know but I'm assuming safely because she called me this morning..." Denise looked around and then continued "...I'm meeting her tonight at eight to get more details about what happened..." Denise took a sip of her lemon water and then continued "...after I brief you guys on the details and you feel..." Denise eyed Derrick and Juka and then continued "...like you don't want to help I'll understand and no hard feelings ok."

Derrick perked up and said "China huh I've never been there. I'm in if we're going there no matter the consequences."

"I'm in too; I got your back Denny." Juka said.

They all looked at each other and with a head nod team Darkghost would take this job pro bono if it meant helping their friend and sister out. No matter the consequences.

<u>7:45pm</u>

Denise sat in the middle of Reading Terminal Market dining hall waiting for Samantha. Emad sat close by within earshot of Denise. Samantha walked in five minutes to eight and looked around to find a familiar face. Denise spotted her and got eye contact and then waved her over to the table.

Denise and Samantha hugged and kissed. They sat down and talked about what they both been up to in the last ten years. Samantha suggested they get something to eat and she will pay the tab. Denise got the drinks since Samantha pick up the food tab. They both ordered seafood; Denise ordered crab cakes, fries and a beer and Samantha ordered king crab legs, shrimp scampi and a glass of white wine. The two ladies ate, drank, and did some more catching up until Denise changed the subject to the reason they were there.

"So girl tell me what happened..." before Samantha could answer Denise continued "...and don't leave anything out because I'm involving some people I really care about and love."

"First I have to tell you about the type of business my father and I are into..." Sammy took a deep breath and then she said "...as you know I work for my father in China at his clothing factory and warehouse. What you don't know is that it's a front for his drug business..."

Denise gasped and said "NO!" but she said it quietly.

Samantha continued "...I know it's not right but..." Samantha paused and looked up at Denise and said "...ok there is no but. Anyway this past Wednesday as you know I was kidnapped around 10:30am

China time from my warehouse with a ransom of 50 million dollars and 20 kilo of heroin…" Samantha held her head down while she allows Denise to soak up what she just told her. Denise didn't know what to think if to believe what Samantha said or think this maybe an act to get her to feel sorry for her and help her out. Nonetheless Samantha continued "…after my father paid the ransom and I was returned, the leader shouted out that it was one of my dad's friend who set this up."

In return Denise said "So do you guys think one of your dad's friends would do something like this?"

"We don't know what to believe we were hoping you and your friends can tell us…" Samantha looked at Denise and then she continued "…my dad friends are in the drug business with him and I think it's plausible that one of them got greedy but my dad don't think it's possible one of them can turn on him."

"Listen Samantha if I take this job it won't be cheap and if we find out who did it what then?"

"Ok money is not an obstacle and if y'all find who did this to my father and I…" Samantha paused "…kill them and we'll pay extra if it hurts when they die."

"Let me discuss this with my friends and if we take the job we'll need half up front and four round trip tickets to China and we need to know everything about your fathers drug business."

Samantha reached into her pocketbook and pulled out a large envelope and handed it to Denise and then said "This is everything you need to know about my father friends but as far as their business is concern I can only tell you that in a more secure place."

"And where is that?"

"My house in Kansas."

"When?"

"We can leave tonight on the red eye out of Philly International."

"I can't do that but I can fly tomorrow morning."

"Early morning?"

"Yes that won't be a problem." Denise replied.

"Well then I'll meet you tomorrow morning at 6:20 boarding is at 7:45 your tickets…"

"What do you mean tickets?" Denise asked.

"…well I figure the gentleman sitting to your right will be joining you…"

Before Denise could say anything Samantha waved her off and said "...I was here earlier and I saw you two together. Anyway as I was saying the envelope you have in front of you has your tickets in it."

"You are full of tricks but don't try and fool me because that wouldn't be nice and I know how to play rough. Ok see you in the morning. By the way his name is Emad. I will formally introduce you two one day soon."

"He's not coming with you?" Samantha asked.

"No he has business somewhere else."

"Well there's four tickets inside the envelope."

"Four?" Denise asked puzzled.

"Remember I saw you earlier. I figured the other two men worked with you as well."

"Very good. See you in the morning goodnight."

"Goodnight."

Denise and Samantha stood up and hug and walked in different directions.

Denise walked by Emad and gave him the head nod for him to follow her. When they got to Emad's car they went over what Denise learned from Samantha and decided that Derrick and Juka will come for the ride out to Kansas. Emad will stay in South Philly and then go to Langley and onto Washington DC. Darkghost might be taking on two jobs but America's interest is priority to Emad and nothing will stop him from protecting her interest not even a friend's friend.

CHAPTER ELEVEN

After a long day Denise still needed to talk to Juka and Derrick about going with her to Kansas tomorrow morning. Juka was out on a date with a young lady he has been dying to take out and Derrick had missed some serious workouts while he was over in Europe and planned on catching up starting tonight. Denise called them on their cell phones and both dreams they had of how their night was going to go went out the window. It was around 11pm when they hooked up at Juka's apartment.

"Damn Denny you really know how to mess up a wet dream. I've been trying to bag Robin for 4 months and now..." Juka paused "... oh well what's up?"

"I need you two to come with me to Kansas for a day to hear about Sammy's father and his business partners. She won't tell me what they're into anywhere else."

"You mean to tell me she needs our help and she won't indulge you here?" Juka asked

"That's right but the way I see it this job could be a big pay day for us all." Samantha said.

"Ok what's the skinny?" Derrick asked.

"Samantha believes her father's friend or friends maybe involved in her kidnapping."

"Why does she believe that?" Derrick asked.

"Well she said when her father and herself were getting away, the kidnappers open fire on them but before they did that one of them shouted out 'this is compliments from your friend' and that was directed at Peter her father."

"Alright I understand now so why the secrecy though?" Juka asked.

"It has to do with the type of business they're into which by the way is drugs. Why else wouldn't her father call the FBI when she was kidnapped?"

This last question was rhetorical and both Juka and Derrick knew it but Derrick had to answer anyway.

"Because maybe they're stupid."

"No I don't think so. For one her father is a graduate of Columbia. And when talking with him, he didn't strike me as such..." Denise explained and then continued "...so how much shall we charge?"

"Didn't you say we have to travel to China?" Derrick asked looking up at the ceiling.

"Yes." Denise answered.

"Well I think we're going to need at least $100,000 plus equipment, food, housing, and airline tickets to wherever we need to go to fully accomplish this job." Derrick recommended.

"And we should get half of the money and all of the pluses before we leave." Juka recommended.

"I believe that's fair. Emad will agree as long as we are good with it. Tomorrow we'll let her know and then we'll take it from there but I think we need to fully hear about their business first." Samantha said.

"No doubt."

"I agree."

Juka, Derrick, and Denise met up with Samantha at Philadelphia International to catch their flight to Wichita Mid-Continent Airport and then onto Samantha's house. The flight was short considering what Darkghost has been through on their last job to Europe. Samantha had a car and driver waiting for them when they arrived in Kansas. The driver was ordered to drive them straight to Becker's Estate.

The Becker's Estate sits on 50 acres of land and consists of a visitor's cabin to the rear about 100yds away, a small pond with Japanese koi fish to the back on the right, and a lake stocked to the gill with fresh water bass and catfish for sport fishing which sat to the far left by the cabin. Basketball and tennis courts as well as a closed-in Olympic size swimming pool for outdoor sporting fun made life sweet at the Becker's mansion. Manicured lawns with exotic flowers from around the continent USA have won annual awards from the American Horticultural Society. I'm telling you this place had all the perks Denise loved; beautiful sites and entertainment.

The group moved through the foyer and as they got to the family room to the right Peter Becker yell out from the top of the staircase "Sammy I'm up here I'll be down in a few."

"Hey daddy we just going to grab something to eat and settle down in the family room."

"Have Alba fix her authentic Ensalada Roja con Pollo dish. Everyone will enjoy it and we can get started while she cooking."

"You guys are in for a treat..." Samantha said to Denise and then said to her father "...well I guess I'll show them to their rooms and meet you in the family room."

"First let's get Alba on the meal." Samantha said out the side of her mouth staring at Denise.

Alba a short Colombian woman around 5 feet tall with jet black wavy hair down her back was at her post as usual; in the kitchen. Watching a Latino soap opera and screaming at the TV as if the cast of the show could hear her.

"Uh huh..." Samantha said clearing her throat and then continued "...you at it again?"

"Sammy! How long have you been here?" Alba said with a strong South American accent.

"Not long just walk through the door..."

The two of them embraced with a hug and then Samantha said "...come I want you to meet some friends of mine. This is Denise, Juka, and Derrick. You guys I would like for y'all to meet Alba South American chef extraordinaire."

"Stop I just cook with love. How do you do?" Alba said with a strong Spanish accent and with her arms open wide for a hug from each one of them. Alba hugged each one at a time and after hugging everyone she said "nice to meet you." and Denise, Juka, and Derrick responded accordingly.

"Daddy ask me to ask you if you didn't mind may you please cook us some of your Ensalada?"

"For you my child I'll cook anything. Now shoo so I can get started right away." Alba said waving her arms at the group and then gave Samantha a little pat on her buttocks.

"Thanks Alba..." Samantha said and then paused and turned to Denise.

"Nice to meet you." Juka said

Samantha continued "...she has been with us since I was twelve and I love her like a mother.

Samantha showed everyone where they would be sleeping for the duration of their stay; two days and one night. The family room was two rooms over from the kitchen which was located to the rear of the house and to the right. Big vaulted ceilings and red oak wood hardwood flooring made the family room majestic. The group made their way to the plush goose down cushioned couch, loveseat, and chairs. Peter followed them in and the meeting began.

"How was your flight you guys?" Peter asked looking at each one individually.

"Good." they all answered simultaneously

"Is there any questions that any of you would like to ask me before we get started with whom, what, and where." Peter asked.

"Yes I do, what type of drugs do you and your friends sell?" Juka asked.

"Heroin." Peter answered.

"How did you get to have all of this and not get caught by now or have you been to prison and you're dumb enough to keep playing this game?" Derrick asked.

"Great planning and great partners. The problem most drug dealers have is trusting the people they work with and in this game you really can't trust anyone. But that's the luxury I have."

"Well at least it maybe a luxury you use to have if what those kidnappers say is true." Denise pointed out.

"I hope he was wrong. You see my partners and I have been doing this for 35 years. I'm tired of this shit and I am ready to get out. Especially now after what happened to Sammy..." Peter paused shaking his head looking at Samantha and then he continued "...my partners and I met when we were in college at Columbia you see Valentin and Jeung were exchange students from Russia and South Korea. It was there when we got the idea to sell drugs. All our families had money so it wasn't really hard getting up the buy money for our first drug buy. Anyway Jeung makes our drugs in South Korea and Valentin runs a candy business in Russia and then shipped to our warehouse in China and then finally it gets here to me and I distribute it throughout three cities here in the States. That's the meat and potatoes of our business. Anything else?"

"Wow that's very interesting Mr. Becker so it seems that we have to go to Russia and China. That can be very pricy sir." Denise said.

"For all your expenses I'm giving you an unlimited credit card and a debit card so you can get cash from any ATM in the world for things you can't use a credit card for. Now what's your base pay?"

"Can you give us a moment to discuss this amongst ourselves?" Denise asked.

"Sure take your time; we'll be in the room across the hall."

25 minutes later

Darkghost entered the room across the hall. Denise tapped on the door jam and said

"Excuse us but we have come to an agreement and will charge $500,000 plus expenses. Is that a problem?"

"Yes that won't be a problem at all. When can you guys get started?" Samantha asked.

"We need to get back to the east coast and speak with our other partner and then we'll get back to you by the middle of the week." Derrick said.

"Well then you guys make yourself to home while you're here and enjoy our hospitality..." Peter paused and sniffed the air and then continued "...it smells like Alba maybe finished with lunch." Peter said

"I'll go check." Samantha said walking out the room.

CHAPTER TWELVE

FBI Headquarters located in the J. Edgar Hoover Building, NW Washington, DC a place Emad know so well after doing business with Director Charles Conover. The inner sanctum of the Domestic Affairs department was as secret as the way the FBI goes about their business with the public. Only Conover and his hand pick staff was allowed pass the two mirrored doors that separated them from the rest of the building. Emad was the only civilian with a swipe card to those doors.

The tall stocky red bearded man I'm meeting with today has a great sense of humor but don't take his humor as a weakness because Charles Conover takes his job very seriously and will do anything to protect America and the honor of the bureau.

Emad and Hallden went to the meeting together on the agencies dime; a helicopter. Just one of the perks of being the best of the best in the kill game Emad enjoyed. Everyone who works at the bureau is always serious it's kind of creepy but Emad has learned how to ignore the sober atmosphere. Conover liked to hold meetings with Emad in his office rather than to have them in the huge conference room. Emad didn't think that this meeting will go without a hitch being that Conover nor Hallden liked each other and he will have to play referee during his time at the Hoover building.

Emad and Hallden after going through security headed for the elevator and took it up to the 5th floor and then walk over to the southwest side of the building. After Emad swiped his card to the mirrored doors, they walked to Conover's corner office. Emad showed Mitchel the office door and Mitchel knocked on the door and entered without Charles answering.

"The last I checked when you knock on a door usually people with intellect will wait for the person inside the room you're wishing to enter to answer. Oh yea I forgot you're without intelligence..." Conover said to Hallden looking him dead in his eyes and then abruptly turned his head and towards Emad and said "...hey there Eli how ya doing?" and then extended his hand to Emad.

"I'm well thank you and yourself?"

"The same as before worried about how to keep our country safer from the terrorist the intelligence community allows to enter and do as they please." Conover said this while pointing his head over at Hallden.

"Whatever Charles as if our beautiful country is in good hands with the bureau when you guys flood our inner cities with drugs." Hallden said pointing his fingers at Conover.

"Wow you guys just can't let up on each other for the better of our country. From my understanding we all want the same thing and from the preliminary briefing you two need each other to accomplish this mission..." Emad paused and looked at both men and crisscross his hands and said "...so shake hands and play nice."

Conover waved his hand at Hallden and said "Have a seat you guys. Does anyone care for any coffee or tea before we get started?"

"I'll take some coffee, black." Emad said.

"I'll take mine black as well." Mitchel said

"Martha may you please get me three black coffees?" Charles said while holding down the intercom button on his phone and then a voice shot back out and said 'I'll bring it in shortly sir'.

"Now what of this drug dealing crew the FBI can't handle?" Mitchel asked Charles.

"It's not that we can't handle them but you guys have assets throughout the world and America need them because this crew is not just here in America but over in Russia and China and South Korea. This crew is major." Charles said eyeing Emad and Mitchel.

"What do we have on them and how do they work?" Emad said.

"As far as we know they are very organized. Their intricate web of business is hard to break through but we believe we may have them peg but we need the intelligence guys with their input to stop them from spreading their poison on our soil..." Charles took a breath and then continued "...ok first thing first the player names are Peter Becker he operates here in America. Then it's Valentin Andreev and he operates we believe out in Russia. And the last piece of the puzzle is Jeung Hyong-Kim he's in South Korea. Very smart men and through our wire taps all we can get is they work together and have a solid bond of trust between them..." now looking at Mitchel, Charles said "...we need you guys to find where they are and Emad..." Charles turned his head towards Emad and said "...you and your team can go into the different locations with the help of both of our agencies and do your thing..." taking his thumb and as if cutting his throat said "... no survivors get it."

Martha tap on the door and entered when Charles told her to. She put the serving tray down on the buffet and exited the office just as swiftly as she entered.

"How soon are you planning on rocking and rolling with this plan?" Emad asked.

"Whenever Mitchel get back to us with the Intel, we'll give you a call and fax over the particulars and then we expect for you to get moving within a reasonable time frame." Charles answered.

"What is the drug of choice?" Mitchel asked.

"Heroin and very pure might I add. We brought some about two weeks ago."

"Ok..." Mitchel said standing next to the buffet retrieving his cup of coffee "...I'll give some of my assets a call overseas and get on this thing pronto..." taking a sip of his coffee and then said "...good coffee."

"I might be over in China by the middle of the week but I'll let y'all know one way or the other and I'll give you both my point of contact over there if and once I get there so if you need me to get started I can handle our problem from there..." Emad mentioned and then paused before he continued "...is there anyway we can do this job without any of your agents getting involved?"

"I think this is big maybe too big for just you four to handle." Hallden explained.

"Listen Eli we know you and your team is good but each agency brings something different to the table and it will be helpful to have different point of views on this one." Conover added.

"Ok we're in and will do our job as usual."

"Sounds good."

"I'm out of here gotta get the boys in motion see you soon." Hallden said and then put his coffee down and walked over to the door and exited the office.

Emad and Charles chatted from a short while longer. Emad left the Hoover building without telling either Hallden or Conover he has a team member who knows Peter Becker and his daughter personally or that Darkghost may be doing a job for them. Hallden knows I know he know of this band of drug dealers and he already has the Intel on them but this is how the CIA likes to play games. They give information when they want to and not when you need it an attribute I seem to have picked up on since I didn't tell Charles I too already heard of them.

Tuesday, June 24th, 7:31am

Since I haven't spent much time with my family I thought I could take this time while the rest of the team was away at the Becker's and have some family quality time. Veronica has been trying to get me to go to Josh & Blisters a gaming restaurant where we could eat, drink, and play games as a family. We decided to go to the one up in NYC instead of the one here in town. Veronica really liked quality time and would make the best of it too.

While driving up to the city we played the license plate game. How you play is: One at a time we take turns finding the alphabet in other cars license plates. The driver can't play. This meant I wasn't playing. Rats. After we get done with the alphabet we do numbers and then when we get done with license plates we do the writings on the side of vehicles. Before you know it time has passed and you'll be at your destination. I love family quality time too.

Philadelphia, Wednesday, June 25th, 9:25am

Darkghost reassembled at the office and Denise explained to Emad what Juka, Derrick, and she have learned at the Becker's and Emad did likewise about his meeting with the agency and the bureau. The next thing they needed to figure out was; which job would they be taking.

"We got the intel on the crew already thanks to the Becker's" Derrick said

"Let's just go kill them all, why waste anyone's time." Juka suggested.

"No way, we're talking about my friend Juka. We just ate at they're house yesterday." Denise said.

"There's no way the FBI & CIA is just going to let us live with this knowledge and be like ok we'll get somebody else to take them out. At this point we have to take the job." Juka explained.

"I believe your right but we can save your friend Denny without both agencies finding out..." Emad paused and then he continued "... remember the Virginia Beach thing?"

The Virginia Beach thing two years ago:

Exhausted from the previous mission of helping Brooklan write her book report on a well-known black novelist, Emad still had the strength to plan his next covert job; dismantling a terrorist group working on blowing up the Hyatt Hotel near Pacific Ave during the most profitable time on the beach; summertime.

This is how it goes. Youth of Ishtar Peoples Republic Army needed to make a statement here in the United States to get the world to notice their struggle in the western part of Asia. At least this is what they believed. Not only were they wrong but will reap the benefit of being stupid.

Emad was able to convince one of the terrorist that being a terrorist isn't what it cracked up to be. By showing him life is something precious and needed to be respected as such. A .40 caliber pistol press against your temple may just persuade anyone.

Al Ahmid Saleem a first Lieutenant in the Ishtar People's Army disguise as a line cook at the Hyatt Hotel was there to set up things for his superiors in the army. He met with them every day after work. Today he will find out that 561 people will perish in an explosion. This number included the guest of the hotel and its staff but he didn't know it also included him; the one.

Derrick and Juka got jobs as dishwashers, so they could keep an eye on Al Ahmid. They worked different shifts being that Al Ahmid cooked lunch and dinner meals. This gave Emad and Denise the freedom to follow Al Ahmid wherever he went after work. Al Ahmid took different routes to his apartment 5 miles west of the beach. One thing he did do the same is stop at the local Wallabee Convenience Store owned by Yusef

Hameed a fellow countrymen from Pakistan. Al Ahmid would spend no longer than 25 minutes in the store talking with Yusef.

What neither Al Ahmid nor Yusef know is that the beautiful long legged black woman who wears pants business suits and regularly shops for snacks and minor household things at the store is really a covert agent surveying the store for points of entry, so that she and her team can come later that night and plant bugs. From previous surveillance Denise spotted a cut out in the ceiling of the bathroom. Mr. Hameed never let any of his patrons' use the stores restroom but when you're a lady with the kind of beauty men usually drool over, you tend to get your way and Mr. Hameed wasn't any different from the other men. After getting permission to use the stores facilities, Denise quickly walked towards the restroom acting as if she couldn't hold it, but once she got inside the bathroom, she pulled out a tape recorder and pushed play. The recording was of her using the toilet.

Once the recording started Denise made her way to the attic and snoop around a bit further. When Denise got up inside the attic she noticed there was a table with four chairs and papers scattered on the table. This meant to Denise that there must be more men or women involved in the terrorist cell here in Virginia Beach or surrounding area. Denise thought to herself 'I have to get over to the table without making noise so I can take pictures of the papers on the table'. Denise has trained and mastered the art of walking silently and that training will come in handy right about now.

Denise tip toed her way over to the table and reached into her jacket pocket and retrieve a miniature camera and took multiple pictures of the papers on the table. While in the attic she could see there was also a roof door. Denise realized she has been up in the attic to long and that her recording will soon stop running. Denise quickly moved down the stairs and put the door back up into the ceiling and flushed the toilet, washes her hands, and exited the restroom. Now it's time to meet up with Emad and the rest of the team. From Denise Intel the best point of entry was through the roof door into the attic and down the hatch from the ceiling to the employees bathroom and she couldn't wait to tell the team of her findings.

"Hey guys I got some serious intel for you. Check this out. As I'm inside the attic I see a table and four chairs..."

"Four, I thought there was only two of them." Derrick stated.

"...hold on that's what I'm getting to next. It seem to me that there maybe 2 others who may be helping them complete their goals. Where they live I don't know they didn't leave any papers of that lying around."

"When we go back tonight to plant the bugs I hope we're not too late in finding the rest of them and their plans for their terrorist attack..." Emad paused and then continued "...what time does Mr. Hameed and the help leave for the night?"

"Well Bruce the guy who does the cooking there and Mr. Hameed usually lock up the store around midnight." Denise explained

"Ok we all need to be ready at 2330hrs. See you guys tonight." Emad commanded

"Later then." Juka said

"Peace." Derrick said

"We gonna get these clowns. Alright see ya then." Denise said.

After planting their bugs Darkghost learned there's actually three other terrorist involved and needed to get to one of the terrorist and try to turn him and the one they most likely will have the best chance at getting to turn is Al Ahmid Saleem.

Tonight when Al Ahmid get off work Darkghost will ambush and kidnap him on Cutler Road before he could get to his residence on Commodore Drive. They will give him a choice and this was the risky part of the mission; give them what they want or die. Al Ahmid chose the former.

Darkghost had everything they needed to take down the Youth of Ishtar Peoples Republic Army. The only problem is that the powers that be wanted all who were involved to be killed but Emad had given Al Ahmid his word and he was a man of his word and no man could make him change that.

Emad devised a plan whereas Al Ahmid would be seen going to work on the day the bomb was to explode as planned by his cohorts but he will be sneaked out by Darkghost before they take out the terrorist.

And then taken into protective custody by Darkghost until they could get him a different identity.

As usual like all of Darkghost plans, this one went without a hitch as well and no one but all of the terrorist were killed. At least that's what the feds thought. Shush I won't tell if you don't. And that was the Virginia Beach thing in a nutshell.

Back to today

"I believe we may be able to pull that off again. When are they supposed to give you a call back about when they want us to get started with the Book Brothers thing?" Denny said.

"Sometime this week. If I had to guess I'd say by today or tomorrow." Emad replied.

"What do you want to do about the Becker's if they want us to get started with their job?" Derrick asked.

"Well our country trumps all. So the Becker's problems are not of our concern anymore as I have previously told you all about what kind of job this next mission is going to be and furthermore they are part of the next mission..." Emad paused and then he continued "...Denny give the Becker's a call and stall them but don't let on to our plans of saving your friend Samantha's life. The agency and the bureau are tapping their phones."

"No problem I'm on it now."

CHAPTER THIRTEEN

Darkghost has made their decision to save Samantha's life and help America by extinguishing the poison corrupting its streets. Only she wouldn't know of this decision to save her life because her father will not be saved. The Book Brothers have done too much dirt in spreading their poison that he couldn't be forgiven. The only reason Emad is allowing Samantha to live is because she is Denise's friend.

After the raid they will take Samantha to a safe location and then she will be given the option to live or die. If she chooses to live, she'll be given a new identity and moved to a town and state she can live out the remainder of her life. And if she chooses the latter, Emad will do the honors and plant a bullet in her forehead right then and there. Samantha will be given 10 minutes to make her decision.

Charles Conover called Emad and gave him the thumbs up on getting started with the next mission. Charles sent a helicopter to get Emad and to bring him to the Hoover building to pick up the plans for the next mission.

Emad inform the rest of his team that they are to be at the office upon his return.

Emad walked through the door to find the team looking quite restless. Derrick was in his rare form as usual telling jokes. Emad listen to a few of his jokes and then had to get to business.

"Ok guys let's get started. There's three parts of this mission in three different location. First we must go to South Korea, and then to Iraq, and lastly we come home for the final stage of our mission. CIA satellite imaging took a picture of the compound we must breach in the first part of the mission…" Emad rolled out a map onto the conference table and then he continued "…but first things first the person we're looking for name is Jeung Hyong-Kim and here's a picture of him…" Emad paused again and reached into the dossier he got from Mitchel and retrieved a photo of Jeung and put it on the table next to the map and then he continued "…burn his face into your memory. Now let's get down to our job. Denny, I need you to post your position to the far right rear of this building…" pointing at the map of the compound "…and Derrick I need you with your sniper rifle on this ridge here near this tree line…" Emad paused and then continues "…once we take out anyone over here that location should be very good for you to see everything that's going on."

"Juka you're going to plant the mines and C4."

"So I'm everyone's eyes?" Derrick questioned.

"Yes, we need your very best on this one. When we get inside no need for radio silence as we usually do but I don't want a lot of chatter. This guy Jeung is nothing to play with; I expect many men at this compound and armed very well. Do not and I mean do not think twice shoot on sight I can't emphasize that enough ok guys?" Emad commanded and then eyed everyone for a response.

Juka and Derrick gave thumbs up with head nods.

"We got you boss." Denise said.

"So we all know what we have to do then and what we need to accomplish?"

"Yea we gonna kill everyone and thing in sight pretty much." Juka confirmed.

"Yea right no captures, I'm good with that." Denise said.

"No sweat off my sleeves, let's get 'er done." Derrick said with a southern hillbilly accent.

"Alright I need you guys to meet me back here at 0300hrs with the gear. We leave for South Korea at 0630 out of Langley. So go get some sleep, you're going to need it."

South Korea, Thursday, June 26th, 6:30pm

Getting into South Korea will not be a task for Darkghost. The agency have arrange for them to use the Falcon X-15. A new state of the art stealth fighter jet that will allow them to fly in cloak mode to avoid detection from radar and satellites. The X-15 has the capabilities to hover or fly. When it's in the hover position the pilot can give a command for the blades to retract by saying Mach 1, and then the X-15 can fly at speeds of up to Mach 1. Voice commanding systems allow only the pilot to give those types of commands. Not only can it carry ten passengers along with its crew but cargo in an excess of two tons. If need be the pilot or navigator can fire Scorpion 55 air to air missiles by giving the jet an order from their helmet mic. And the Falcon X-15 is packing 10 of those missiles.

Darkghost will be put down about 2 klicks out of Inch'on South Korea in the Yellow Sea and then make their way to the shore. Emad and his team will have to track through jungles in order to reach Inch'on where there will be a Humvee waiting for them with their equipment. Darkghost will have a 3hr ride to Jeung drug compound. After that a four and an half hour return for extraction or be left there to fend for themselves without the help of any CIA assets.

"Eli you have 5 minutes until jump zone." the captain of the stealth jet announced

"Thanks captain. Ok guys get ready for the jump."

The jet came to a slow stop and then hovered over the water and then the captain began talking over the beeping noise coming from the jet.

"Ok Eli this is it see you guys in nine hours at the extract point. Good hunting."

"On the count of three we jump starting with you." Emad pointing at Juka.

"1, 2, 3, go..." Emad eyeing Denise and said "...go..." next he hit Derrick on his back and said "...go..." and then he said to the captain "...don't be late."

Emad jump and splashed into the Yellow Sea.

Darkghost treaded in the Yellow Sea in a circle before they started to swim towards the shore. They reached the shore in about a half an hour.

The team exited the sea with guns drawn. Emad waved Juka to go ahead with two fingers and Juka moved quickly through the sand followed by Denise and then Derrick and Emad picking up the rear. When everyone was in the woods they rested for 5 minutes. Juka pulled out a pictured map of the jungle the CIA satellite took. Darkghost began their track through the forest with Juka running point.

A Humvee was waiting for Darkghost, after they had tracked through the forest.

"Derrick drive and Juka you navigate and Denny and I will get the weapons ready." Emad commanded.

Darkghost rode for three hours and stopped 1 klick outside of the compound where Jeung was held up.

"Fan out and approach with caution we're in the danger zone now. This is where we make our money people. Remember shoot first." Emad said.

Head nods from everyone in confirmation. Denise took the far left flank with Juka to her right and Emad approaching up the middle and Derrick to his right.

Darkghost walked slowly through the wooded area everyone in the ready position to shoot. Derrick spotted a man sitting up in a tree. He froze in his tracks. While squatting, Derrick took aim at the man's head and pulled the trigger.

"One down." Derrick said from his post on the ridge.

Still moving forward Juka looked down his sights and found another man leaning on a tree sleeping. Just as Juka got to him, the man had awaken and looked Juka dead in his eyes. Before he could rise his weapon Juka stepped forward quickly and side stepped to his left and disarmed the insurgent, spun him around and with his K-bar knife slit the insurgent's throat. At the same moment Juka was handling his problem, Emad had shot two men smoking a cigarette and holding a conversation. Darkghost reached the compound and Emad called everyone except Derrick to his location. When they gathered together Emad had Juka to give him the map of the compound.

"Listen up Juka from the Intel we have the electrical box is over there..." Emad said pointing to his left and then he continued *"...and we need C4 at all these location here..."* now pointing at different spots on the map *"...Denny I need you to cover him on the left and Derrick you got the center and I'll take the right. After you get done planting C4 light the red smoke. This will be your signal Derrick to hit all the red dots and then we go in and kill everyone no survivors. I repeat no survivors..."* Emad said looking at everyone in their eyes *"...ok Denny let us take our positions now."*

Denise radioed in about two minutes after she left.

"You're up Juka let's go." Emad commanded.

Emad followed Juka looking through his scope and Denny panned her rifle in a sweeping motion. This was a prime time for Darkghost to do this because 90% of the people at the compound were asleep and the 10% that wasn't well four of them were dead. And the rest will soon be dead too.

Juka walked in a crouched position until he got to the first building. He reached around to his backpack he was wearing and pulled out a claymore mine and inserted it into the ground. Just as he was about to move on to the next site he heard a whistling noise and then a groan from a man. When he turned his head towards the groan the man fell right in front of him.

"Get moving Juka we got your back." Denny said.

"Affirmative." Juka replied.

Juka set the timer on the mine and moved on. Before he could get to the next building all hell broke out. Three men came out of a building screaming and shooting in the direction of Juka. A siren sounded and lights to the compound lit up the area. Within seconds Derrick had shot each of the three men in their heads and body.

"Move in, move in. Derrick take the rear and kill everything that comes out. Denny get the left side and Juka you and I will take the middle." Emad commanded.

The gun fight ensued and Darkghost got the upper hand. And just as fast as it got started is just as fast as it stopped.

"Did anyone see Jeung?" Emad asked.

"No." Denny answered.

"Negative." Juka said.

"I never saw him in my sights." Derrick said.

"Let's search the area and do it quickly we have a plane to catch." Emad commanded.

"Hey over here." Juka called out.

When everyone got to the area of the claymore blast they could see a tunnel that wasn't there before.

"Ok Juka go inside and see if there's anyone down there." Emad said.

Upon searching Juka found Jeung. Apparently, Jeung had an underground escape route but when the claymore mine was blown he was trapped inside and killed.

"Back to the beach." Emad commanded.

One down.

CHAPTER FOURTEEN

South Korea, Friday, June 27th, 1:23am

The Falcon X-15 wiz away from the Yellow Sea beach outside of Inch'on South Korea with Darkghost safely aboard and headed west.

Valentin was supposed to shut business down at the Yaroslavl candy factory but he still had dope that could be processed. He had planned to go behind his partners back and sell to the connect he had in Miami. With Ivan missing as so what Valentin thought, he let Gregori run the factory without him supervising and went to al Basrah to take care of the family petroleum business.

The Falcon zoomed up to the city of al Basrah and set down near the petroleum refinery owned by the Andreev family. Just two klicks away and the moon shining bright team Darkghost was the last of the Joint Task Force (JTF) to make its way to a safe house set up by the agency. Around 0300hrs Darkghost will attack the refinery with the help of the other agents from both the CIA and the FBI.

Because there were no survivors in the Jeung raid, Valentin didn't know of the raid nor do he know that there's a joint task force being form by the CIA, FBI, and Darkghost which he never heard of in the first place that want to kill him and destroy his drug empire.

Charles and Mitchel will be safely sitting in the Situation Room back in the USA. Commanders these days aren't what they use to be back when they fought with the troops. Today they would just get in the way because most of them didn't even have military training anyway.

"Now listen up everyone as you all know, the refinery is two klicks away northwest of us. We are going to split up into four teams. Alphas, Bravos, Charley, and Deltas. Agent Longton will team up with my team and we'll be the Alphas..." Emad said pointing at agent Longton. While looking at the rest of agents with eye contact he continued by saying each agent name "...and agents Thompson, Fevlum, George, Peters and Lofton will be the Bravos. Agents Herrs, Kellmon, Ling, Briggs and Blensaw will be Charley..."

"I don't like Charley can we be the Deltas?" Kellmon said interrupting Emad.

Emad ignored him and continued "...lastly we have agents Harry, Jeffries, Laws, Freemin, and West. You guys will be Deltas..." Emad paused and looked around the room and then he continued while picking up a basket "...inside this basket I have pieces of paper numbering from one to five. Each team will take turns pulling one piece of paper individually."

"Why are we doing this?" Agent Fevlum asked.

"It's for when we're out there and one of us need to communicate we won't have to say our names. The ideal is for all of us to make it out but if one of us shall happen to fall and the enemy takes his or her equipment and we are still talking, he or she won't know our names. Are we all on the same page now?" Emad asked looking around the room and then he continued "...this is how it works I'll pull first..." Emad reached into the basket and pulled a piece of paper out, read it and said "...my number is three, so when talking on the com I'll say 'Alpha Three' y'all get it?"

The room started buzzing and Emad let the rest of his team pick a number and then the rest of the agents chose a number one team at a time. After each team finished choosing Emad had everyone surround the long rectangle shape table sitting in the middle of the room. On the table was a map of the refinery. Emad then continued with his instructions.

"Deltas you guys take the northeast section here..." Emad pointing at a section of the map and then said "...Bravos y'all take the southeast here."

"Is that a tower?" Thompson asked.

"Yes it is and most likely there will be a man or two in there. Be careful. You may want to take out whoever is in there first. Is there anyone on your team who's a good shot?" Emad asked.

"Lofton, that'll be your job, you're probably the best shot amongst us on this team. Does anyone disagree?" George said looking at his teammates. No one from the Bravos disagree.

"Cool then it's on you Lofton. Are you game? Emad asked.

"I'm gamed and ready to get it on sir." Lofton said enthusiastically.

"Ok then we need for Charley to take care of the southwest." Emad said.

"What of this petroleum thing a majig?" Laws asked.

"I don't think we want to be planting any C4 or any type of explosives next to it." Freemin said.

"And last but definitely not least the Alphas. We will take the northwest side and remember gentlemen we are here to protect the children of our country and the interest of our country as well. You are to shoot to kill no prisoners we have no room on the airplane. You WILL give up your seat if you decide to be a saint because today isn't the day for that. So if any of you can't do that let us know now so we can excuse you now." Emad looked at the faces around the table and no one moved.

"Ok then, everyone should be studying your section on the map and then go get some rest. We have a big day ahead of us." Emad ordered.

Each separate team gathered together and surrounded their section of the map. Everyone had a voice and gave input on how to go about conquering the mission at hand.

The CIA previously has had several safe houses in the area. The one the task force is meeting in and three more within two miles in different directions. Darkghost will stay in the meeting safe house and the rest of task force will split up and go to their assigned house. Approximately 2:30 am each team will converge on the petroleum refinery and set up about one city block away.

Iraq, Saturday, June 28th, 2:24am

"Delta One to Alpha Three." Agent Ling spoke into his microphone attached to his helmet.

"This is Alpha Three go ahead Delta One." Emad responded.

"Team Delta is a go."

"Ten four Delta one."

"This is Bravo One the Bravos are lock and loaded and ready to go. Bravo one out." Thompson reported.

"Affirmative Bravo One." Emad said.

Dead silence for a few minutes.

"Charley is here sorry for the delay. Charley One out." Jeffries reported.

"Glad to have you with us Charley. Radio silence until we go in 5 minutes. Let's synchronize our watches now it's oh three hundred hours in 5, 4,3,2,1 synch. Timers set for 5 minutes in 5, 4,3,2,1 set. Happy hunting gentlemen."

Dead silence for 5 minutes and on the 5th minute each team started moving quickly towards the refinery. Once inside the refinery Agent Lofton took aim at the tower personnel and shot both men in the head and body with his M4 rifle. Gun fights erupted throughout the refinery grounds but the task force had the upper hand because of the element of surprise.

"What is going on?" Valentin asked as he ran out of his room. All he heard was gunfire and didn't know which direction the shooting was coming from. The worker he was talking to just hunch his shoulders and looked at Valentin with fear in his eyes. When Valentin turned around he saw another worker running towards him.

"It's the cops and they are all over the place." the worker said frantically waving his arm over his head around in circle.

"Ok both of you follow me." Valentin ordered.

Outside on the southeast Agent Fevlum took a round in his left bicep and was leaning on the outside wall of the infirmary.

"Bravo Four is hit but I'm pressing forward."

"What's your twenty?" Peters asked.

"Infirmary. How ironic." Fevlum replied.

Denise looked over to Juka and motion for him to cover her. She was ready to storm into one of the housing units. Bullets ricocheted all around her. There was a guard with a MAC 10 spraying the area. And then all of a sudden the guard stopped shooting.

"Alpha One to Alpha Two and Five move out." Derrick said. He had a bead on the gunman and neither Denny nor Juka knew of it.

Denny turned the corner and shot the door of its hinges and then pressed her body up against the wall waiting for return fire but there was none.

Juka ran inside the housing unit firing his Remington shotgun. No one was in the room. Denny followed him inside. After scanning the room Denny motioned Juka over to the door on her right as if she heard something. When Juka got to the door he put his left hand up and made a fist, telling Denny to wait. Then he motioned for her to go in first after he knocked down the door.

Six men were on the other side and when Juka knocked the door down gunfire rang out. Juka did all he could to get out of the way of the bullets but one had his name on it and hit him in the hip. It was a grazing bullet wound but hurt like hell and Juka let out a howl.

"Can you run?" Denny said showing Juka two grenades.

"Yea."

Denny counted down from three with her fingers and Juka took off running for the door to get outside. Denny rolled both grenades into the room and just as she got to the door they exploded. Blowing the backroom off the building. No survivors.

Emad and Longton were already inside the warehouse, left of the building Denny and Juka had entered. Longton and Emad were pinned down by Valentin and his group.

Valentin was angry and told his men "I will kill them slowly when we catch them". He had two problems; one, he was running out of ammo and two; he had to get through Emad to get more.

Over on the northeast side. Agents Blensaw and Briggs was in an intense gun battle with workers from the kitchen and guards from the refinery.

Back on the northwest side of the refinery.

"I have had enough of this shit. I'm blowing this building up. Do you have any more grenades?" Longton said.

"Yes, I have three." Emad answered.

"Ok, I have two. Let's waste them all."

"STOP!" Derrick said into his helmet mic as he came running up to Emad and Longton. Derrick continued "1and 5 is on the other side of the warehouse and some of the petroleum is stored there."

"Well how else will we get to them?" Longton asked.

"We have to use these..." Emad said holding up his rifle "...or our hands but no explosives." Emad explained.

The three of them sat there for a while thinking with bullets ricocheting all around them. As if a light bulb lit up inside Emad head.

"We can't just sit here taking all this heat. Why aren't they scared of the petroleum exploding when we return fire?" Emad asked.

"Because there's probably no petroleum in the barrels." Derrick answered.

"Alpha 1 do you copy?" Emad asked.

"Alpha 1 here go ahead." Denise responded.

"Is five with you?"

"Yes."

"Ok we need you guys to split up and each one take a corner of the warehouse in the rear and give it all you got. Do you copy?"

"Affirmative. Moving out right now call you back when we get there copy."

"Copy."

Emad covered up his mic attached to his helmet with his hand.

"Listen up when they start firing at the corners. We'll give you cover fire..." Emad said whispering to Longton pointing at Derrick and himself "...so you can get over to their left flank. And once you're safely there we'll do the same for Derrick on the right. Y'all understand where I'm coming from."

"Sounds like a plan. Let's make it happen." Longton said.

When Denise and Juka opened fire on the outside rear corners of the warehouse Emad gave the go ahead for Longton to make his move. Projectiles bounced off the ground at Longton feet. One by one both men made it safely to their positions.

"Alpha Five do you have any C4?" Emad said.

"Yes sir I do." Juka answered.

"I need a hole in that wall back there now..."

"I'm on it."

"...2 and 4 we need to advance when you hear the explosion copy?"

"Copy." Derrick replied.

"Copy." Longton responded.

One minute later a big explosion rocked the warehouse and Emad, Derrick and Longton all stood up and started firing and walking towards Valentin position. With nowhere to go Valentin surrendered.

"Who are you guys? And what do you want from me?" Valentin asked.

"It doesn't even matter." Emad said.

Emad walked up to Valentin with his .45 in his hand and shot Valentin right in the head at point blank range. Valentin body dropped to the ground with force. Emad turned around and told everyone to move out.

In total the task force lost five agents; Ling, Kellmon, West, Harry, and Lofton. All five were good family men with children. May they rest in peace?

Two down.

CHAPTER FIFTEEN

Outside the Petroleum Refinery

After the mission was completed the joint task force of Darkghost and both CIA and FBI agents had to meet their transport two klicks west of the refinery and compound. Emad had Juka get the Situation Room on the radio so he could inform them of their progress in the mission.

"Sit Room this is Juka do you copy?"

After a few tries a voice came out of the receiver.

"Go ahead Juka."

Emad didn't recognize the voice but he knew the line they were using was secure.

"The mission is a success need evacuation in 20 minutes over."

"Standby." The voice ordered.

After a few moments a voice began to speak again.

"Juka your transport is on its way as planned..." this voice Emad recognized to be Mitchel Hallden's "...there will be two transports and their ETA to you is in 23 minutes. Will wait only two minutes after arrival. So get your ass there and don't be late. Do you copy?"

"Copy." Juka responded.

"Sit Room out."

"Juka we got to hurry. Do we need to carry you or can you keep up?" Emad asked.

"I'm good; the question is can y'all keep up with me?" Juka snapped back.

Emad turned away from his teammates and spoke into his headset microphone.

"All agents, I repeat all agents move out to the evacuation point ASAP, our target has been hit..." Emad said calmly but with urgency in his voice. *"...Sit Room has been radioed and the bird is on its way. ETA in 20 minutes. Wait time is two. So move out now."*

Darkghost along with Agent Longton ran through the streets of al Basrah and the rest of the JTF pulled up the rear.

When they were about a quarter of a mile away from the refinery Iraqi soldiers dressed in commando fatigues and armed with out of date AK-47 blocked their path to their extraction point. Before the JTF could catch up with Darkghost, the Iraqi soldiers opened fire upon them and everyone took cover. Some men dropped where they were and others used the closest building as a shield. JTF returned fire and all hell broke out. With outdated weapons the soldiers held off the JTF at bay.

"I have had enough of this shit." Derrick said. Derrick pulled two grenades from his flap jacket and rolled them towards the soldiers.

"That'll fix 'em." Derrick barked.

"Everybody use all of your explosives now or..." Emad didn't have time to finish his sentence because the two grenades Derrick rolled had exploded.

All at once the members of the joint task force rolled and threw all what was left of their grenades. Massive explosions erupted and the Iraqi soldier's gunfire stopped.

"Move we have no time." Emad commanded.

The team rushed around the walls which held their cover and proceeded to run through and over the rubble of the buildings their grenades had caused.

"Look!" Juka said pointing up at the Falcon X-15 as it hovered over the extraction point.

"We got one minute!" Denise shouted.

"Big Bird, I repeat Big Bird, we are here." Emad said into his helmet microphone.

"Big Bird and Sylvester is here and we hear you loud and clear." The captain with the call sign of Big Bird said with a deep baritone voice that crackled over the receiver.

Darkghost and the rest of the JTF needed to get to the rooftop next to the building that had been bombed in another battle.

Within seconds Darkghost and the rest of the JTF had reached the rooftop. Emad, Denise, Juka, Derrick, Longton, and the rest of the Deltas that had survived the raid loaded into one of the helicopter and the rest of the JTF boarded into the other. When the stealth helicopter holding Emad and his team took to the air bullets ricocheted off the rooftop.

"I guess they don't know who they're fucking with." Captain Woodard said.

"I don't believe they do." The navigator said with a broad smile.

Captain Woodard banked the Falcon left and brought the X-15 around pointing at the insurgents and shot two missiles at the roof opposite of the building where the joint task force team had been extracted. Before the building could finish crumbling, both X-15 with its human cargo safely strapped in, zoomed away leaving just a blur of red flames and smoke.

"Sit Room this is Big Bird, we have our cargo and we're en route to homeland. Big Bird out." Captain Woodard said into his headset.

"Sit Room, Sylvester has its cargo and we're right beside Big Bird. Sylvester out." Captain Pierce said into his headset.

"Big Bird and Sylvester we copy god speed on your way in. Have Emad give the D.O. a call. Sit Room out." The voice from earlier replied.

"Emad, Hallden wants you to call him..." Woodard said as he was holding his cell phone up and handing it back to Emad he continued "...its secure the D.O. gave it to me before we left." Woodard reassured Emad.

Emad unstrapped himself from his seat and walked forward to the cockpit.

"Just push the number 5 button; he set the speed Dial to a secure number back at the Situation Room." Woodard said as he gave Emad the phone.

Emad did exactly as he was instructed to do and after three rings Hallden answered.

"Emad I need for you and your team to get one days rest and then head out to Minnesota. We'll have a jet waiting for you in Langley. You guys will be leaving at 5am. Hold on..."

"Hello hello." Emad said after a few moments of dead air. Emad could also hear mumbling in the background.

"Now where was I, oh yea, you will be brief once you land there by Special Agent Howard Crews on the whereabouts of your next targets. We'll talk on the other side of this thing. Good hunting."

"Thanks good sleeping."

Click.

Dial tone.

Hallden was fuming because he hated for people to hang up the phone before he did.

Emad returned to his seat and motion for his team to lean in by waving his hand at them.

"What is it now boss?" Juka said as he leaned in.

"Check this we get one days rest and then we have to be at Langley the next morning."

"Not counting today right." Denise asked.

"Yes not counting today. So get some rest, hit the bank, have a fun day because we'll be hunting the next day." Emad answered.

"Cool, I can finally get some workout done." Derrick said flexing his muscle as if he had a dumbbell doing curls.

"Why doesn't everyone come by my house for a barbeque?" Juka said.

"You know I have a big family man they can eat you out of a house and a home." Emad said.

"I haven't seen the kids in a while it'll be fun."

"Those bad behind kids, shoot you should be glad." Denise said laughing.

"Hey you're talking about my family now."

Everyone busted out into laughter. Soon the jet will land and the joint task force that took out a part of the worst drug dealing gang will go their separate way. At least some of them will. Darkghost still have one more threat to America to take out. And friend or not the problem will be solved.

CHAPTER SIXTEEN

Minnesota climate today seemed quite warm, around 72 degrees. The cabin in which the Becker's were held up in had shutters that banged loudly against the outer wall. There was no movement inside as if everyone was scared that they might be seen.

Peter Becker hired former military men to protect his daughter and himself. At least that's what he thought. One stayed inside with the Becker's and one on the front porch and one out back. The other two roamed the perimeter keeping an eye out for anyone or anything that might want to creep up and attack with surprise. All of them were strapped with automated weapons and enough ammunition to handle any intruders. Even military personnel.

Kata and his crew have been together for five years and spent time together in the military in different armed forces. Captain Woodear trained his men in the elite unit of special ops soldiers to out think your opponent with your mind and never stop until they are dead. Two men heard that message loud and clear.

"I hate this." Peter said pulling back the curtains and looking out the window in the front room.

"I know dad but this is something we have to do." Samantha replied.

"Something has happened to Jay..." Peter paused and rubbed his rough beard since he haven't shaved in two days and then turn around to look at Samantha then he continued "...he hasn't answered his phone or called me back since this morning..." Shaking his head Peter then continued "...and Valentin hasn't returned my calls either. What the hell is going on?" Peter asked rhetorically.

"Dad stop worrying and come sit next to me..." Samantha said and waved her hand and patted the cushion of the old couch next to her. When Peter sat down, Samantha continued "...we don't know actually what happened to them or if anything has happened to them. Right now all we know is that Uncle Jay and Uncle Valentin haven't called you back and..."

"Wait a minute you get kidnapped and Jay and Valentin disappear and you're trying to tell me that this is a coincidence." Peter said cutting Samantha off.

"I don't know dad, I mean it is kind of fishy but look at us now we're in hiding with armed men." Samantha said pointing toward the next room but didn't know that the armed man her father had hired was standing in the doorway.

"Excuse me Mr. Becker our arrangements for our next location has been confirmed." Kata said.

"Thank you we'll be ready when the time comes." Peter replied to his hired help and then looked at Samantha and said "...let just drop this conversation and stop assuming that nothing has happened to them. We both know they would have called by now and me taking this type of precaution is warranted."

"I guess you're right dad."

"You guess?"

"No, you're right. Where are we going next?" Samantha asked.

"First we're going to Texas and then our final location is Colombia. I have an associate there that can help us out." Peter Becker answered.

"Which one Texas or Colombia?"

"Colombia."

Kata covered his earpiece to listen to what his cohorts had to say.

"I read you loud and clear. I'm on my way."

"Is there a problem?" Samantha asked.

"Nothing I can't handle..." Kata snapped back at Samantha. "...just sit tight and I'll be back in a flash."

Kata walked out onto the raggedy porch where one of his men was standing.

"Keep your eyes open I think we may have company."

"My eyes are always open." Gorilla Red responded.

The broken down house the Becker's took refuge in was surrounded by dense trees and being that it was summertime foliage was thick. Kata looked up ahead as he walked off the porch and saw one of his men waving his hand for him to come over to where he was.

"About 100 yards south through there I saw two men hanging out." Wallace said.

"Take me to them…" Kata said looking at Wallace and then looking towards Sean he said "…stay here."

After about six minutes Kata and Wallace came upon a big red pine tree and hid behind it. Wallace handed Kata the binoculars as they knelt down.

"What do you think Kata?"

"I think you should go get Red and have Star on high alert…" Kata paused a second and as Wallace was about to leave Kata reached out and grab his arm and said "…double time it and alert the Becker's we may have to leave at once and bring back some rope and duct tape…" Kata eyed Black and then said "…do you read me?"

"Yes sir I'm on it." Wallace responded.

Kata stayed behind and kept the binoculars trained on the two men and surveyed the area looking for any other surprises.

Running fast through woods, Wallace ran up to Gorilla Red and asked "Where is Star?"

"He's inside with the Becker's. Why?"

"We have some visitors about a hundred yards that way. Kata want you and me to come back so we can handle the situation."

"Star I need you to come out to the porch." Red said into his walkie talkie.

"On my way." Star responded.

"What's up?" Star asked as he came out on the porch.

Wallace motioned Star off the porch and said "You two have to stay here while me and Red go handle a problem out in the woods. Kata's orders." Wallace said in a low voice but not whispering.

"No problem." Sean said.

"Star get the Becker's ready just in case we have to leave in a rush."

Star walked back onto the porch and into the house. Once inside he made the Becker's aware of what's going on and had them pack. Blue Star took his post inside with Peter and Samantha Becker and Sean roamed around the cabin, while Gorilla Red and Wallace returned to where Kata was waiting.

93

"What we're going to do is surround them. As far as I can see they're here by themselves. Red you come in from the left and Black you from the right..." Kata paused and looked up at the sky and then continued "...I want to capture them and see if we can get some information as to why they are here..." while pointing at his shoulder Kata continued "...shoulder wounds and no head shots Red."

"Damn." Red snapped.

With a pat on their backs Red and Wallace were on their way. The two FBI agents were not on point and didn't know they were being watched. When they found out it was too late. Before either one of them could pull his weapon from its holster, Red and Wallace had shot both of them in both shoulders.

Kata walked up to them and all three men help the agents off the ground.

"Take them inside their tents." Kata ordered.

Once inside the agents hands were bonded and their mouths duct tapped. The three men walked back outside.

"Red you stay in here with me and Wallace you clean up outside and keep watch."

Kata and Red return to the tent and Kata started the interrogation.

"What agency are you guys from?"

The bigger agent just stared at Kata like he wasn't there and wouldn't answer him but the smaller of the two did have something to say.

"We're agents from the b..."

"What are you saying?" The bigger one said cutting the smaller one off.

"Listen Pat he's going to kill us anyway but at least if we cooperate maybe he would give my family a message..." and then the smaller one looked at Kata and said "...if I tell you what you want to know will you at least do that for me?"

"I tell you this if you tell me what I want to know I'll kill you fast and let you leave a message for your agency, but if you don't I'll let the animals eat your remains and I promise you will have a slow painful death." Kata paused to let what he said marinate for a second and then he continued "...so what's it going to be, curtain number one, the fast death or curtain number two, the slow death?" Kata said with a smirk on his face.

"Ask your questions." The smaller agent said.

"No, you can't we took an oath." Special Agent Pat Garret said.

"You get the slow death." Kata said and slapped Special Agent Pat in the face and shot him in the knee and then he continued with his questioning "...now where was I, oh yea I assume you're from the FBI, but what I need to know is how long do we have before your back-up comes?"

"Yes you're right about that and you have 20 to 30 minutes before they get here. Now can you write down a note for me and mail it to my family." Agent Remington said.

"Hold your horses we have time for two more question. In what direction are they coming and how many?"

"East and Northwest. About ten agents from both directions. Now will you write my note for me?"

"Sure where's the paper and pen?"

Agent Karl Remington pointed over to his knapsack and Kata retrieved the pen and paper from it. Remington spoke clearly and quickly and Kata wrote just as fast. When they were done Kata shot Remington in his head and ordered Red to cut Special Agent Pat Garret heart out of his chest.

Red quickly walked over to Agent Garret and pushed him to the floor and tapes his mouth and then began to cut his heart out while he was still alive.

Both men rushed out the tent and ran through the woods along with Wallace heading towards the Becker's house on the other side.

Kata walked through the door and had a talked with the Becker's.

"We have to all leave at once."

"Is everything ready for us in Texas?" Peter asked.

"Yes it is, we have to leave right now let's go." Kata said with urgency in his voice and then he continued talking to his team "...do as we plan and set the timer for an hour from now."

Within minutes everyone was in their vehicles and traveling away from Minnesota and onto Texas.

CHAPTER SEVENTEEN

<u>*Hulseman Street- South Philadelphia, Sunday, June 29*</u>th

We really need this day of rest before we hunt down the final piece of the Book Brothers. This one won't be as easy as the other two not saying that the mission we perform earlier were by far easy.

Jeung Hyong-Kim thought he could hide in his native country and be protected by the forest that surrounded his compound. His tunnels help us with his demise.

Now let us briefly discuss Mr. Valentin Andreev. His wife tries to have him assassinated. His cousin Gregori had one of his best friend's daughter kidnapped in the attempt to break up the bond the Book Brothers had because of jealousy. Why didn't he just shut shop down? So greed was his demise.

With Valentin's death Ivan can run the family business and do fair business with the United States.

<u>*5:23am*</u>

As I said before my home office is my sanctuary. Veronica is getting a bit tired of my business schedule and our children miss their dad greatly.

"What's that I smell?" Veronica said as she reached in for a kiss on Emad's cheek.

"Only my famous chocolate chip pancakes…" Emad replied and turned to return a kiss back to Veronica but on her lips and then sighed before he continued "...I'm also making homefries, sausages, beef bacon, and omelets to order..." Emad said pointing at each item.

"Wow you should be home more often."

"Not finished. Check this babe; over there I got my oranges out for freshly squeeze orange juice."

"Damn baby the kids are going to be happy and mommy is happy too..." Veronica gave Emad a long wet kiss and then said "...and mommy is going to show daddy just how happy she is tonight."

"Shoot with this kind of treatment I should do this more often."

Both Emad and Veronica laughed out loud.

"I wonder who will come downstairs first." Veronica said.

"My bet is on Tre'. You know that boy can eat." Emad suggested.

"Guess whose home and guess who's coming next week?" Veronica asked.

"Evan!"

"No, Askia and Shafiq and my mom next weekend."

"Mother Cruz huh. Ok then in that case..."

Before Emad could finish his thought Askia came into the kitchen. This also saved him from saying something he would later regret.

"What up Pops?" Askia said walking towards Emad and gave him a handshake with hug and a kiss on the cheek.

"Hey son how yer doing?" Emad replied then took his son's hand as they embraced.

"I'm good. Need some help with breakfast?" Askia said while he was walking over to Veronica to give her a hug and kiss.

"Yes you can start the sausages. They're over there on the island." Emad said pointing to his right.

"Should I put the oven on three hundred and fifty degrees?"

"No, three hundred is good enough."

"Well is there anything I can do Mr. Chef?" Veronica asked.

"Okay mom, dad and I can handle it."

"I wasn't talking to you but I'll let you guys do y'all thing and get out the way."

"Thanks mom this give me a chance to talk to Pop about something." Askia said.

Soon as Veronica left the kitchen, the noise of footsteps stomping down the stairs filled the air. The chance of Askia having father and son bonding time went out the window.

"Daddy, daddy, daddy." Elaine, Tre'shawn, and Brooklan said as they ran towards Emad and nearly knock him down.

"Hey my babies. Whoooa, I miss y'all too but I'm cooking and if you want to help wash your hands if you haven't already, brush your teeth and when you do that then you can come back and help. Ok."

"Yes but daddy I have something for you." Elaine said.

"I do too can I show mine first." Tre'shawn said.

"Do as I ask and after breakfast y'all can show me at the same time."

"Come on y'all so we can come back and help and no fighting." Brooklan astonished.

"Man now I know why I moved to New York. No one can ever get any sleep around here." Shafiq said.

"And good morning to you too Fiq." Askia said.

"I'm sorry good morning Pop. What's up ugly?"

"Ugly, we have the same face."

"Good morning son. Boy do I miss all of this. How long are you two here for?" Emad asked.

"I'm here for the week." Shafiq said.

"I'm leaving in the morning." Askia replied.

"Well Juka is having a barbecue later and then I'm leaving on a business trip. Are you two coming?" Emad asked.

"Yes sir."

"I'll be there. We haven't seen Juka in a long time." Askia said looking at Shafiq.

"We need to talk individually later." Emad commanded.

"Around what time because I'm going to see Veronica around 2." Shafiq replied.

"After the twins show me their gifts you and I can talk." Emad said to Shafiq.

"Anytime Pop I already told you I needed to speak to you." Askia reminded Emad.

"Good lets finish cooking so we can get this day rolling."

The twins wrestled down the stairs to be first to the kitchen, with Brooklan as their mediator. Even Ashantia and Taavetti were in tow.

As you can see my home life can be a bit much but I won't trade it for nothing.

Breakfast went by smoothly and so did my talks with my older twin boys. Next, we got ready for Juka's barbecue. This day has been fun and relaxing considering where I've been the last two weeks.

When the evening was over I had to get the family back home and have a meeting with my team about the next part of our mission which by the way we dubbed "Operation America First".

Veronica wasn't too happy about this but I'll make it up to her tonight.

Emad's Home Office

I had some emails I needed to check before we could start our briefing. Even though I freelance there was an email from yourboss@ FBI.org. This is Mitchel's way of control.

"Well from the email I receive from Mitchel we are still a go for tomorrow." Emad said.

"What time are we leaving and where are we leaving from." Denise asked.

"The same place as usual and we are out at oh five hundred hours…" Emad paused and look around the room to make sure everyone was on the same page and then he continued "…get home and get some sleep because we don't come back home until we get this one."

"Are we still doing the Va Beach thing with Denny's friend?" Derrick asked.

Emad looked over at Denise.

"Denny do think your friend will have a problem with us saving only her life and not her father's?" Emad asked.

"How would you feel if someone gave you that same ultimatum? Of course she'll be upset but she will have to make that decision when the time comes." Denise replied.

"I see your point but you know how this outfit runs. No one is above our goal and I told you that when you started with me…" Emad paused and looked everyone in the eyes and then he continued "…I told all of you this before you started with me that no one is above America's interest and no one will get in my way of protecting that interest. Right or wrong?"

Head nods in agreement from all of Darkghost all in unison.

"Well then let's get back on track and complete this mission." Emad said.

Just when Emad had finished speaking those words there was a knock on his outside office door.

"Come in." Emad answered.

"Hello everyone."

"All of you remember Agent Longton?" Emad asked.

"Yes I remember him that's not the question that comes to my mind. It's why you are here Agent Longton?" Juka questioned.

"I asked him to come and I know I didn't ask you guys about this but I figured we can use all the help we can get on this one being that this Peter Becker guy is using ex-military personnel for his protection."

"What we going up against our own people and we're using someone we barely even know? You can't be serious Eli?" Denise said.

"How do the saying go 'serious as a heart attack' listen guys Agent Longton is a good agent and we worked good together in Iraq so it was obviously the best decision since we do need help on this one..." Emad said and then open his desk draw and pulled out some folders and then said "...here is the mission dossier read them tonight and be prepared for tomorrows mission. Sleep well everyone."

"Wait, what's your first name, cause I'm not gonna just call you Agent Longton?" Juka asked.

"It's Marcus." Agent Longton answered.

"Marcus, I'm Juka that's Derrick and the mean one is Denise. She takes some getting used to but she'll come around soon give her some time."

Special Agent Marcus S. Longton graduated magna cum laude from Princeton University. He also graduated third of his class at the academy. Very smart with common sense and resilience. He won't give up until the fight is done. The qualities Emad look for when choosing a new member of Darkghost.

Agent Longton worked a high profile case in which he profiled a serial killer. The serial killer killed men with the last name that started with an "R". And after two weeks of hunting the killer, the FBI was able to capture the serial killer they dubbed James "the Name" Franklen.

Agent Longton was promoted to Special Agent because of his efforts in the capture and prosecution of the most sought after criminal in the metro Montgomery, Alabama area has seen to date.

Once the meeting was over Emad turned his attention to his wife. Emad and Veronica both needed this time and Veronica made the most of their time.

She had previously brought a sexy teddy but hadn't had the chance to wear it for Emad. Veronica strolled out the bathroom looking and smelling good. Her olive skin glowed. Hair flowing down her back.

Emad tried to be cool and stay put on the bed until Veronica made her way to him. Once Veronica reached the bed Emad grabbed arm gently and pulled her onto the bed. He rubbed the side of her face up to her hair and then pulled her hair to open her neck for a kiss. Veronica responded with moans of pleasure and then pushed Emad onto his back. Veronica nibbled on her husband's nipples and then grabbed his penis, which had already gained an erection. She proceeded to give Emad oral pleasure while she twisted her body until she was sitting on his chest. Emad pulled Veronica by the waist so that her buttocks were buried into his face. This went on for the next five minutes. Veronica hopped up and then squatted on Emad's lap. Once Emad was inside her she let out a loud moan and then they made passionate love all night long.

Because he hadn't spent quality time with Veronica, Emad turned his home and cell phone off and Darkghost didn't have the full Intel they wanted to pursue Peter and Samantha Becker because of this action. All they had was the location of their last sighting. Nor did they know that the men that were protecting them had killed two FBI agents and had fled Middle River. Darkghost will pursue their prey nonetheless, intel or not.

4:46am

Darkghost met at their usual clandestine place. Once all members had assembled, they loaded into the Falcon X-15 and made haste towards Minnesota.

The Becker's had a 6 hour jump but they were traveling by vehicle and Darkghost had a jet at their disposal.

When they arrived at the FBI surveillance camp ninety-eight yards outside of the Becker's hideout. Emad gave the reins to Marcus. The addition of ex-FBI Special Agent Marcus S. Longton to Darkghost paid off immediately. Now they have a detective on the payroll.

"From what I discern and the violence here, I can pretty much say this is the work of some mercenaries, the Becker's military men did this." Marcus said.

"Ex-military men." Juka corrected.

"They cut out this agent's heart." Derrick added.

"Denny and Derrick recon 100 yards radius and make it fast." Emad commanded.

"On it." Denny said.

Derrick gave a head nod of confirmation.

"We need to move quickly these military, excuse me ex-military…" Marcus said looking at Juka after he corrected himself and then he continued "…will stop at nothing. The Peter Becker must be paying them a hell of a lot of money." Marcus said.

"A lot more we're getting paid to kill them all." Emad replied.

"But we doing our job for the country we love and they're doing it for the love of money." Juka added.

"Eli you guys need to get over here now." Denny said over the radio.

"What's your twenty?" Emad asked.

"Ninety-eight yards north."

"On the way."

Emad, Derrick, and Marcus ran out the tent and headed north. When they got to Denny's location they could now see a smoldering shell of a house as if it has been blown up with C4 or someone blew the propane gas tank outside.

"These big red pine made it hard for us to see the smoke when we came up and the smoke we did smell was masked perfectly by the Becker's protection with the fire they started at the campsite. They even contained the campfire so it will burn then smolder. I'm going to have fun hunting these guys." Emad said with a grin and then paused before he spoke again "…Derrick and Juka take the left side of the cabin and head around back. Denny and Marcus y'all take the right. Move." Emad ordered.

Darkghost converge on the smoldering shack bent over with weapons eye level and everyone did as Emad had ordered.

"Eli I have two sets of tire marks over here and they looked to be going southwest through there." Denny said.

"Juka go to the Humvee and get the scanner so we can find out what vehicle these tire tracks match." Emad ordered.

After scanning the tire tracks, Darkghost knew what kind of vehicles they were hunting.

"Everyone back to the Humvee. Move!" Emad ordered angrily.

All at once Emad realize they might be far behind the Becker's and time is of the essence right now. Darkghost ran expeditiously towards the FBI campsite. Even though the woods were thick with foliage, Darkghost made it back to the campsite within three minutes.

"Derrick you drive and I need you to do your thing. Juka check what could possibly be their next destination and then plot a course that will intersect them." Emad ordered.

"By the look of both smolders I'll say we're about six to seven hours behind." Marcus added.

"Ok that's good to know it cuts a lot of time down from me trying to guess where they might be." Juka said.

Silence fills the Humvee for a while and the intensity was thick in the air. No one seems nervous, just anxious to catch the bad guys.

"I got it from what we assume to be the time they left and the direction they were going when they left, I'll say they are going towards Texas. Right now they might be in South Dakota. Depending on if they went around and started going east or straightening out west and then we're talking about the west coast but if they kept going south I would say they going to Texas." Juka advised.

"I say south. They're heading for the border to hide in Mexico. What do you think Eli?" Denny asked.

"Well Marcus here is the criminal profiler and detective but my bet is south." Emad suggested.

"Definitely south." Marcus added.

"Does anyone want my opinion?" Derrick asked.

"No, just drive." Denny joked.

"Ok then plotting a course that will get us to Texas quicker than the normal course, one might take." Juka stated.

Juka tapped on his laptop and after a few hits.

"Bingo, take interstate thirty-five south." Juka ordered.

"If I was them I would stay off the main roads and that will slow them down and that will be their downfall. Juka how far are we to I-35." Emad said.

"A half an hour away."

"Derrick we need to be on that interstate within fifteen minutes." Emad commanded.

"I'm shooting for ten." Derrick replied and then pressed hard down on the gas pedal.

The Humvee engine roared and Darkghost was coasting at one hundred miles per hour within twenty seconds.

"Going at the rate of speed we're going, our eta to Texas is oh one-hundred hours tomorrow." Juka proclaimed.

CHAPTER EIGHTEEN

Racing to beat the Becker's to Texas, Emad called in a favor from his old buddy; he knew when he was stationed down in Corpus Christi.

"Hello."
"Jimmy!" Emad said.
"Hello."
"Jimbo its Eli."
"Eli, man how ya been?" James Moore asked.
"I'm good and you?"
"I'm great." James answered.
"Look, Jimbo I don't mean to be short but I'm in a rush and need a favor. Do I have any credits down there?" Emad asked.
"Sure, what can I do for you?"
"Listen, I'm looking for two Suburban's traveling together..." Emad paused to get his thoughts together so that he'll be very precise about his description of the Becker's and their entourage and then he continued "... most likely the SUV is black. There will be one woman, an older gentlemen and men that probably look like mercenary. From the tire tracks at the sight our surveillance team was watching. It's probably a four to five combat man team. Can you help me with this?" Emad asked Jimmy.
"I'm on it. Give me an half an hour to get things up and running and then I'll get back in touch with you."
"Thanks bro. I'll call you back in forty-five. Peace."
"Peace." Jimmy replied.

When Darkghost cross the borders into Missouri, Emad called Jimmy back and got the answer he wanted. Jimmy set up a network of men and women to do surveillance across the Oklahoma and Texas border. If or when the Becker's and their entourage enter Texas they will be watched and not even know it. Not only did Jimmy cover the main roads but he mostly covered the back roads.

While traveling to their destination, a light bulb went off in Peter Becker's head. He remembered that one of his old associate owned a private airplane strip just across the Oklahoma border into Texas. Peter had given a discount on a big drug package in lieu that if one day he needed a favor the associate would repay. That day has come. Now back to the light bulb.

Peter wanted repayment now. He thought about flying into San Antonio once he got into Texas and then onto Colombia. The gentleman in Colombia Peter has asked for help has mastered the art of not being found and therefore eluded capture from American authorities. Peter wants to learn this art form, because he knows in order to run and not be found, he must master this same art form.

Darkghost has been chasing the Book Brothers and fatigue is starting to set in. Emad know if he slow down the Becker's will get away and not pay the ultimate price for being on the wrong side of the law.

Denise wanted so badly for her friend she went to school with to accept Emad offer and live. But something in her made her believe that Samantha will fight for her father and pay the same price as he will.

The Humvee hummed down the interstate at a high rate of speed. The FBI had given Darkghost a Blue light to put on the dashboard so the state and local police wouldn't bother them as they pursued their prey.

Emad and the rest of Darkghost even the new member viewed this chase sort of as a game. And none of them care for losing this game.

After speaking with his associate Peter directed the driver of his Suburban to the small airstrip just over the border about 10 miles into Texas.

"How long will it take for us to get to our destination dad?"

"Well the G4 is fueled up and the pilot is waiting for us, so we'll be in the air about fifteen minutes after reaching the airstrip."

"And then we'll be heading towards San Antonio or Colombia?" Samantha asked.

"First we make a pit stop in San Antonio and then onto Colombia." Peter replied.

The Becker's were spotted by one of Jimmy's lookout. Jimmy call Emad immediately.

"Go ahead Jimmy what's up?" Emad said as he answered his phone.

"How far out are you from the border?" Jimmy asked Emad.

"Twenty-five maybe thirty minutes."

"Get your ass to the Whitetail Airport. Its west of Vernon. Are you past I-44?"

"No."

"Your friends are heading towards the airport. I think they're flying out." Jimmy speculated.

Emad covered the receiver of the phone and looked over to Derrick.

"Forty-four coming up Derrick take forty-four south and step on it we're not far behind."

"Jimmy is you still there?"

"Yea go ahead."

"Can you stall them?"

"I'll tell my people to throw a roadblock up but don't detain. How that sound?"

"My man Jimbo thanks. I owe you one."

"Man it's my pleasure. Happy hunting brother."

Click.

"It looks like the Becker's are trying to fly out of Texas and most likely they'll be heading south of course." Emad said to his team.

"What's the plan boss?" Juka asked.

"Jimmy going to try and stall them so we can catch up and do our thing. If he can't and they take to the sky we gonna need their flight plans." Emad explained to the team.

"Just in case we don't get there in time. Do you think it will be wise to get the X-15 down here to that airport so we can keep close behind?" Denise asked.

"Yes and no. If the Falcon get there before they arrive it could spook them and then we'll be chasing them farther into Texas. That's the no.

But if it get there just after they leave then it'll be good for us." Emad answered.

"What if we have the Falcon come into Wichita, which isn't far from Vernon? How fast can we get the Falcon down here?" Marcus asked.

"You know what, that's a great ideal. Juka get Mitchel Hallden's assistant Stewart on the phone and have him to get authorization for the Falcon to be sent down to Wichita Airport. Tell him we need it at our disposal and no question asked." Emad ordered.

"I'm on it boss." Juka complied.

Stewart wasted no time in trying to get the approval from Mitchel to send the stealth helicopter down to Wichita Falls Airport for Darkghost's disposal.

"What's up Stewart?" Juka answered his phone.

"The X-15 will be down there in about forty minutes. That's the best I can do. Is that good enough?" Stewart questioned.

"It's going to have to be thanks."

"No problem, you guys just do what you do best and that will show your gratitude. Good hunting."

Click.

"Forty minutes. That's the best he could do Eli." Juka proclaimed.

"Alright, then we have to get to Wichita and wait." Emad sighed.

James Moore's people tried to stall the Becker's and their entourage for about a half an hour with no success. But they were able slow them down some and give Darkghost about twenty minutes of relief.

Peter, Samantha, and their mercenary protection team parked their Suburban's on the tarmac and exited the vehicles with quick efficiency. The Becker's didn't pack much luggage, so they were able to get across the tarmac and onto the jet expeditiously.

As promised the G4 jet was fueled. The pilot and his navigator had already done the preflight inspections, checked NOTAMs and the weather. The pilot was told to be extra careful and fly as high as possible.

"My name is Jack Grum, I'm your pilot."

"Take off now!" Peter scolded the pilot.

"As soon as you guys are all buckled up we can take off." Jack snapped back.

"Just do as I say!" Peter shouted.

"You're the boss. David lets bypass the checklist and prepare for takeoff. Not far to Pleasanton." Jack the pilot ordered his navigator.

"Pleasanton?" Peter asked bewildered.

"San Antonio is a military town especially Air Force and Army. Whoever flies into that city have to get clearance from the military. Which mean manifestos for everyone and thing that comes in. And if you don't have the proper paperwork, security will detain. Do you want that?" Jack said.

"No, fly us into Pleasanton."

Jack and David both flipped switches. The G4 engine roared with a putter but the sound to Peter was sweet. He knew this meant they would be in the air in a matter of seconds. "Almost there" Peter thought to himself.

The jet slowly crawled up the runway trying to gain momentum for flight. Kata looked out the window and saw a SUV speeding up behind and then multiple bullets ricocheted off the runway. But no sound of gunshots, which meant whoever was shooting at the G4 jet were using silencers.

"Aim for the wheels." Emad commanded.

"I'll try for the engine." Denise remarked as she hanged out the window firing at the right wing of the G4.

"Hurry up they are gaining on us." Kata said to the pilot.

Jack pulled on the throttle and increased his speed. The nose of the G4 rose and then the jet took to the air. Peter let out a sigh of relief and sunk into his seat. Everyone looked exhausted. Kata advised everyone to take a nap, since they will be in the air for an hour and a half.

CHAPTER NINETEEN

Whitetail Airport

"Damn it, Derrick take us to the airport office. We need to find out their flight plans if they made any." Juka suggested.

"Good idea. Denny you go inside with Marcus and get the info and make it quick. We're short on time."

"Shall we use force if necessary?" Marcus asked.

"Use as much force as necessary." Emad replied.

The office to the airport was located on the far northeast side of the runway. The building looked shabby with the blinds shut tight. Music blared loudly of rock and roll. Inside the office sat a short petite young lady in front of a computer, speed typing. Sitting across from her was a medium built man smoking a cigar. Both individuals were oblivious to what just happened outside.

Headlights shined brightly through the cracks of the blinds. Sherman stood up and motioned for Susan to stop typing.

"Who the hell is this? Did someone make appointment for a flight tonight and you didn't tell me?" Sherman said frowning at Susan.

"No, I don't know who this could be."

The bell above the door to the office rang and Denise and Marcus walked through with smiles on both their faces. They both quickly swept the room with their eyes as to ascertain who or what is in the office.

"Hello my name is Freda Long and this is my husband Thomas. I notice a plane just took off. Is someone else here who can fly us to Arizona? To be exact Tempe, Arizona." Denise asked.

"Well I would but we're kind of busy right now, but..." Sherman responded.

"We don't have time for this..." Marcus interjected pulling out his .45 handgun and pointing it at Susan while looking at Sherman and then he continued "...listen we need the flight plans of that airplane that just took off and we need it immediately."

"Wa wa wait a second..." Sherman said holding up his hand and then he reached over to his desk and grabbed some papers and said "...they're going to Pleasanton here."

Sherman handed out the papers to Denise. Denise snatched the paperwork and briefly scanned the writings to make sure they were flight plans. Marcus followed her with his .45 trained on Sherman as they walked out the door just as quickly as they walked in.

"Juka here's the flight plans." Denise said while handing the flight plans.

"You have any problems?" Emad said in a low voice to Marcus.

"None, the gentleman inside was very cooperative when I put this in his secretary face." Marcus proclaimed showing Emad his pistol with a slight grin on his face.

"Okay Juka where are they going?" Derrick asked.

"San Antonio."

"Derrick get us to Wichita so we can intercept them in the X-15." Emad commanded.

"Denise do you think you can drive from here?" Derrick asked.

"Yeah, let's switch seats."

"Feeling a bit groggy boss." Derrick added.

"No problem you have driven a long way we need you rested. Denny step on it."

"Will do." Denise responded.

And just like that the Humvee spun out and Darkghost hit the road again in pursuit of the Becker's.

"Who the hell was that?" Peter's voice boomed and filled the airplane as he looked at Kata.

"It beats me. I know they weren't the cops." Kata replied.

"And how do you know that?" Samantha asked.

"If it was the cops they would have had more cars chasing and their lights would've been on."

"I tend to believe your right..." Peter paused rubbing his chin and then blurted out "...merks for the government."

"Yeah most likely an undercover group our government put together." Kata agreed.

"They will pursue us until they succeed in our capture." Samantha said.

"Or dead." Peter added.

During the ride into Wichita Falls Airport, Emad called Director Charles Conover to see if he could get authorization for Darkghost to bypass security and go straight to the tarmac where the Falcon X-15 is waiting.

Ring.

Ring.

"This is Eli go ahead Charles."

"We got you a pass. Airport security has a description of your Humvee and was told not to stop or try to detain you. And they were also told that you guys would be armed to the teeth. When you get to the airport, go to the South maintenance gate. You can get entry there to the tarmac. The Falcon will be waiting there too."

"Thanks Charley."

"Happy hunting."

Click.

"Denny we have the go ahead, follow the signs to the south maintenance gate. The Falcon will be there waiting for us." Emad instructed.

The Humvee tires screeched as it moved through the terminal. Denise laid on the horn as they passed parked taxis waiting for fares. The south gate came up fast and Denise had no trouble maneuvering the SUV around a moving car and turned into the gate and onto the tarmac. The Humvee shrieked to a halt.

"I got the gear." Marcus shouted.

"Everyone grab something and move." Emad added.

All five members reached into the back of the Humvee one by one and grab a piece of gear and ran across the tarmac and into the Falcon X-15.

"Take off, take off and make it fast. Head towards San Antonio." Derrick ordered the pilot.

"Set our heading towards San Antonio. Do you know where in San Antonio?" The pilot asked.

"Here's the flight plans." Juka said as he handed the paperwork over to Captain Woodard of the Air Force.

After looking over the flight plans thoroughly Captain Woodard smiled widely.

"Emad." Woodard called out.

"What's up Cap?" Emad answered.

"It's no way they are flying into San Antonio. Look at this right here..." Woodard pointed at a word on the flight plans and then continued "...Pleasanton Municipal Airport is not in San Antonio nor is Castroville Municipal Airport. Pleasanton about thirty-five to forty miles south of San Antonio and Castroville is about thirty miles west. This flight plan is misleading to the untrained eye..."

"Well you got a handle on it Cap let me get out of your way. Good job." Emad commended.

Pleasanton Municipal Airport-4:23am

"Mr. Becker we are starting our final approach."

"Thank you Jack."

"Alright gentlemen this is where we make our money. Be prepared for the worse from here on out. Stay alert. The Becker's and our survival depends on us being at our best. When we exit the plane I will take point, Red you're to my right, Wallace to the left, and Blue and Sean you two bring up the rear."

The G4 brakes activated and then the tires locked. Once the jet slowed, the pilot steered it off the runway and onto the tarmac. The side door open slowly and came to rest upon tarmac.

Kata was the first one out, followed by Wallace and then Gorilla Red. Next, Samantha with her father close behind. As ordered Blue and Sean brought up the rear.

Peter's connection had an all-black Hummer H2 limousine waiting just off the tarmac. Inside the limo were all the amenities that came with a stretch limousine of this size.

Expeditiously the group jogged towards the limo. Kata team was in their positions as ordered with weapons held across their bodies in the ready position. The entourage split up once they got to the limo. Kata took Peter by the arm and shoved him into the limo. Red grabbed Samantha and did the same. Everyone yelled 'go' to the driver.

Castroville Municipal Airport-4:22am

Emad didn't want to call ahead to either airport because the chase was exciting. And the job of catching Peter Becker and killing him was Darkghost job alone. From here on out Darkghost will ask for help only from the agency or the bureau.

"Eli get ready you have one minute until we land."

"I copy that Cap..." Emad said into the overhead microphone and then he looked at Derrick and continued *"...Derrick you're with me when we land. Everyone else stays put but when it's time to move be ready if they're here..."* Emad looked up and hit the overhead button to activate the microphone and said *"...Captain Woodard."*

"Go ahead Eli."

"Get as close as possible to the office."

"Already on it sir."

After several seconds the stealth helicopter jerked. Emad knew this meant the Falcon had landed. Derrick slid the side door open and he and Emad exited the X-15 and ran over to the office.

Derrick busted through the door first. Two men about average height were standing with their pistols drawn. Derrick quickly pulled his M16 rifle up and paned it from one man to the other.

Emad came up from behind and stood next to Derrick on his right side with one hand on his shoulder and the other on his sidearm still holstered.

"What do you want?" the man standing in front of Emad said.

"Information. We're with the United States government what branch is not of your concern. What is though is if you have given refuge to drug dealers we are chasing. Now my man is going to lower his weapon..." while Emad was talking he was tapping Derrick on his shoulder and then he continued talking to the men standing across from him "...all we want to know is if anyone has landed here anytime within the last hour."

After speaking Emad crossed his arms and waited for a response.

"No sir. Now you men just get on out of here before we start filling you up with lead. I know the law around these parts and if a man trespasses on your land we have a right to shoot 'em right between the eyes." The other man said.

"Sir before your finger pull on that trigger my man will have killed both of you so please don't test him because he's dying to kill someone. Thanks for the info but if I find out you're lying we'll be back and not to talk..." Emad looked over at Derrick and said "...move out."

Emad turned around and walked out the door. Derrick backed out steering the men down.

"We have to hurry and get to the next airport before we lose them." Emad expressed.

Interstate 37-4:34am

"Where are we going?" Peter asked the driver.

"I was ordered to bring you to San Antonio, where you will be safe until your departure tomorrow." Hector the driver answered with a Spanish accent.

"How long will it take us to get there?" Samantha asked.

"About twenty-five minutes. Relax you are safe now, I will take care of you."

"We'll relax when we're in Colombia." Peter interjected.

"Suit yourself."

Peter looked over at Samantha and said "We're almost there baby just take it easy."

"I'm fine dad don't worry about me."

The H2 was quiet the rest of the way to San Antonio: the first step to refuge.

Pleasanton Municipal Airport air space-4:36am

"Pleasanton Municipal this is foxtrot x-ray one fife do you copy."

"Go ahead foxtrot x-ray one fife."

"My name is Captain Woodard of the United States Air Force to whom am I speaking to?

"*Local air traffic controller Bart Vincent.*"

"*Mr. Vincent may I please speak to your watch supervisor.*"

"*Foxtrot x-ray one fife do you wish to declare an emergency?*"

"*No, I need to speak to your watch sup it's a matter of national security.*"

"*Standby.*"

Bart snapped his fingers and waved his hand at his watch supervisor Henry Knobs, which meant for his supervisor to hurry over fast. Bart briefly explained to Henry who was on the line.

"*Foxtrot x-ray one fife this is watch supervisor Henry Knobs go ahead.*"

"*Sorry for being brief but I'm requesting information on a G4 jet landing about a half an hour ago carry about seven people. This information is of national security please do not give me a hard time.*"

"*Yes what about them?*"

"*Exactly how long ago did they land? What are they driving and which direction did they travel? Over.*

"*As a matter of fact they landed about fifteen minutes ago. I don't know what they were driving or what direction they went. I can find out if you want.*"

"*Please if you can sir. We will be landing in five minutes a call will be coming in as we speak to clear all airspace for us and make a runway available.*"

"*I just got that call before you radio the tower. I was order to give you any and everything. Come in on runway five and I'll have that info before you hit the tarmac. Over.*"

"*Thanks Mr. Knobs your country owes you. Foxtrot x-ray one fife out.*"

The Falcon hovered over runway five. The side door slid open and five individual rope and Darkghost gear was thrown out. Each member of Darkghost descended from the helicopter.

Once on the runway everyone grab a piece of the gear and ran towards the tarmac where there was a black Suburban waiting.

Henry and two airport security guards was standing next to one of the Suburban's Mitchel had there for them.

"Is your name Emad?" Henry said to Derrick.

"No, that's him." Derrick responded pointing at Emad.

"Commander, I'm Henry Knobs. This is the information you ask for. Hope it help you guys out."

"Thanks Mr. Knobs." Emad replied.

San Antonio-5:05am

One third of the Book Brothers was running for his and his daughter lives. It seems like an eternity for them to get to San Antonio. Peter's lifeline had set up a refuge near Lincoln Park, so he and his daughter along with their entourage could lay low for a couple of days until they can get out of the states.

"My boss said you guys should wear the clothes he put in the closets and if you need anything just call this number and someone will be here to assist you." Hector instructed Peter and then handed him a note with numbers on it.

"Did he say how long it will be until we can get out?" Samantha asked.

"No, but you will be safe here. Call that number if you need anything and don't go outside with all these people…" Hector pointed around the room at everyone and then he continued "…you will only bring suspension…" Hector said looking at Peter as if Samantha didn't existed and then he continued "…I must go now adios."

Hector quickly walked out the door with a stone look on his face. Samantha shivered and felt the disrespect Hector had shown her and Peter her father had felt it too but they were in no position to act on that emotion. Had it been any other situation Samantha would had attack Hector and earned his respect or try like hell to beat it out of him.

"Sweetie go take a shower or bath and I'll go see what's for breakfast in frig." Peter kissed Samantha on the forehead as he dismissed her to the bathroom.

"Yeah I'm in dire need of a deep washing and from the smell of things we all do." Samantha snapped back with a smile.

The entourage settled in on the furniture looking wore out. Kata wasn't used to running; he and his team would've preferred to go head up with whoever was chasing them. Even if it meant fighting the law.

"Okay men look alive we been through way worse than this." Kata said.

"This running is for the birds Sarge." Wallace shot back.

"Listen this is what we have to do to keep them alive and get paid. This is the business we chose men so suck it up now."

"I'm with you Sarge." Gorilla Red interjected.

"Me too Sarge." Star added.

"I'm just saying I am tired of running that's all brothers." Wallace added.

"Let's get this money and whoever gets in our way of that, will pay with their life…" Kata paused for a second and then said "…Sean and Red you two got first watch, so go get cleaned up and grab some breakfast. The rest of us get some rest after breakfast." Kata ordered.

<u>5:15am</u>

Darkghost split into two teams. Juka and Denise were in the lead black Suburban and the second team followed in a white Suburban. The two teams communicated with one another through ear microphone, which looked like Bluetooth accessory for cell phones.

"Marcus, if we want to track someone in a big city like this one. How do we go about doing so without them finding out?" Juka asked.

"Short of putting the local or state police on alert, we can check the video footage from cameras on traffic lights, highway overpass, and satellites."

"Juka, can you hack into the state and local police database to pull up the footage we need."

"Can an eagle fly? I'm on it Eli give me a couple of minutes."

"My man. In the meantime Marcus we need two rooms near this interstate. I have to call Hallden."

The Suburban Darkghost got from Mitchel was buzzing with activity. Marcus was talking to a lady at the front desk of a small motel two exits away. Juka had finally hacked into the database of both the state and local police. Emad loathe giving Mitchel updates on his team progress but that's the only way the bureau will use Darkghost in this fight against America's criminals.

"Take the next left Denny and the motel is on the right." Marcus said.

"I'm ready Eli whenever you are."

"Good job. We'll wait until we get into the room."

Within minutes Darkghost had pulled into the motel's parking lot, two cars deep.

"I feel like I'm worthless. Hey I'll get the keys, whew, this is too much excitement." Derrick jested.

"Just go get the room cards knucklehead." Denise joked.

"I'm going, I'm going."

Inside Motel Royale office smelled of cigarettes. The walls were stained with nicotine. Wallpaper barely hung onto the walls and the carpet had missing fibers so that it looked like bald spots on the floor. A skinny kid worked the desk. Derrick checked the team in and got out of the office as fast as he could.

Once inside the room Emad and Juka scanned the cameras on interstate thirty-seven. Watch supervisor Henry of the air traffic controller gave a good description of the limo, along with the time the Becker's and their entourage landed and left the airport. Henry information was spot on, down to the direction they went into.

"From the info Henry gathered the Becker's landed at oh four twenty-five hours. Giving them time to get to their vehicle and getting into San Antonio about twenty minutes before we even hit the interstate." Emad explained.

"So I'll rewind the footage back to about oh four forty."

"Stop right there!" Emad said loudly.

"Is that the limo?" Derrick asked.

"Can you zoom in close? Need to try to see inside the limo or get the license plate number." Emad questioned.

"Yes and give me a second annnd gotcha. Boy am I good." Juka boasted.

"Yes, you are my young padawan student." Derrick commented.

"Now get a close up of their plates and let's see who the limo is registered to..." Emad stood up and walked over to the window and cracked the mini blind and peeked out the window, while still looking out the window Emad continued "...Denny get on the phone with the MVC in Austin. Ask to speak with a lady named Camille Rogers. She's the site supervisor..." and then Emad walked over to the table "...give her this access code..." Emad wrote down some numbers on a notepad courtesy of the motel management and handed it to Denise and then continued "...and she'll give you any information we need on any vehicle in the United States that's registered. Before you hang up with her, tell her I said hello and thanks."

"No problem." Denise replied.

"Eli we got them." Juka said.

"Well at least the vicinity they're in." Marcus added.

"What's the vicinity?" Emad asked.

"Jefferson Heights." Juka replied.

"Good work gentlemen. Juka, find out if there's any abandoned homes or homes up for sale."

"I'm on it."

"Why abandoned or homes for sale?" Marcus asked.

"The paperwork for a house sold might not be downloaded into the system if it was just sold. Let's say yesterday. And if the house is abandoned that could be great for hiding out if it's in a secluded spot." Emad explained.

"On the site I'm on gives me a list of homes on the market in Jefferson Heights. Can you pass me those blank cds?" Juka asked Marcus.

"Where?"

"Right behind you in that bag over there…" Juka said pointing to his right and then he continued "…I need to save this list to a cd so I can print it out at the front desk. Motels usually have computers with printers." Juka said with sarcasm in his tone but smiled as if he was joking.

"Here you go."

"Thanks. Soon as this is finished, I'll do the abandoned homes list and then go down to the front desk."

"Ms. Rogers sends her love…" Denise cut in on the conversation and then continued "…okay the black H2 with Texas tags Zulu Lima Zero Four Seven Niner is registered to the Gomez Limousine Services, owned by a Mr. Juan Gomez. The location of the business is on the other side of San Antonio near Monticello Park. I have the address here."

"Listen up everyone, Derrick, Marcus and I, will be going to the Monticello Park section to find this Gomez Limo Services. Juka stay here and keep working on the housing list." Emad ordered.

"Denny I expect dinner to be ready by the time we get back." Derrick joked.

"Anything you say sir." Juka said with hint of sarcasm.

"Whatever don't be cowboys just because we're in Texas." Emad added.

"I'll drive this time. I already GPS'd the Park." Marcus said.

Monticello Park

Gomez Limousine Services was located near the business district of Monticello Park section of the city. Marcus was having a hard time finding a place to park the Suburban. After riding around in circles, a spot opened about three city blocks east of the limo service. Walking in a fast pace, the three man team tried to blend in with the rest of pedestrians. All three men had concealed handguns under their left arm. Darkghost stood outside of the building to get a feeling of the area surrounding the office. Emad didn't want to seem suspicious so after one minute had past he walked through the door and went straight to the receptionist.

"Hello my name is Eli and if it's possible may I speak to your boss."

"May I ask what's does it concern?" Mary Spencer asked.

"We go way back and since I was in town I thought maybe I'll surprise him with a visit." Emad replied.

"Well if you want to have a seat you can wait."

"So he's in his office now?"

"Yes he is."

"Thanks. Marcus you get her."

Within an instance Mary Spencer was sitting at her desk with a big gun pointed at her. She froze like a deer in headlights.

"Move." Emad ordered Derrick.

Derrick opened the door quickly with one gun in his right hand. Emad right on his heels with both hands on his gun high by his head. Coming through the door both men aimed their pistol at the three men sitting in the office.

"Okay listen up, we are only here for information. Make this hard and people will die. Starting with him." Emad said pointing his .45 at the gentleman sitting in front of Mr. Gomez to his left.

"What type of information are you talking about, Mr.?" Mr. Gomez responded.

"You rented out a black H2 Hummer limousine. It picked up seven people at the Pleasanton Airport and dropped them off in the Jefferson Heights section of this city. What is the exact address of the drop-off?" Emad asked.

"I can't give you that information."

Emad put two bullets into the back of the man's head; he had his .45 aimed towards. Mr. Gomez gasped and stood up in front of his desk.

"Next it'll be the receptionist and then so on and so on, do you get my drift Mr. Gomez."

"You're killing me sir. You don't understand if I give you this information he will kill me worse than what you will."

"And how do you know how I'm going to kill you. Oh, just because I have this gun in my hand you assume this is the way you'll die if you don't give me what I want. That's a bad assumption Mr. Gomez..." Emad paused and walked around the desk and sat down on the edge to Gomez's left. Emad leaned in to whisper into Juan's ear "...if you give me what I want, I can put you into witness protection."

"They will find me."

"Derrick." Emad said.

"Nooo!" Juan shouted.

Derrick tapped the neck of the man sitting in front of him with two bullets.

"Okay, okay deal. All I know is the street and that's the truth. Canton Street and that's all I know." Gomez said leaned over with his hands on his head.

Emad jumped up and shot Juan Gomez in his face and when Mary started to run towards her boss, Marcus shot her in her back, sending her flying into the office desk.

"Move out." Emad ordered.

Jefferson Heights

On the way back to the motel Emad called Juka to give him the info he abstracted from Juan Gomez. Motel Royale wasn't too far from Jefferson Heights and when Emad and his two teammates returned from Gomez Limo Services they started to put together a plan of how to go about locating and killing the Becker's and their entourage.

"First thing first, Juka did you locate the house." Emad said.

"I'm on that Eli. It took me some time to patch through to the satellite to get good look at the street live. When I get that you'll be the first to know. But I did locate three empty houses on that street. Here's the list." Juka answered and handed Emad a sheet of lined paper with addresses on it.

"Thanks, while we wait for the other info, Denny recon Canton Street." Emad ordered.

"What am I looking for?"

"Any pertinent information regarding which one of these houses…" Emad handed the list to Denny and then continued "…would be the best location to set up shop when we get the actual location of the Becker's hideout."

"No problem." Denise replied while grabbing her jacket and keys off the table.

"Wait…" Emad said looking at Denise and then continued "… hang out in the area for the day. And be ready for the real estate agent with the keys of the house you recommend."

"I like how you think boss." Marcus said.

"If you like that then you'll love this. We'll pose as movers…" Emad paused and looked at Derrick and said "…Derrick that means we're going to need a moving truck."

"Dah." Derrick blurted.

"Don't be a smart ass." Emad joked back.

"May I leave now?" Denise said sounding impatient.

"Go on and I shouldn't have to say this but careful." Emad said hurrying his words because Denise was rushing out the door.

Canton Street near the Becker's hideout

Darkghost had moved into their stakeout house without any detection. Denise will remain on recon duty until nine o'clock in the evening.

Samantha and her father haven't been outside of their hideout for twenty-four hours and Samantha is getting restless. She wants to take the chance of going out but Peter and Kata have forbidden her to do so.

Samantha disobedience has put her father and her life in jeopardy, along with the men who is protecting them.

Two hours after the last time they had a discussion about her leaving the house Samantha snuck out to go for a walk. Their worst fears came to reality. Denise spotted Samantha and tailed her back to the hideout.

Denise immediately called Emad and reported what she observed and Darkghost snapped into action. Being that the Becker's hideout was perpendicular to Darkghost's house, setting up a sting to take the Becker's out, became much easier than Emad expected.

"The house across the street to our right is our target. From what I have ascertained, is there's two entry points we need to cover; the front door and the rear door. Now the rear door is located more west of the house. Whereas the front is centered to the house. There's eleven windows; four in the front, two on each side, and three in the rear." Denise instructed while showing the team a sketch she had drawn while on recon.

"The problem is getting to the rear of the house, how do we go about doing that?" Marcus asked.

"The Becker's share a backyard with their neighbor behind them. So whoever has the job of covering the rear can gain entry through that way."

"The job is yours." Emad ordered pointing at Denise.

"No problem, I got it…" Denise replied and then she continued "…as you all could see when y'all came onto the street; there are a lot of cars out there we can use for cover fire."

"But our mission is to kill Peter and Samantha. We need to get inside the house or draw them out Master Yoda." Derrick reminded everyone.

"Juka, you got watch. If anyone comes or goes, we need to know immediately." Emad ordered Juka ignoring Derrick's comment.

"Of course Eli, I'm on it." Juka replied.

"We also need to monitor their conversations and see what they're talking about." Marcus added.

"Very good thinking my young padawan warrior." Derrick agreed.

"Derrick quit with the Star Wars rhetoric. Do you have anything in your bag that will help with that?" Emad asked.

"Fortunately I do…" Marcus said grabbing and then reaching into his duffel bag and retrieve a box. When he open the box he continued "…these babies here can attach to any surface and transmit sound from up to seventy-five yards radius and send it back to this control. Neat huh?"

"Well Derrick you can help him with planting the bugs…" Emad ordered and then continued "…I'll take second watch. Is everyone clear on what they are doing tonight?"

Everyone confirmed by nodding their heads.

The team was busying themselves with getting ready for an attack on the Becker's hideout. From information the bugs planted by Derrick and Marcus, the Becker's are leaving the hideout tonight.

"If we stick to what we planned our mission will be a success. Don't forget there are ex-military men inside that house. But they are the enemy. And we fight for what is good. Bring it in guys for a group prayer." Emad said.

After prayer the team walked out the door. Denise and Juka walked over to their rental car. Juka got into the driver's seat and Denise into the passengers. They drove around the corner to drop Denise off so she can cover the rear. Juka then drove back around the corner and parked the car on the side street. He exited the car and walked around the corner to attack the hideout from the east.

The neighborhood was quiet at this time of day with little or no movement from the citizens that lived in the community. Looking through a pair of binoculars Emad could see Juka turning the corner and dispatched Marcus to his post.

What was good about the house that Darkghost chose to set up their stakeout in is this. Part of the roof is flat.

Derrick needed this type of roof so he can do his job as a sniper.

As usual Emad liked to have a broad view of what's going on so he liked to attack from the middle.

Darkghost had covered all their bases as so they believed. What they didn't expect is the neighbor that shared the backyard with the hideout is workers of the man hiding the Becker's.

Darkghost was being set up and walking into a death trap. Their own Intel was deceitful. Peter and Samantha had already left and what Darkghost was listening to was a recording of them in the house.

When Samantha went on her walk she had saw Denise before Denise saw her and acted like she didn't. When she returned to the hideout she reported this to her father. Kata quickly put a plan in play to get them out.

First he had Peter to call his contact. From him he learned there's an underground tunnel from their house to the house they share a yard with. Secondly, he figure that they would be bugged and told the Becker's and his men they needed to record themselves talking about a fake plan of escape. Finally, plant his booby traps inside the house. When whoever came busting through the door they will set off a chain of explosions throughout the house.

"All units check in." Emad commanded.

"Bravo is a go." Juka said.

"Sparrow is a go." Denise said.

"Charley is ready." Derrick said.

"Delta is a go." Marcus said.

"Alpha is a go. Everybody move in." Emad ordered.

As Denise moved in she had noticed all the mini blinds were left open and could see inside the house.

"Abort, abort. It's a trap." Denise shouted into her earpiece.

Juka had already reached the porch and Derrick had shot the doorknob off the door which set off the chain of explosion. Juka was blown off the porch and into a parked car. Juka lie limp on the sidewalk. Marcus ran towards him shouting "…someone call an ambulance".

Emad whipped out his cell phone and dial nine one one. Smoldering embers had attached itself to Denise's jacket on her back. Marcus looked up for Denise and noticed she was on fire and tackled her to put the flames out that had erupted on her. Once Marcus had distinguished the flames on Denise he looked towards Juka. Emad was already attending to Juka's wound.

"We need to get him to the hospital." Emad said.

"No, no hospital. I'm okay, just help me up." Juka stated.

"Let's get him inside…" Emad said looking at Marcus "…and no one talks to the police but me. Understand. Marcus get on the horn and call Mitchel and express to him how we need to keep the crime scene in our control."

"I'm on it."

"I'll get the car and then go get the Suburban." Derrick added.

"Denny go with Derrick we're going to need that rental car back. Marcus and I will stay with Juka, now hurry."

Fire trucks siren blared loudly off in a distant and getting closer with every second. First on the scene was a patrol police officer. He jumps out his car with his gun in his hand aimed at Emad.

"Hold your fire I'm FBI." Emad said holding a badge for the officer to see.

"Don't you move a muscle. Turn around and put your hands on that car." Officer Gland commanded.

"I'm not putting my hands on nothing but you can come take a look at my badge. I'm on orders from the bureau and this situation is of national security. If you want to lose your job, detain me much longer."

"Let me see that." Officer Gland said as he snatched the badge from Emad hand and jump back.

"What the hell is going on around here?" Officer Gland added as he gave Emad his credentials back.

"I am not of any liberty to discuss the nature of the raid. You can keep people back and wait for instructions from your Lieu. I have a hurt man in the house that needs medical attention…"

Derrick came screeching around the corner and slammed on the brakes five yards away from Emad and Officer Gland.

"Wait that's my man…" Emad said to Gland holding up his right hand. "…Derrick get the door, Marcus and I will get Juka."

When Marcus and Emad came out with Juka, Denise was just pulling up in the rental car.

"We need to hurry and get the hell out of here before someone figure out who we are and want to talk to us." Denise said.

"Denise we need you to stop by the pharmacy and get supplies and plenty of pain killers. And then meet us at the motel." Marcus asked.

"I'm on it. See you guys at the motel."

"Not us, I need you here to preserve the crime scene." Emad said to Marcus.

With that Denise punched the word 'pharmacy' into her GPS and hit search. While waiting for the results Denise drove in the direction of the motel.

Since Derrick was doing the driving Emad tended to Juka's wounds. They needed to hurry and get him back to the motel, before he loses too much blood. Emad was good at working on combat injuries. Even though he's a little rusty since his days in the Navy Seals.

"Hang in there Juka we're almost there."

"Man don't mess me up Eli."

"How do you mess up ugly?"

"Derrick you got a lot of nerve talking about ugly."

"I can get more girls than you."

"Yeah more ugly girls. Ugh." Juka let out a moan and held his side.

"Beauty is in the eye of the beholder." Derrick kept talking trying to keep Juka's mind off the pain he was feeling.

Emad looked down at Juka and saw that he had his eyes closed. He then caught eye contact with Derrick in the rear view mirror and waved his hand at him for him to keep Juka talking. Emad knew they had a close bond since they found out that each have one parent from the same city in Spain: Cordova.

Derrick started speaking Spanish and Juka laughed at his jokes. Derrick was talking about the newest member of the crew. Not in a bad way but it was funny nonetheless. Even Marcus had to laugh. This made Juka laugh more when he chimed in speaking Spanish on one of Derrick's jokes. Derrick had forgotten they still had their earpieces in their ears until Marcus started speaking and he could hear him.

"Why you never said you speak Spanish?"

"You never asked." Marcus replied to Derrick question.

"Get ready fellas we're about to pull up to the motel."

"Denny are you there?"

"Yeah Eli, go ahead."

"What's your twenty?"

"I'm on my way to the room with the supplies. I'll be there in ten minutes Eli."

"We're here already, see you when you get here."

CHAPTER TWENTY

Royale Motel

"Marcus and I will go back to the crime scene and do our investigation. You guys keep an eye on Juka and warn us of any changes."

"You guys be careful. I'll update y'all every half an hour on Juka." Denise replied.

Becker's Hideout

The fire department had put the fire out by the time Emad and Marcus got to the house. And yellow crime scene tape had been taped around the perimeter of the property. Two police officers stood guard and were ordered to only allow Emad and Marcus entrance to the property.

"How you doing officer?" Emad said holding out his badge and then he continued "...I'm Special Agent McWhorter and this is Special Agent Longton we're here to investigate this crime scene.

"I need to see your credentials as well sir..." Officer Norwood asked looking at Marcus and then continued "...thanks sir. Do you men need us to stand guard?"

"No we'll be alright, thank you." Marcus said.

"Alright then we're out. You men have a good day."

"Thanks y'all do the same."

Emad had already started up the few steps of what was left of a porch when he turned and waved goodbye to the officers. Once on the porch Emad could see right through the house. Marcus joined him and stumbled on a loose floor board.

"What kind of explosive do you think they used for this."

"I don't know until we take a further look inside. We need to find the accelerator of the fire."

"I'll take this side of the house and you can take that side if you like." Marcus suggested.

"Why don't you go through the house and I follow your lead."

This is what made Emad a great leader. Knowing the right man for the job. And being that this wasn't Marcus' first rodeo he quickly but methodically moved through the house with ease. Emad was impressed by how he went about his business.

"Here, this is the detonator. They used a remote trigger and by the way the blast looked they must have used plastic C4."

"Remote."

"Yeah this means they were close by and saw or was warned that we were coming."

"If they were warned then we have someone on the inside betraying us."

"Shit this could get real messy if that's the case."

"What sparked Denny to yell out? Let me call her…" Emad hit a button on his earpiece and then continued *"…Denny is you there?"*

"Go ahead Eli."

"What did you see to make you scream out for us to abort?"

"The house behind the Becker's house; someone was in the basement window with something in his or her hand. I had got a funny gut feeling something was wrong. Why you ask?"

"It looks like you may be right because Marcus found what started the explosions. We need to go next door so get your ass here on the double. Derrick how's Juka doing?"

"He's resting but I think he'll pull through just fine."

"Thanks keep me posted."

"Will do. Hey Eli…"

"You don't have to say it bro; we will."

"Come on Marcus lets hang out back until Denny gets here."

Denny exited the truck with her weapon drawn and walked over to Emad and Marcus. Both men pulled out their weapons from their holsters. Everyone held their guns low as they walked up to the back door of the house directly behind the Becker's. Emad motioned for Marcus to check the basement door to see if it was locked. Emad and Denny covered him by pointing their weapons at the windows on the first floor. The basement door was lock. Marcus put up one finger to indicate to give him a second to pick the lock. Marcus reached into one of his pocket to his flap jacket and pulled out a lock picking kit. It took him all of one minute to pick the lock and then motion to Emad that he was finished.

They approached the basement slowly. Marcus swung the door open and Denny jumped in the doorway pointing her gun inside the basement. Marcus was first to enter with Emad following closely. Denny pulled up the rear and held guard at the door until Marcus and Emad could secure the room and find a light.

"Close the door Denny." Emad said as he turned on the light to the basement and then he continued whispering low "…lets secure the house first and then we can investigate."

"This is how the Becker's got out without us seeing them." Marcus said pointing at a door.

The door was connected to the outside but under the surface of the ground. Emad waved his hand at the door and everyone got into position to storm the door. Denny checked the door to see if it was lock. It was unlock. So she swung it open. Emad went high and Marcus went low but no one was in the tunnel. They both moved back into the basement and Denny closed and locked the door.

Emad motioned for them to move upstairs to secure the rest of the house. Emad went up the steps first and burst through the door. No human sounds coming from anywhere of the house. Only a TV on in the living room tuned to a Latino station. Emad waved his left hand for them to follow him into the house. Room by room they secure the house until all rooms were secured.

Now Marcus can get to business of searching the house for evidence of who may have lived here.

"From what I have ascertained; I would say these people are Colombian. Check out the clothing left in the closet and the art work on the wall." Marcus said.

"Yeah and…" Emad answered.

"They're all South American things."

"But you said specifically Colombian not South American."

"The reason I say Colombian is because the picture over there is of the Andes Mountains. And they're in Colombia."

"I agree this note here…" Denise held out a piece of paper with Spanish writing on it and continued "…is a list of Spanish ingredients written in Colombian to make an authentic Colombian dish."

"Are you thinking what I'm thinking?" Marcus asked.

"I'm already ahead of you." Emad said as he pulled out his cell phone and hit speed dial number five.

"Stewart, I need you to find out if there were any flights out of the San Antonio area going to Colombia, South America. I need that information like yesterday."

"Give me ten seconds hold on…"

There was a short paused and Emad could hear keys being struck rapidly on a keyboard.

"Eli you there…"

"Yes Stewart go ahead."

"A private jet left out of Castroville Municipal Airport four hours ago heading towards Colombia."

"Okay can you scramble the X-15 and have it meet us at Lackland Air Force Base within one hour."

"Captain Woodard never left the area. That will be no problem."

"I owe you big time Stewie."

"Just doing my job. Good hunting Eli."

Click. Dial tone.

"Let's get out of here and get back to the room and pick up the rest of the team."

"What about Juka?" Denise asked looking concerned.

"If I know Juka we'll have to tie him down to keep him from not coming with us. I prefer for him to come if he can help and not hinder our mission."

<u>*Royale Motel*</u>

"Juka how do you feel?"

"I'm good Eli, what's up?"

"We're going to Colombia. Can you help with the mission?"

"I'm a little soar but I can move and who else is going to help with the computer analysis stuff."

"Team vote. All for Juka staying on the mission raise your hand."

Every member of Darkghost raised a hand and Derrick raised both of his and waved them above his head. Everybody laughed and Darkghost commenced preparing to meet their transport.

"Michael we need someone to pick up the black truck and someone to drop off the rental car." Marcus asked Stewart's colleague.

"I'll take care of it."

"Thanks Mike."

"May I drive this time?" Marcus asked the team.

"You got the keys right. I'm glad someone else wants to drive." Derrick said.

"Load up people it's time to move." Emad ordered.

CHAPTER TWENTY-ONE

Colombia

Peter and Samantha have been running and now feel as though they can relax and take a breather. This place they have taken refuge in will be their home for the unforeseeable future. They were greeted by the man who made their escape from the United States government possible. The private jet they used landed in a clearing at the foothills of the mountain.

"Julio." Peter walked towards the man he was talking too with open arms.

"Peter, how was your flight?"

The two men embraced and looked at each other before Peter spoke again.

"It was fine thank you how is your father? I hear his health is failing…"

"He's a strong man and will recover soon. Who is this may I ask?"

"Where are my manners…?" Peter turned to his daughter and said "I will like for you to meet my daughter Samantha. Samantha this is Mr. Julio Cartagena."

Julio walked over to Samantha and took her hand into his and kissed it and then said "…Nice to meet you…" and then Julio turned to Peter with Samantha hand still in his and said "…you never said how beautiful your daughter is she's breath taking.

"Thank you sir and it's nice to meet you as well." Samantha returned the compliment.

"Call me Julio. Your father and I go way back. So feel at home and worry no more."

"Julio I would also like to thank you for all your help you have given me and my daughter."

"Shush no more talks of gratitude let's get you to my home. There you can wash and change your clothes if you like."

"Sure."

"You have no need for your men now you can dispose of them if you want."

"If it's all the same to you I'll like to keep them around a little while longer. At least until they have rested for a day or two. All of us are a bit fatigue and could use some much needed sleep."

"As you wish..." Julio said and then extended his hand and said "...this way please."

Cumaribo, Colombia

Stewart and his colleague Michael were working their assets hard in Colombia. Their assets job was to find the private jet that transported the Becker's and their protection and where they are hiding.

"Hello."

"Eli, my asset has located the jet, I gave her your number. She'll be calling you in a second. Her name is Maria."

"Thanks Stewart."

Emad closed his phone and stood up and walked towards the cockpit.

Ring.

Ring.

"Hello." Emad answered his cell phone covering his left ear.

"Hello, am I speaking with Eli?"

"Yes this is he. Is this Maria?"

"Yes. Time is of the essence I have the location of the private jet you seek. About twenty-two miles south of a small village town name Cumaribo there is a tree line. I will be there in fifteen minutes. I will only wait five minutes until I leave."

"We will be there."

"Good here is the coordinates..."

135

"Wait one sec let me put you on speakerphone for my pilot."

"Hurry."

Emad removed the phone from his ear and hit the speakerphone icon button on his phone and said *"...Maria can you hear me?"*

"Yes I can."

"Go ahead Maria."

While Maria was giving the coordinates to Captain Woodard, Emad walked back to his seat and buckled himself down and Captain Woodard punched the numbers into the navcom computer simultaneously. Once Maria was done giving the coordinates, Captain Woodard said 'initiate mach1' and the blades of the helicopter retracted and the wings extended from the side of the Falcon X-15. Like a lightning strike the stealth helicopter accelerated instantaneously.

Within seventeen minutes the X-15 had traveled to the coordinates. Captain Woodard said 'stop mach1' and the nose of the Falcon rose to the sky to slow it down. The wings retracted and the blades popped out. The Falcon X-15 was now hovering over the coordinates Maria had given to Woodard.

"Emad we're here. Call me ten minutes before extraction and I'll be here at this very same spot. Good hunting sir." Woodard said into the overhead microphone.

"Thanks Cap..." Emad replied into the intercom.

Darkghost unfastened their seatbelts in unison. Derrick was the first to the side door. He opened the door and grabbed five separate ropes that were anchored to the deck and threw them out the door. Denise and Marcus threw the tactical gear and weapons out the other side door.

One by one the each team member moved down an individual rope until they reached the ground. Emad gave Captain Woodard the okay to leave with a thumbs up signal with his hand. After gathering their gear Darkghost turned their attention to the tree line off to their left. Juka reached into his backpack and grabbed a pair of binoculars and handed them to Emad. Emad panned the tree line side to side. On his second time through he saw a light flickering and pointed to his right towards it and said *"...over there move out..."* and just like that Darkghost was on the move again chasing the Becker's.

Maria had an older model Lincoln Navigator parked on a hidden trail thirty yards away. The woods were dense this time of the year. The tall trees full of foliage will provide good cover for Darkghost in case anyone was probing from above.

Once we got to Maria she explained that we had to get out of the woods quickly because thieves hanged out in them. She said 'they would soon learn of our presence and attack in large numbers'. We moved expeditiously towards the waiting vehicle.

Maria drove America's protectors to a safe house fifteen miles west of their drop off point. Fatigue has finally set in but you couldn't tell because everyone looked stoic which made the Navigator quiet on the ride to the safe house.

"Listen up everyone we all need a shower and some rest. So let unpacked and get to it. We need to have clear heads for tomorrows hunt."

"That's an order Denny." Derrick said smiling and waving his hand back and forth past his face with his nose turned up.

"You should go first I smell you over here." Denise replied and then everyone laughed.

Next morning

Emad and Denise were dress for the day's recon surveillance before the rest of the team had even gotten up. Both dressed in black fatigues. Denise hair was tied back and covered with a black cotton scarf. Emad donned a black scully and stood up from the table to retrieve a cup of coffee. A large table length map shielded the badly stained wood tabletop.

Denise peered over the map with intensity. She felt at home prepping for the days battle of hide and seek. Recon was her specialty and pleasure.

Emad returned with two cups of coffee and sat quietly as Denise study the terrain surrounding the highlighted x which represented Mr. Cartagena drug field and lab.

"I believe if we come in from here…" Denise said while pointing at a spot on the map and then she continued "…and here, we'll be able to search more of the grounds quicker. But if one of us can get over here…" once again Denise pointed at the map "…and place some high resolution cameras we'll be able to see who comes and goes and what time if they have any shift change."

"I'll do that and you and Juka pair up. Derrick and Marcus can take this area over here…" Emad took his right pointer finger and circled an area on the map and then he continued "…while you and Juka get this area."

The bathroom door shut loudly and Juka sprang to his feet with a surprised look on his face. He had slept hard the night before due to his injury but now felt rejuvenated. Marcus rub his eyes, stretch and yarned and then stumbled over to the coffee maker.

"Are you guys serious? We're here to do a job and y'all slept in like we're on vacation."

"Denny just read your map and don't worry about our sleeping habits." Derrick responded as he stepped out of the bathroom.

"No she's right we have business to do so snap to it men we have a long day ahead of us." Emad concluded.

"No problem boss ready in ten minutes. That'll give me time enough to get this coffee into my system and a shower." Marcus said.

"I just need a shower and I'm ready to go." Juka added.

Derrick said nothing just pointed at himself and then the bathroom, after which he hunch his shoulders. The team busy themselves with getting ready for the days task; recon. Once the rest of the team was showered and dress they went over the recon game plan.

Moments later Maria stopped by the safe house bearing supplies. Emad had given her a list of things they will need for the upcoming fight with the drug cartel that was supporting Peter Becker.

"It wasn't easy getting these things on such a short notice but I have succeeded. Check everything out to make sure I got what you needed."

"Yo Derrick and Denny come check this stuff out while I call Conover to give him our update." Emad asked.

Emad called Conover and gave a brief update of Darkghost progress. Derrick as usual made jokes about the second rate weapons of foreign countries but in the end always approved of them. Derrick could use anything and make it work to Darkghost benefit.

"Everything looks good Eli." Derrick confirmed.

"Okay guys pack it up and get ready to move out."

Cartagena Main house

"We never really had a chance to really get to know one another. Please make yourself at home…" Julio said to Peter pointing at the all-white satin armchair in his study. Peter pulled up his pants legs and sat down with his right leg crossed over his left and then Julio continued "…we will go visit with my father later. He has told me many things about you and your partners…"

"I figured this much and by the way your treating me I assume he has told you good things about us." Peter interjected.

"Yes mostly good. He liked the way you guys got started and how he helped you with that."

"Your father was very generous to us and we reciprocated with good deed. Anytime your father has called on us for any type of job we came through for him as well as he has for us. Like now."

"Yes, yes I know and we need your partner Valentin to do something for us in Russia.

"I'm sorry to say this but I believe Valentin may be dead."

"And why do you say this?"

"He hasn't returned any of my phone calls and I can't reach any of his contacts. And I fear the same fate has fallen upon Jeung."

"Do you believe the people who were chasing you in America may have something to do with this?"

"There's a good chance that America's government may be behind all of this."

"Well if they come here we will have a big surprise for them…" Julio said and started laughing loudly and then he continued "…come I have something my father wanted you to see."

Andes Mountain Foothills

"No one need to play hero today let's just do our jobs and make it back to the house safely." Emad said looking his teammates individually in the eyes.

Everyone shook their heads in agreement and went their separate ways. Emad was the only one working alone and he had the most dangerous job to do. He had to set motion sensors outside the perimeter of the main house that would remotely activate two .50 cal rifles pointed at the exit of the driveway to the main house. The rifles are accompanied with two hundred rounds each that will fire every five seconds. Once Darkghost set the weapons anyone tripping the sensors will start the weapon and get torn in half. Darkghost will be waiting on the other side of the main house ground for anyone to venture into the woods, because that would seem to be the only way out.

Emad needed to get as close to the main house without being detected. He quietly thanked his commanding officer for his Navy Seals training and proceeded with the task at hand. Emad slivered all around the driveway without detection until he had succeeded. Once he was finished he radioed his men asking of their progress.

"Alpha to Bravo and Charley can you hear me?" Emad whispered into his earpiece microphone.

"Bravo here go ahead." Derrick whispered.

"Charley here go ahead." Marcus whispered.

"What's your progress?"

"Denny is placing our last camera now." Derrick answered.

"Juka is finishing up as well."

"Meet me back at the outer tree line. Alpha out."

"Affirmative, Charley out."

"Gotcha, Bravo out."

While Derrick and Denny were creeping back to the rendezvous they were being followed. Two of Felipe's men had spotted them finishing up and began to follow them to see where they were heading. They were so busy keeping their eyes on Derrick and Denny that they didn't know that they were being watched.

"Bravo this is Charley you have two stragglers on your six. Don't stop. Keep moving west and you'll bring them to us. Do you copy?" Juka said while leaning against a tree following the two soldiers with his scoped rifle.

"Copy. On our way." Derrick replied.

Derrick and Denny didn't break stride but started to ease west without the enemy soldiers noticing. Juka and Marcus got themselves into better positions to attack the soldiers.

"What's going on?" Emad asked.

"Nothing we can't handle boss you keep going and we'll meet you 'cha there." Juka responded.

"Very good. Hurry it up and get a move on."

"We copy. Now can we get back to business?"

"Alpha out."

The Charley team was waiting ten yards ahead and was on both sides of the path hiding behind trees. When Bravo passed by, Marcus counted down from twenty. Just as he got to one, the soldiers appeared. Juka attacked from the rear with a garrote. As he was strangling one soldier, Marcus jumped out from the front and had cut the throat of the other soldier and covered his mouth while stabbing him twice on the way to the ground. Juka undid his garrote from the soldier's neck and Marcus wiped his blade off on the soldier's jacket he had killed. This was Marcus first hand to hand fight he had killed someone.

*"On our way Alpha. Charley out…" Juka confirmed and then he continued talking to Marcus in Spanish "…*so how did it feel killing up close and personal?"

"I'm not giving it any second thought. Let's just meet with the others." Marcus replied in English.

CHAPTER TWENTY-TWO

"What happened back there?" Emad questioned his team and stared at each one in the eyes.

"I guess we were a little sloppy and didn't see the two men who were following us." Derrick explained.

"Sloppy huh. In this game sloppy gets you killed and I shouldn't have to explain that to any one of you…"

"No harm, no foul boss. Can we drop it and get back to business?" Juka asked with that's enough voice.

"Yea you're right but no more sloppy work agreed?"

"Sure." Denny answered.

"No problem." Derrick added.

Just as Emad was about to command Juka to the monitors, he was already on his way to the table. Juka reached behind the three monitors sitting on the table and flip the switches to the on position.

"All three monitors is on and transmitting clearly." Juka said holding his hand up for a high five from whoever was standing behind him.

"We are going to watch for only twelve hours and then we go in. In the meantime let us check our weapons and gear. You all know the routine, every hour someone relieve the man or woman at the monitors."

"But captain I can't hold her." Derrick said in a Scotty from Star Trek voice and shaking Denny.

"Fool get your hands off me. Damn you always playing around."

"Yea right but you still love me right." Derrick replied puckering his lips for a kiss.

Slap!!!

"Damn Denny you didn't have to hit me that hard."

"You better be glad I didn't punch you."

"Settle down children." Marcus added.

"Come on guys we got work to do." Emad ordered.

Cartagena Cartel Main house

Oblivious to what had transpired outside the walls on the main house grounds, Julio and Peter exited the house en route to visit with Felipe. As they walked towards the car, Julio clapped his hands and snapped his fingers for his workers to move quicker. The women asses he patted as he walked by them. He enjoyed being in charge without his father around.

Felipe didn't like his son mistreating or flirting with the help. He always said "we have bitches for that" and if you were caught going against his words, you would find yourself in the basement flogging room. And no one was exempt from that room not even Julio, who found himself to be in that room quite often when he was a youngster.

"How far is Felipe from here?" Peter asked.

"Not far. Father didn't want to stay on grounds while he was recovering. So we had a small house built for him about three kilometers south of here. We'll be there shortly."

"Great haven't seen your father in many years I am excited to see my old friend."

"As he is to see you as well."

"We are here just over that ridge."

The small cottage sat behind some wild cashew trees. The cottage was built from native lumber milled in the Cartagena Cartel lumber mill. A half mooned gravel driveway paved the way to the front door. One large thick paned window acted as the right wall in the front of the house.

A man sat in the tree just as you came onto the property armed with an AK-47 assault rifle. Two men sat on the porch each with an Excaliber 28 gauge shotgun leaned up against the house. Men patrolled the property holding small automatic weapons and a sidearm holstered under their arms.

"Don't forget to blink your headlights three times fast Pedro."

"Yes sir, Mr. Julio."

"Why is that?" Peter asked.

"If we do not they will shoot at us."

"Who will shoot at us?"

"The men protecting my father."

Pedro did as he was told and the car was allowed to pass without incident. Pedro parked the car just off to the side of the house.

"Mr. Julio, how are you doing today?"

'Mr. Julio."

"I'm fine Camilo…" Julio answered and waved at Alex before he continued "…this is Peter he's a good friend of the family. He'll be staying with us for a moment. Peter this is Alex and Camilo."

"Nice to meet you." Peter said extending his hand in greeting the men.

"Come your father has just finishing eating and now reading the newspaper." Camlio said briefly.

Once on the porch Peter could see Felipe sitting in a lounge chair reading. A big grin came across Felipe face and he tried to get up and greet his friend.

"Felipe!"

"Peter!"

The two men embrace each other. Felipe grab Peter by his shoulders and patted him on one side.

"How's your health my good friend?"

"I am fine Peter let us talk about other things. Julio excuse us we have some catching up to do."

"Sure poppa I'll be back in an hour to retrieve Peter."

"Thanks Julio." Peter said a shook Julio hand as he walked out the door.

"So tell me who are these people chasing you?"

Peter explained the whole ordeal to Felipe. How he believes the people that are chasing him might be the people he tried to hire to find the people who kidnapped his daughter Samantha.

Felipe told Peter he shouldn't worry because he had a plan that will work and get rid of those people.

"Okay guys it's time to load up and move out."

"Not without prayer we won't." Denise said.

"Bow your heads." Juka snapped.

"Marcus since you pretty new with us. May you please lead us in prayer?"

Marcus prayer was short and to the point. He asked God to protect them and their families as well as their enemy families from evildoers. And to make them victorious in their quest for what they believe was right.

"Amen."

"Now move out!" Emad commanded.

Darkghost were minutes away from ridding the earth of some foul people. When they get to the main house they will split into two teams; Emad and Derrick represented Alpha unit and Denise and Marcus was Bravo. Juka stayed at the safe house to man the monitors, so he could tell both units of anyone trying to get an upper hand on them.

The Alpha unit will ready the .50 cal rifle. Bravo will cover to make sure no stragglers will get out on the north side of the grounds.

"Alpha 1 to Bravo 1 do you read me?" Emad radioed.

"Loud and clear Alpha 1." Denise answered.

"Are you in position?"

"In position and lock and loaded. We're ready sir."

"The gun is on get ready for some fireworks." Derrick explained.

A patrol guard walked through a sensor beam and the weapon started firing. Instantly the guard's torso was cut in half from his sternum down and flew into the side of the main house. Denise cut the power to the main house and yard. The generator kicked in and a loud warning alarm sounded and men came running out from all over shouting and firing into the direction of the two .50 cal weapons.

Derrick took aim and started sniping one soldier after the next. On the other side Marcus was covering Denise as she made her way into the main house. Emad had already breeched the compound main house.

"I'm inside moving through the lower part of the house." Denise reported.

"Watch your six Bravo 1…" Emad said.

"No one followed her from out here." Marcus reassured.

"*Everybody must be outside because I cleared five rooms without any resistance.*" *Denise explained.*

Just then a man came from around the corner yelling Spanish profane words and firing in Emad directions. Emad relaxed his body so that he would fall to the floor and shot three times into the soldier's head.

"*Bravo 1 have you found the Becker's?*"

"*No!*"

"*Keep looking they haven't left.*"

"*I'm moving t…*"

Denise was punch into her face before she could finish her sentence.

"*Bravo 1 are you okay?*" *Emad paused and then continued* "*…something is wrong Bravo 1 isn't answering. Juka guide me to her last location.*"

"*Take the next left and go down one flight to your left and she's right there.*"

Denise didn't have a chance to respond because a man twice her size was all over her and had knocked her headset off her head. When Denise hit the ground she tried to point her gun at the man but he had smacked the gun out her hand. Then he picked her up by her throat and belt buckle and threw her across the room. Denise back smashed into the wall and she fell to the floor. Denise shook her head as if she was clearing out the cobwebs. The man stood back and waved Denise towards himself. She stumbled to her feet and wipe blood from her eyebrow and mouth. Denise took two steps and the man charged her. Bad move. Denise slid on the floor knocking his feet from under him. His face slammed into the floor and Denise jump to her feet and onto his back.

"I'm going to choke the life out of you asshole." Denise said while applying a kimura choke hold.

The man was too strong for Denise and wiggled out from her grasp. When he turned over he had a gun in his hand ready to fire bullets into Denise body.

"Move!"

Emad ran into the room and fired five shots into the man body.

"Are you okay Denny?"

"I'm okay I had it under control. Thanks anyway." Denise said smiling.

"I believe the Becker's are upstairs. Come on we got to move."

Peter and Samantha were trying to figure out how they could get outside and into the woods.

"Give me a second, here Wallace give me a hand."

Wallace and Kata tied several sheets together and anchored them to the solid oak wood bed frame. Kata broke out a window and tossed the sheets out of it. He and his men covered the Becker's as they shimmied down the sheets to the ground. The Becker's and their entourage had escaped minus Red and Wallace.

"You should be ashamed of yourself."

Red head snapped around and he raised his gun and started firing. Emad and Denise hit the ground and returned fire. Red and Wallace took cover as well.

"You get paid for what you do. How are you better than me?" Red shouted.

"You know better than to help out criminals. You fought for America and now you're helping to destroy her."

"America never paid me this much money baby and that's what it's all about right."

Wallace tried to go for the sheets and Emad shot him in his back. Wallace fell to the ground and his head splattered against the brick path.

"Why don't we settle this like real soldiers?" Red asked.

"And how do we go about that?"

"Hand to hand with knives combat."

"Sure, come out slowly and throw down your weapon."

Both men side stepped until they were out in the open. Each man had his gun pointed at the other.

"Are you ready?"

"On three drop your weapon." Emad said.

"Three!" Red said quickly and dropped his weapon and lunge towards Emad.

Emad stepped to the side and Denise shot Red two times in the chest. Red dropped to his knees with his open widely and a shock expression on his face.

"Who said you were a soldier. I have no honor for a man without honor."

Emad then turned away from Red as he fell over to the floor.

"I got five rabbits going east." Derrick said

"*Can you hit them from where you are?*" Emad asked.

"*That's a negative; I repeat I have no shot.*"

"Denny hurry down the sheets I'll cover you..." Emad said to Denise and then he continued "...*Marcus stay in position and take out anything that comes your way.*"

"*Roger that.*"

"*Denny and I will go after the rabbits. Derrick go help Marcus. Five more minutes gentlemen and head back to camp. Alpha 1 out.*"

"*Roger that.*"

"*Copy.*"

When Denise touch the ground Emad did the same as she did. Denise covered Emad until he reached the ground.

"Move!" Emad said.

Emad and Denise ran fast through the woods scanning the trees for any movement.

"Over there." Denise said pointing to her right.

Emad and Denise both kneeled down on one knee and fired their guns. A firefight ensued with Kata and his remaining men. Emad could hear bullets wiz by his from behind. Extra gun fire came from the right side of Denise.

"Where the hell are they? And why are they helping us?" Denise asked Emad with a shock look in her face.

One by one Kata's last two men was gunned down. He stood alone as the Becker's only protection.

"*Did you guys think I was going to let you have all the fun?*" Derrick said.

"Damn it Derrick you were supposed to be helping Marcus." Emad said angrily.

"*I'm here too let's kill these bastards and go home.*"

INTERLUDE

STAY TUNED FOR THE NEXT CHAPTER
CHRISTIAN'S MOVE

BOOK TWO: The Past

CHRISTIAN'S MOVE

In times of war and uncertainty there is a special breed of Warrior ready to answer our Nation's call. A common man with uncommon desires forged by adversity he stands alongside America's finest Special Operation Forces to serve his Country, the American people, and protect their way of Life. - Navy Seals Creed

"I'm hit!" Denise yelled out.

"Denny!" Emad shouted.

"Where ya hit at Denny?" Derrick asked.

"My left arm…" Denise replied with a moan and then she continued "…I can still use my sidearm."

"Ammo check." Emad asked.

"I have one full clip and about a half clip I'm using." Marcus said.

"I have two clips in my pocket and I just reloaded my sidearm."

"I'm good Eli I just reloaded too and I have one full left." Derrick added.

"Good, Denny you stay low. Derrick and Marcus let's plow the roads."

With that all three men stood up and pulled the triggers on their respective weapons, while walking forward and sweeping their weapons in a side to side motion. Darkghost continued to fire into the direction of the Becker's and their protection.

After the smoke cleared and Darkghost had done enough damage, Emad sent Marcus and Derrick in to see if there were any survivors or dead bodies. He preferred dead bodies.

"Derrick report." Emad barked into his headset microphone.

"There's nothing here Eli."

"We hit nothing it's as if we were firing at no one." Marcus added.

Emad paused then said *"Okay men after you clean up, lets meet up at the rendezvous spot and I'll get Denny."*

"Roger that." Derrick responded.

"I can't believe this shit they got away. This Kata character is becoming a real pain in the ass." Marcus said.

"I know he's a real Houdini." Derrick replied.

Derrick and Marcus looked at each other and began to run east towards the rendezvous. Denise had positioned herself against a large tree and had been listening to the conversation between her teammates via her headset.

Colombia

"Dad, slow down I don't think they're behind us." Samantha said breathing hard out of breathe.

153

"Baby we have to keep moving." Peter reminded his daughter.

"Listen, you two I will get you to safety. This has been more than I have expected. Eli will not stop hunting us until he has killed all of us or just you two. I've lost too many men and now it's time for y'all to pay me."

"The job is not over until I say so." Peter demanded.

"You have a choice Mr. Becker either pay me or I kill you myself." Kata said and then pulled the slide on his 45 Beretta chambering a bullet and then pointing it at Peter's forehead.

"Does it look like I have the money on me...?" Peter said with beads of sweat starting to swell up on his forehead and then he continued "... if you want your money come to Korea with us.

Peter knew where Jeung kept his money but he didn't know his friend was dead. Peter did have his suspensions of both Valentin and Jeung being murdered by the same people hunting him but he had no proof of his suspensions.

"I can promise you this Mr. Becker..." Kata said and then pulled his weapon out and put it to Peter's head and then he continued "... you won't see Korea."

Kata pulled the trigger on his 45 Beretta pistol and blew Peter's brains out the back of his head. Samantha screamed "NO!" and then made a move towards Kata with no avail because he put two bullets in her forehead. Kata turned and ran away from the dead bodies.

Langley, VA 1985

After a long and intense meetings between the President of the United States Alex Cooper and the Director of the CIA Cameron Justice along with the Secretary of the Navy Admiral Cornelius Woodear Sr. a decision was made on making elite soldiers. President Cooper agreed to allow five individuals selected by Director Justice to be trained at a clandestine location only he and the CIA knows about and after this intense training to be enlisted into the Navy and then trained by Navy Seals instructors at another secretive location that only he and Secretary Woodear knows about.

These five men and women will protect America from all criminals both foreign and domestic. These five people will be America's killing squad trained in counterterrorism and have the ability to be effective anywhere in the world and in any kind of weather conditions.

"Have you any candidates in mind you would like to start this project off with?" Cooper asked.

"Yes sir, a candidate. He signed up two weeks ago and we've done a background check on him and so far everything seems to be okay." Justice replied.

"Good, when will you talk to him?"

"I have my people picking him up as we speak."

"So you just assumed I'll be okay with this partnership huh?"

"Well Mr. President with all the intel we have about upcoming attacks on us and our allies' sir, we just thought you would be ready to do something offensive to counter them sir."

"What time will your first interview with this candidate be conducted?" Woodear asked.

"Well its nine thirty now. We should have him here and ready to talk by three o'clock this afternoon sir."

"Well, then men that give us time to have lunch and get back to meet our first guinea pig." Cooper said with smirk.

"Sorry sir but you will not meet our guinea pig nor will he meet you sir." Justice said.

"Excuse me and why not?"

"Sir this is a secretive project that we can't let anyone know that the President of the United States of America the most powerful nation in the world knew anything about what we're going to do with each candidate..." Woodear looked at President Cooper and Director Justice and then with a matter of fact tone "...it's for your safety and your administration as well sir." Woodear explained.

"Oh I see. Very well then I expect a photo of him and an outline of his background on my desk by this evening."

"I can do better than that sir..." Justice reached into his briefcase and then said "...this is yours sir." Justice slid a dossier of their potential candidate over to President Cooper.

"You're full of surprises Mr. Justice don't make it a habit."

"Yes sir I won't sir."

<u>*1500 hrs.*</u>

"Mr. Emad Elijah McWhorter I presume?" Justice asked.

"Yes sir, but what is this all about?"

"You did apply to the agency yes?"

"Yes I did but I never got an acceptance letter. I was just sitting in my living room and your people just whisked me away and no one will tell me what's going on."

"You do understand this is the Central Intelligence Agency and sometime we have a tendency to just act and then explain our action…" Justice paused and steered Emad in his eyes and then he continued "…well then let's get to it. The reason why you're here is because your country needs you Mr. McWhorter." Justice paused again to let what he said sank in for a minute and then he said "…we are starting a new team of men and women. You have the background we believe we need in our leader of this team. First things first, you have to pass our psyche test and then a physical. After which you will be taken away and your identity change. You will not be able to speak or see your family. You will be dead to your family for seven years. What do you think about all of this?"

"Wow I need more time to think about this sir." Emad said rubbing his goatee.

"Of course you do."

"I'll be back tomorrow with my answer."

"No you won't, you have until sixteen hundred hours or four o'clock civilian time. You can take a walk and call your family but don't mention this job to them. And Mr. McWhorter we have ways of knowing if you tell them anything."

"I imagine you do sir."

"Okay then I'll see you back here in forty minutes."

<u>*1600 hrs.*</u>

"I'm ready sir when do I get started?"

"Now…" Justice walked over to the door and knocked on it and a man entered the room, Justice continued "…this is Agent Roberts he will take you to your room so you can get settled in. Once you're settled, we need to talk more details."

After Director Justice finished his statement he waved his hand for Emad to exit the room and follow Agent Roberts to his temporary room. Emad got settled in quite fast because he had nothing with him when he was whisk away from his home in Monmouth County, New Jersey.

Emad found his way back to the conference room. Upon entering the conference room he noticed the vaulted ceilings and beige painted walls which gave off a solemn feeling to Emad. Now for the first time today he could really take in his surroundings. He didn't notice earlier in the afternoon that there were paintings on the wall and the paintings were of lights at the end of a tunnel and these paintings were on every wall in different shades of black and gray. Or that the only chairs with cushions on them, were the two chairs that sat at both ends of the long oval wood grain table.

"You will have to ask our interior decorator that one." Cameron answered.

"Oh I didn't know you were standing there."

"From here on out you don't ever do that again." Cameron scolded.

"Do what?" Emad asked with a puzzling look on his face.

"Say what's on your mind out loud got it."

"Yes sir."

"Okay details, this is what your training will consist of. First we will get you mentally tough. You will also learn the art of being more than one person and deception will become your lover. You will be able to relax your mind and body at will. Endure pain at a high level. Hand to hand combat with and without weapons. How to love and hate your enemy. How to get men and women to do your bidding. You will learn how to use different types of weapons. Both close and mid-range weapons as well as long range weapons. Emad if you give one hundred percent of yourself to this program. You will become the best CIA agent on this planet..." Cameron Justice paused to let Emad think and then he continued "...and this is a two year program with us."

"What do you mean by with us as if I have to go somewhere else?"

"Like I said two years with us and then two years with the United States Navy in their Navy Seals training program.

"Wow!"

"Yes wow."

With this Cameron reached under the table and pressed a button. A man in a lab coat walked into the room without knocking. Emad turned around in his chair but before he could react, two other men barge in behind the doctor and snatched Emad out of his chair. Emad wiggled and tried to fight them off without any success.

"Take it easy young man and this will be over shortly…" Dr. Xavier Wilcox said to Emad and then he looked over at the two men and said "…take him to treatment room number five.

"No, no, no. Get your hands off me. Director Justice, why are you doing this to me?"

"Shut up and do as you're told. You belong to me now…" Cameron slapped Emad in his face and then he continued "…there is no escape…"

Emad eyes opened wide with a shocked look on his face.

"Go on get him out of here." Cameron said to the men holding Emad.

The doctor quickly walked over to Emad and stuck a needle in his neck. Emad's body went limp and he became unconscious.

CHAPTER TWENTY-THREE

<u>Monmouth County, 1981</u>

I'm seventeen years old and about to graduate from high school. I decided to join the police force and stay close to my family. My mother wanted me to go to school and become an engineer since I'm good with my hands and putting things together. My true passion is detecting things and figuring out how something happened.

So there I was at the police academy. Training was a breeze and I graduated at the top of my class. I really excelled in all aspects of training but being a leader I loved the most.

My first day on the job I was bright eyed and bushy tailed. I couldn't wait to catch some bad guys. They partner me up with this old Black guy named Gus Johnson. Now Gus didn't take any shit from anyone but was loved by everyone. He was two years away from retirement. Every day before our shift would start, Gus would say to me 'young man you better listen to me today and watch how I do things' as if I wasn't doing that already.

"Young man, you better listen to me today and watch how I do things." Gus admonished.

"GJ, every day you say that to me. I'm six months on the job and my arrest records are higher than any other rookie on the force and some veterans."

"Every day there's something different on the job. I want to keep you on your toes."

"Thanks for everything GJ. Tomorrow I take the detective tests."

"Are you nervous?"

"Just a tad bit."

"You shouldn't have anything to worry about. You're probably the smartest cop in the department..." Gus said and threw the car keys and continued "...why don't you drive today and don't drive like it's your car."

"What do you mean?"

"I see how you drive and it looks scary."

"I'll take it easy on ya."

From that day I drove the patrol car while Gus rode shotgun. It took eight months after I passed the detective's test before I'd left patrol for the detective's office. There weren't a lot of bad crimes in my hometown like murder, rape, and burglary. After being on the job as a detective for about one year I realized if I want to become a great detective, I'm going to have to apply for a position in another city. So I applied for a detective's position in both Essex and Camden Counties. Camden's high murder rate and lack of detectives made it easy for me to get the job there.

Once I accepted the job in Camden, New Jersey I needed to find an apartment. Being that I've always been able to find my way around anywhere once I have a map, I made mental notes of surrounding towns and places of attraction.

The City of Camden Police Department had a great deal of cold cases or what you may call unsolved mysteries. So fortunately for me they put me in homicide or more specifically: cold case squad.

"Detective McWhorter if you're finished with getting your desk together I would like to see you in my office." Lieutenant Foster Parrish said.

"No problem sir I'm right behind you."

The Lieu was a big guy and he never raised his voice in anger, but got his point across very well. He would just stare at you with those piercing eyes and telepathically you knew what he wanted you to do. No one didn't mind coming into his office because it was one of the most comfortable offices one had ever been inside. Soft green painted walls, King Arthur arm chairs and a chaise lounge chair anyone could use at any time of the day and as long as he wasn't in it of course.

"Close the door behind you and have a seat."

"Thanks."

"Since this is your first day here, I'll take it easy on you…" Lieutenant Parrish reached into his left bottom desk drawer and grabbed some manila folders and tossed them at Emad and then he continued "…here's three cases you can start on today. If you need anything you can ask Detective Valucci who you'll be partnering up with. Can you open the door …" Parrish pointed at the door and when Emad opened the door Parrish yelled "…Valucci get your butt in here!"

Detective Marco Valucci a two year veteran slow jogged to the office. His medium built frame weaved around desks and chairs and then he skipped up the staircase by taking two steps at a time to reach the Lieu's office. Very athletic and muscular due to his daily kick boxing training regimen he does at Heathcoat School of Boxing located across the Delaware River in Philadelphia.

"Lieu you call me?" Marco said as he got to the door.

"Come on in I want you to meet your new partner. This is Emad McWhorter show him around the squad room and then you guys get started on those cases I gave him."

The two detectives extended their hands at each and then firmly shook hands. Parrish gave them a little peep talk and then dismissed them to get started on their cases.

"McWhorter." Parrish called.

Emad stopped and looked back.

"Welcome to cold case squad and Little Beirut."

So there I was sitting at my new desk looking over a case I've received second handed. I opened the folder to find out that this case has been cold for four months and the first detectives on the case had no leads. I looked up and caught eye contact from Detective Marco whose desk was sitting straight across from mine.

"So what 'cha got there…" Detective Marco paused I guess trying to remember my name "…Emad right?"

"Yes, and you're Marco right. Well, two school girls found a man's body while walking home from school. The detectives working the case ID'd him as being Jonathan Booker a twenty-two year old college senior at Penn State University planning on becoming a meteorologist. He's Black 5'10", 192lbs, red hair, light-skinned with green eyes…" Emad flipped a page up and kept reading never looking up at Marco "…apparently the man's throat was cut with a smoothed edge knife.

The only evidence left behind by his attacker was some footprints and a bloody torn t-shirt."

"Was there a weapon found?" Marco asked.

"No, they didn't find a weapon but there was evidence that he fought his attacker."

"What's the evidence of that?"

"The coroner found skin under his finger nails on both hands."

"Since the Lieu gave you the folder, how do you want to work this?" Marco asked.

"I was thinking we need to find out why he was where he was found and then who was with him." Emad replied.

"We need to speak to the detectives who worked the case first. Tell me their names?"

"Let me see, oh Vincent Martin and Gregory Gimms."

"Well then this will be interesting." Marco said with a slight grin on his face.

"What do you mean?"

"Wait and see. Come on they're in homicide."

"I thought this was homicide."

"Yes but all our cases are unsolved."

No shit after talking with Martin and Gimms I could see why this case wasn't solved. Martin is too silly and goofy, while Gimms is sloppy. I'm willing to bet my check that they couldn't solve a jay walking case.

My partner and I started out by going to Jonathan family's house in Upper Darby, Pa. At his mother's house we found out after she ragged our asses and then the department's ass for being sloppy that Jonathan had two friends and one was his roommate and the other was his girlfriend of two and half years. We left there and went to the university to question his friends.

I suggested to Marco that we should change the way we look before questioning Jonathan's friends. The reason why is because we both still looked young and could pass for being college students. Students will feel more comfortable talking to other students than cops. Marco agreed and we went shopping for some college garb. After shopping we drove forty minutes to Penn State.

Upon getting there I asked for directions to the senior dorms. A tall muscular gentleman pointed me in the right direction. I think he plays sports by the way he was holding on to his football. Anyways when we got to the dorms there was a gathering of students out front. So we split up to work the crowd faster. As I was asking around for Jonathan Booker, a young lady stopped me and said to me 'I thought I knew all of Jonathan's friends, how do you know him'. I told her we were old friends and I was looking for him because I haven't heard from him in a few months.

The young lady and I started bumping gums and she turned out to be Jonathan's ex-girlfriend Katharine. About five minutes into our conversation she opened up like a book just as I expected. She told me Jonathan was cheating on her with a girl from Cherry Hill, New Jersey but he didn't know she knew because she had been following him around secretly. She also told me where in Cherry Hill the young lady lived and gave me a distinctive description of her.

"What's the note pad for? Are you a cop?" Katharine asked.

"Yes, I'm Detective Emad McWhorter working on Jonathan's murder. Will you please help me solve his murder?"

"Why didn't you just say that? I loved him of course I'll help in any way I can. What do you need to know?"

"Well I think you have been very helpful with the information you have given me so far but if you happen to think of anything else here's my phone number at the department..." Emad wrote his name and number and gave it Katharine and then he continued "...don't worry we are going to find out who did this."

After I finished speaking with Katharine I found Marco and we walked back to the car. I asked Marco to drive while I looked for the so called girl Jonathan was cheating with address on my map. Next, we found a pay phone so we can call the lieutenant to ask him to call ahead to Cherry Hill Police Department to let them know we will be in town questioning some suspects. Just some professional courtesy between police departments we like to do when working in someone else's backyard. Parrish didn't ask any question but simply said "No problem" and then hung up the phone.

"So what 'cha find out." Marco asked.

"Jonathan was cheating on his girlfriend with a girl who lives at this address..." Emad pulled out his small note pad from his inside jacket pocket. He flipped it open and gave it to Marco "...she didn't know her name but gave me a description of her..." Emad added moving behind Marco's left shoulder and pointing at the note pad "...I was thinking when we get there and knock on the door let's just see who answers the door."

"And if it's not her?"

"Then we ask if the girl who fits the description is there."

451 Lincoln Avenue

Knock

Knock

Footsteps loudly approached the door.

"Who is it?" a voice spoke from behind the door.

"The police ma'am."

"Oh…"

The door swung open and a beautiful full figured white woman stood before us.

"Hello ma'am I am Detective Valucci and this is my partner Detective McWhorter…" Marco said holding up his badge and identification and I did as well "…may we please come in and ask you some questions about Jonathan Booker?"

"I was wondering when you guys were gonna come by."

"What do you mean Ms." Emad said.

"Johnny and I were seeing each other but his mother didn't approve nor did my parents. And being that I was with him on the night he was murdered I just thought you guys would be stopping by to question me. Come on in and have a seat. May I get you guys something to drink."

"No ma'am we're fine. By the way what's your name?" Emad answered and asked.

"Katharine Stein."

"What did you guys do that night?" Valucci asked.

"We caught a movie and then went on a walk."

"Did you see anyone acting suspiciously while y'all were together?"

"No but we ran into my ex-boyfriend and his friends while we were at the movies."

"How did your ex-boyfriend act when seeing you with another man?" Emad asked.

"Normally Bradford would just keep doing what he was doing when he saw me with someone else but this time he was angry and let it be known that he didn't approve of us being together."

"Why because Jonathan was Black?" Emad asked.

"Yes I don't know if you notice or not but this area is not into race mixing."

"Well I can't say that I have. What's Bradford full name and address?" Valucci asked.

"He lives four houses down to the right when you walk out and his last name is Dumalles."

"Does he work or go to college?"

"He works at the car repair shop on thirty-eight."

"Do you know the name of the shop?" Marco asked.

"O'Brian or O'Brime, all I know is it starts with an Oh and it's on thirty-eight."

"Thank you very much and if you can think of anything else please give me or Detective Valucci a call." Emad said while handing Katharine a note with their information on it.

"I hope y'all solve this because Jonathan was a really nice guy."

"We'll do our best ma'am. You have a nice day." Valucci said.

"You do the same." Katharine replied.

Marco and I paid Bradford a visit at his home first and that meeting proved fruitful. I notice he was lying about his whereabouts on the day of Jonathan's murder. Marco and I agreed we needed to get him down to the department. So we asked our lieutenant to get us a warrant for his arrest.

Once we got him on our turf we had no problem breaking Bradford. He even admitted to some rapes of young girls in surrounding neighborhoods.

Being on the job really took another meaning when I solved this case. But the most rewarding part of the case was when I was able to tell Jonathan's parents we found and arrested their son's murderer. The Booker's was also pleased to hear we got a confession and the district attorney's office was asking for the maximum sentence to be served being that it was a hate crime.

After a few years of this type of work I got bored and needed more. So I applied to the Central Intelligence Agency.

CHAPTER TWENTY-FOUR

<u>*Berlin, August 1986*</u>

It was cold, cloudy and windy and the evening was young. I finally reach my destination after driving about ten miles from town. I had a meet and greet with an associate of an international terrorist named Christian. We don't have any photos of Christian and anyone that gets close to him is murdered or never heard of again.

What is a meet and greet you ask. A meet and greet is when one person has something that another person wants. Someone who mutually knows the two people puts them together. At the meeting both parties must present partially of what they offer and gives each party a chance to feel the other party out. Therefore, we call this type of meeting a meet and greet.

Now you're probably thinking, what is the product I am trying to sell? Well if you must know. Forrest O'Hagan is an international criminal looking to buy a list of hack codes to access the CIA databanks. Mr. O'Hagan wanted to hack into the CIA databanks to retrieve locations of their safe houses.

Word got out about a rogue CIA agent, wanting to get even with the agency. This so called rogue agent stole a list of CIA hack codes to safe houses throughout Eastern Europe and Asia. Now he wants to sell this list on the black market to the highest bidder. Bidding had started at one point two million dollars. Our dear Mr. O'Hagan would not bid but offered a price of twenty-one million dollars. Forrest O'Hagan wasn't the type of man you can easily turn down and he never takes no for an answer.

For some time now Mr. O'Hagan has been able to slip capture from any justice department and during his time on the loose he has rain havoc in the form of terrorism with Christian's help and no country is excluded from his evil doings.

Okay back to what I was saying. An asset to the agency has set this meeting up. But one thing I've learned during my training is that you should never trust anyone. Not even a so called asset to the agency. So I came to the meet and greet with a fellow agent by the name of Tristan Thomas.

We arrived one hour early before the actual time of the meeting to make sure there wasn't any traps or people hiding anywhere. My partner was driving and had parked the car on the road instead of in the driveway. When we exited the car the wind was so strong I could hardly keep my fedora on my head. As we approached the altbau style house I could see there was a light illuminating from right side of the house. We surveyed the area surrounding the house and notice there weren't anyone hiding in wait. After about fifty minutes has past Tristan and I continued our approach cautiously. I knocked twice, paused and then three rapid knocks in succession as per the orders of the man we're meeting. The door swung open and a man standing 5'10", with a muscular body built, and blonde shaggy hair hanging on his shoulder answered the door. From the photos I've seen of Forrest O'Hagan, this man match his description.

"Mr. Jack Joshua." the stranger said holding out his hand for a handshake.

"Yes and your Mr. Forrest O'Hagan?" Jack Joshua asked and took the stranger's hand and shook it.

"No, I'm not Mr. O'Hagan…" the stranger said still holding Jack's hand "…he had another engagement to attend. I'm Maxwell, Mr. O'Hagan assistant he asked me to stand in for him and do the deal."

Maxwell gently pulled Jack through the threshold by his hand and Tristan followed closely behind.

"This is my assistant Simon he'll be joining us." Jack said.

Maxwell motioned for one of his men to come over and frisk the two men. Maxwell's man found a .40 caliber Beretta pistol on Simon and a Glock 9mm on Jack. He handed both weapons to his boss.

"No need for these at our meeting. You men can retrieve your weapons before you leave." Maxwell said and directed the men to the study room by extending his hand and asked if they would care for anything to drink. Jack and Tristan both declined.

"How nice it was for Phillip to arrange this meeting."

"Yes it was but I thought he and Forrest will be here for this meet and greet." Jack replied.

"Yes that was the first idea, but why do we need an audience of Phillip's kind anyway? He'll just get in our way don't you agree?"

"It really doesn't matter. Let's get started, do you have the cash?" Jack said stopping in his tracks.

"Yes it's over there…" Maxwell said pointing over to the desk.

Jack could see a large piece of luggage sitting on the desk.

"Will you please open the case so Simon can examine the contents?" Jack said.

"I have the cash. Do you have the sample of the list?"

"Yes I do and while he's examining the cash…" Jack said pointing at Simon "…you can take a look at the partial list." Jack had the disc in his hand and raised it up shaking his hand.

"And when do I get a chance to view the complete list?"

"You will be able to view the complete list at our next meeting."

"Very well then follow me."

Jack and Maxwell walked together over to the desk and Maxwell popped the locks to the luggage. Thousand dollar bills looked back at them from the luggage. Jack handed Maxwell a cd disc and Simon started thumbing through the bills to see if all of them were real. Maxwell gave the disc to one of his men sitting at a small desk with a desktop computer.

"It looks good boss." Maxwell's computer geek said after seven minutes had past.

"Are we good then?" Jack asked.

"Yes we are. Now when can we get the list and do the exchange?"

"How soon will you be ready with all of the cash?"

"Give me a call in twenty minutes…" Maxwell said holding out his business card "…and the time is seven forty-two. That gives you until five after to call me. And if I don't hear from you in the next twenty minutes you can keep running but you will not be able to hide. And when we find you we'll not only kill you but everyone you love and they die first while you watch. Do we understand each other Mr. Joshua?"

"Perfectly, and Mr. O'Hagan must attend or there will be no deal. Do you understand me Mr. Maxwell?" Jack answered.

Maxwell smiled and showed Jack and Simon the door. As soon as they walked out the house, Emad looked at Tristan and said 'We have to hurry and get our people into position'. Tristan gave him a head nod in agreement. The safe house was ten minutes away which gave them enough time to get the complete disc together and put a tracker in it so they could follow the disc and retrieve it from whoever had it in their possession and make their arrest. Emad was hoping that that someone would be Forrest O'Hagan.

Nine minutes later

There was no time to waste, the agents working on the disc had to hurry and get it ready before Emad had to call Maxwell back. This is the first time the agency had gotten this close to capturing Forrest. Agent Parker finished the disc two minutes shy of the set time for Emad to call Maxwell for the place of the meeting at 8:00pm.

Ring

Ring

"Mr. Joshua, you are a man of your word so far." Maxwell answered his phone.

"Well let's see if you're a man of your word. Do you have all the cash and where will you like to make the swap?"

"The Europa Center closes at nine. Its fifteen miles south from my location. I'll see you there around eight thirty."

"And Mr. O'Hagan?"

"Yes he will be at the swap."

Click

"Do we have anyone near there?" Emad asked.

"I'm already on it Emad…" Tristan said while dialing a number on the phone.

Ring

Ring

"Hello, Jensen Holt Center, how may I direct your call?" Jamie Lovington said.

"This is Agent Tristan Thomas access code echo zeta five two, code word of the day is sun burn."
"How may I help you Agent Thomas?"
"I need five agents for back-up at the Europa Center in fifteen minutes. They need to cover all the exits. Forrest O'Hagan will be there around eight thirty tonight."
"Agents will be dispatched in five minutes."
Click
"Here's the disc Emad. Good luck." Agent Parker said.
"Eli we have to hurry." Tristan said with his left hand on the door knob and waving his right hand.

Europa Center

Europa Center has exits throughout the mall that could be readily accessed. The mall isn't how you would think of a mall with all the clothing stores and eateries encased in glass walls and such. No this mall had some clothes stores and eateries but what made this mall unique is that it also has an apartment block included. This will make it hard for us to contain Forrest and his henchmen.

Having the extra agents to cover the exits will help us out a great deal. All agents was given a short lesson on Mr. O'Hagan which they listen to on their way over to the mall along with the most resent photos we have of him.

As I previously said before we couldn't take Mr. O'Hagan for the average crook or terrorist. He has been able to avoid capture the last five plus years and if we want to get him this time we have to bait him out carefully. The last run in with Forrest left three agents dead and ten maimed and hospitalized. This guy was ruthless and he will do anything to avoid going to prison. But he knew there will be no prison term for him. He has cause to many deaths and destroyed millions of dollars in property lose. Forrest O'Hagan will be put to death either by hanging, firing squad, electric chair, lethal injection, or a United States government agent.

Every possible exit was covered by an agent disguised as a taxi cab driver and each agent was strapped with a .38 caliber pistol. Emad and

Tristan waited for Forrest and Maxwell and whoever they brought with them outside of a small shoe store near one of the two inner courtyards.

Okay here's the op. Two things you already know; one, we're using the previously mention hack codes to bait Forrest out of hiding and two, once the disc is used the tracker is turned on and then we can zero in on his location.

What you don't know is why. When we find his hideout we can search it and maybe find out how he will attack Disney World.

We also know Forrest won't show up for the swap. It's too risky for him and he won't take the chance of being captured. Remember he's a very intelligent criminal. When we exit the mall along with Maxwell and his colleagues, there will be an agent to follow him. Each agent is under strict orders to follow only and report. All the other agents not involve with the initial tailing of Maxwell will get into position and be ready for handoff so Maxwell won't get suspicious of the tails. Sounds like a plan huh? Well let's see if it works.

"Are all agents in positions?" Tristan spoke into his microphone covered by his fist.

One by one each agent sounded off. Tristan stuffed his earpiece into his shirt and then exited the restroom and walked over to where Emad was posted up.

"Here they come." Emad said motioning with his head to his left as Tristan approached.

"Mr. Joshua do you have the completed list?" Maxwell asked without any pleasantries.

"Yes and where's the money and Mr. O'Hagan?" Emad said looking from side to side.

"Walk with me to my car." Maxwell replied and motioned with his hand pointing to his right.

Emad and Tristan walked with Maxwell and his entourage with Emad shoulder to shoulder to Maxwell. As they got to Maxwell Mercedes Benz Maxwell turned to Emad and said "If you don't mind may you please let my associate here examine the disc?"

"Once I see Mr. O'Hagan."

"You won't see Mr. O'Hagan."

Two men approached Emad and Tristan from their rear and put pistols on their backs.

"Get in the car and don't make me ask you again."

CHAPTER TWENTY-FIVE

<u>*Berlin, August 1986*</u>

Time is of the essence, Tristan and I needed to move fast to get out of our situation. The main thing now is to remain calm and ascertain what they will do now: kill, trade, or release us. My gut feeling is that they will kill us. I know Tristan is thinking the same thing, I only hope he keep his temper intact.

Tristan has been a bad mother shut your mouth agent since he graduated from the academy. He came through the same program as did I, only he was second. Tristan was born on a potato farm in De Moines, Iowa with a father who believed in hard work and education. He grew up an only child because his twin sister had died when they were two years old.

"If you both remain calm and do as we say, you'll both live and be rich men." Maxwell said.

"You want us to trust you but where is your trust of us." Emad replied showing his bonded hands.

Maxwell laughed and Emad responded very quickly. Emad elbow surprised the guard sitting to his right when it came up fast and strong to his chin. The guard pulled the trigger on his pistol as Emad leaned back and the bullet went through the top of the driver's side back door. Emad grabbed his wrist and twisting it, taking the gun and backslapped the guard with the gun knocking him out. Emad immediately pointed the gun at Maxwell. Tristan reacted simultaneously by kicking the gun hand of the guard sitting in front of him with his left foot, knocking the gun from his hand and then coming back with another kick to his face. Both guards were slumped over and their guns were now in Tristan's and Emad's possession. Now Tristan had his gun trained on the driver. All this had happened before Maxwell could react from the front seat.

"Pull over!" Emad shouted to the driver.

"Now if you don't mind Mr. Maxwell could you please give us the key to our restraints?" Tristan firmly said.

After taking off their handcuffs, Emad reached over the guard sitting next to him and opened the car door and pushed him out. While Tristan covering Emad, Emad grabbed the other guard and did the same with him.

"Now this is what's going to happen Mr. Maxwell, your driver has three seconds to take his gun out and toss it back here and then he can jump out the car or get a bullet in his head, one..." Tristan said.

Before Tristan could get to the count of two the driver was moving and had retrieved his gun from its holster and tossed it into the back seat. Tristan exited the car and pointed his gun at the driver. He also wiped his brow to tell the other agents to stay back. While Tristan was ordering the driver to get out the car, Emad had Maxwell covered. Tristan then slid into the driver's seat and drove off. Emad took out his knife and cut the fabric to the back seat.

"Lean your head back..." Emad said to Maxwell and then he continued "...I am going to blindfold you now."

"Mr. Joshua you will regret this one day." Maxwell said confidently.

CHAPTER TWENTY-SIX

My Navy Seals training was long and gruesome on top of my CIA training. In all I've been training for a little over five years. Part of my CIA training consisted of me running covert missions and now I get the chance to use all my abilities. I am mentally and physically ready for anything the world of terrorism has to offer.

Derrick was on his first enlistment when we met for the first time. Unlike Derrick my training was done in a secretive location. Just so happens Derrick and I were assigned to the same unit. We didn't quite hit it off at first because of his views on women. As you know I have a sister but what you don't know is that I also have four other sisters. I was raised in a two parent home with a father who showed little interest in me. My second oldest sister who taught me how to swim was also like a second mother. Having two women and three girls in the same house gave me a great sense of respect for women.

Derrick kept everyone on their toes in our unit with his practical jokes and pranks. He would string up buckets of water over doorways that would drop down on whoever walked through the door or put black grease inside someone's cap that would run down their face when they sweat.

Outside of Derrick's views of women we became close because he showed the same dedication towards the interest of the United States and the protection of its citizens. His importance to her became very clear on our first mission together. For the most part of our lives we would just hang out until our unit is called in to rescue or destroy. Today we're rescuing and destroying.

The Mayor of Milwaukee, Wisconsin Joseph Vincent is good friends with President Alex Cooper and their daughters have become friends as well. While on vacation for spring break in New Zealand Megan Cooper and Daisy Vincent disappeared. The President wasted no time calling in a favor from his good friend Cameron Justice director of the CIA. Even though Alex Cooper was no longer the current president he still had pull.

Cameron immediately put his assets in Australia to work. The assets found out that there's a secretive and exclusive organization for the wealthy that buy and sell young girls. Intel also found out that a sheik in Pakistan is part of this organization and has brought the President's and Mayor's daughters.

"Here's a chance for us to use our guys" Cameron said.

"How ironic it would be that our President who okayed the program will be needing them first…" Cornelius Woodear Sr. replied and he then continued after a short giggle "…I'll get the unit on it right away. Send me the Intel."

"It's already on its way."

"See ya around Cam."

"Take care Woody."

Beep

Beep

"Honey I got to go. Command is paging me." Emad said.

"Give me a kiss and be careful." Veronica replied.

"Love baby."

"I love you too."

Beep

Beep

Beep

"Damn it's about time." Kata said out loud to himself.

Beep

Beep

Beep

"Yeah it's time to rock and roll." Tristan said jumping up from the table of a date he had with his future wife.

"What the fuck is going on?" Melissa said.

"I'll explain another time." Tristan answered and kissed his date on the cheek before he ran out the restaurant.

Beep
Beep
Beep
"Hell yeah!" Derrick said.

"Boy you better watch your mouth before I wash it for you." Grandma Pearl chastised.

"Sorry Nana for my language but I have to go. I'll watch T.V. with you when I get back. Love you."

"Love you too…" Grandma Pearl replied and then said to herself "…every time that thing goes off he got to leave."

Along with the special soldiers that were called in there were five other soldiers in the unit as well. This would be their first time working together since the elite soldiers have been added to the unit and the soberness of the elite soldiers has infected the rest of the unit.

"Attention on deck!" Seaman Nebs said.

"As you were men…" Lieutenant Commander Woodear II said and then he continued "…our transport is on the tarmac now for our next mission. I will brief you while we're en route to our destination. So grab your gear and double time it out to the tarmac and board the transport."

With that said all of the soldier's boots hit the deck and mission "Liberate" was under way. Once in the air Cornelius Woodear II started briefing his men.

"Listen up we have three main targets. First two targets is our top priority and they're the daughters of President Alex Cooper and the Mayor of Milwaukee Joseph Vincent. The two girls were kidnapped by some pirates while they were on a cruise ship sailing around New Zealand. After that they were sold to a sheik in Pakistan to be his sex slaves…" Woodear paused and then looked to his left and then he continued "…Nebs if you will please. Seaman Nebs is passing out photos of our targets. We are to save and rescue the girls. The third target is the sheik himself and his name is Ali Jabbar Albin. We are going to do this one by the numbers. No mistakes allowed is that understood?"

"Yes sir!" every special ops soldier said in accordance.

"Very good then, here's your orders. Thomas, McWhorter, Fields, Smith, and Jacob, you men are to take out the Sheik and your team will be known as Zulu. As for the rest of you men, your orders are to get the girls and your call sign will be Tango. Does anyone have any questions?"

There was silence for about eight seconds.

"Ok then, Seaman Nebs if you don't mind will you please put the map of the palace up on the screen."

"Yes sir." Nebs replied.

"As you all can see here's the palace. To the east of the palace is a small section of a mountain. We will put you down on the east side of the mountain over here..." Woodear paused and pointed at the mountains on the screen and then he continued "...making your way west..." Woodear said dragging his finger across the screen "...you can gain cover here. And it's here the two teams will split and get ready to enter the palace and complete your orders. Does anyone have any question?"

The transport fell silent and Woodear continued.

"Good, happy hunting men and Godspeed." Woodear added.

CHAPTER TWENTY-SEVEN

Ali Jabbar Albin palace was located in a secluded area near the Karakoram Mountains. He had his palace built here so the mountains could give him some type of protection from foreign governments. The transport put the unit down approximately a half a klick away from the sheiks palace on the other side of a small part of the mountain. The unit had to climb up and then descend from the mountain in order to approach the palace safely. The temperatures of the mountain were close to below freezing at this time of the night. Emad and his team had prepared themselves for this type of terrain. Once they got up and over the mountain, infrared readings of anyone moving around the palace were transmitted down to the unit from drones flying above. Isn't technology sweet? Emad positioned his men to avoid most of the palace security. Quickly the unit moved forward through the sand crotched down low so they wouldn't be detected by the palace's security.

"Tango you are cleared to move into position." Fields directed while looking at the infrared imaging of the palace on his DT-6 handheld computer.

"We're moving out."

"Once you get into position pop red flare." Emad ordered.

"Roger that Zulu leader."

Tango team moved north to get into position. Every member from both teams had a security agent in their sights.

"Zulu leader, this is Tango."

"Go ahead Tango."

"We're in position and ready to pop red flare."
"Switch from night vision. Tango you have a go."
Phoosh

The sky glowed red and all the security agents scrambled disoriented. Both teams moved in killing the palace's security in their sights. Emad and his team made it to the palace without a scratch. They made their entrance to the palace via one of the east side doors. Jacob ducked his head in the door first and then gave a thumb up. Smith rolled a grenade down the corridor adjacent to the door. One by one the team entered the palace covering each other with McWhorter at point and Thomas taking up the rear. McWhorter found the first marble column and kneeled behind it for cover. In a sweeping motion with his MK 20 McWhorter surveyed the large room and motion for his team to proceed.

Security guards jumped out from behind a wall and started shooting towards Emad and his team. The fire fight was intense and Emad and his team found themselves pinned down.

"We're wasting time use your grenades." Emad commanded looking at Smith.

Within seconds Smith tossed three grenades into the direction of the guards.

Boom

Boom

Boom

"Move!"

Team Tango

Derrick Varnell is the team lead of Tango and was also running point. Tango had made their way into the palace via a northern entrance. Since Zulu was causing the most raucous, there were only two guards to watch the girls and the rest had left to help out on the east side of the palace.

"We have a total of ten minutes. Johnson I want you to secure that corridor…" Petty Officer 3rd Class Varnell ordered pointing to his right and then he continued "…and Wiggins you secure this corridor…"

Petty Officer 3rd Class Varnell barked pointing to his left and yet again he continued "…Parker you're with me."

After giving his teammates their orders Petty Officer 3rd Class Varnell gave a motion with his hands for them to move by waving his hand forward. The only thing standing in between Varnell and the girls were these two guards. Varnell made quick work of them by shooting both men in their foreheads with his MK-20. Parker grabbed the keys to the cell and gave them to Varnell. Parker then got into position to cover Varnell as he breached the doorway which led down to where the slaves were being kept.

They made their way down the steep staircase which seems as if they had stepped into the twilight zone. Once they reached the bottom of the staircase they noticed the walls were moldy and wet and the floor was uneven sand. Lights blanked off and on and they could see their breath as if they had enter a walk in freezer. When they reached the first cell Varnell called out the President's daughter name.

"United States Navy is Megan Cooper in there!" Varnell shouted.

"She's not down here. They took her and Daisy away last night." A voice spoke from behind the cell door.

"We are here to rescue you all. Can you go unlock all the doors with the girls in them and bring them to the staircase?" Varnell said after he opened the cell door.

"Yes."

"And do it as fast as you can because we are press for time."

"Chief this is Petty Officer Varnell do you read me?"

"Yes go ahead."

"They moved the priorities last night. We need to find them. Copy."

"Copy. Do you have an ideal where they are?"

"Not yet, on my way to find them."

"Make it fast Petty Officer."

"I'm on it Chief."

Intel didn't know the sheik had moved the President's and Mayor's daughters up in another room because he was preparing them for shipment to a friend of his in Eastern Europe. The girls thought it was last night when the other girls were removed from the dungeon but in fact it had been three days ago. The sheik didn't want Megan or Daisy to look to bad when he shipped them off.

The last three nights Megan and Daisy had been put up in a lavish Arabia style room complete with all the trimmings. They ate well and were bathed thoroughly everyday by other slaves. Everyone in the palace knew that they were off limits. Not even the sheik had touched them sexually. They would be just right for his friend. It was well known throughout the world that both girls had made a pact with one another to keep themselves only for their future husbands.

"Is that everyone?" Parker asked.

"Yes, except for the two girls they took last night." Misty replied.

"Johnson and Wiggins this is Varnell. Do you read me?"

"Johnson here go ahead."

"Wiggins here go ahead."

"Meet us at the top of the staircase to the dungeon. Do you copy?"

"Copy."

"Copy."

4 minutes later

"Parker and I will go find the two priorities while y'all get the other girls to safety." Petty Officer Derrick Varnell said.

"You only have ten more minutes until the transport leaves." Seaman Justice Wiggins added.

"I know that just get them to safety."

Back to team Zulu

"The sheik should be trying to get to his evac spot now. Kata what's our evac time?" Emad asked.

"We got seven minutes."

"Kata you're with me. The rest of you stay here for three more minutes and then get to the evac spot." Emad ordered.

The sheik had a stairway that led to his helipad from his private room on the west side of the palace. Upon reaching the helipad, Albin and his protection team engaged Emad and Kata. Kata squeezed his trigger first and shot two of the sheik's personal protection men in their chest. Emad followed with a precise shot to the third man forehead. Both men approached Ali Jabbar Albin.

"How could you ever believe you will get away with taking our President's daughter?" Emad asked.

And before Ali Jabbar Albin could answer, Emad shot him twice in the face.

"Move." Emad said to Kata while running away.

Kata stayed and stared at the sheik before he shot him two more times in his chest.

"Stupid Arab." Kata said looking down at Alban's dead body.

"Kata lets go and that's an order." Emad said with bass in his voice.

Team Tango

Time was pressing for Varnell and Parker to find the two main principle reasons for them being there. Very quickly but cautiously they ran up two flights of stairs. The girls were hiding in a large lavished room.

Scared from the noise of gun fire the girls hid in a closet clinging onto each other. When Parker opened the door to the closet and raised his weapon both girls screamed in astonishment.

"We are here to rescue you. Come with me, I'm Petty Officer 3rd Class Garner Parker of the United States Navy ma'am."

"Help us please!" Daisy said.

"That's why we're here ma'am."

"We don't have much time come quickly with us."

Parker grabbed Daisy by the arm and Varnell did the same with Megan. The four of them running quickly to reach the transport before the charges were set off in the palace. The first set of semtex explosives exploded on the other side of the palace just as the foursome reached the main floor.

"Varnell what's your position?" Emad asked.

"We got the main cargo and on our way to you sir."

"You better double time it Petty Officer."

"Roger that."

No one on Emad's team life was lost in the rescue and raid of Ali Jabbar Albin's palace, except for Ali Jabbar Albin and his guards. The elite soldiers have proven their worth.

CHAPTER TWENTY-EIGHT

Corpus Christi Naval Base

When my unit returned from our first mission we were full of confidence. I was still excited and needed some alone time to evaluate myself and my team. So I headed to this small lake outside of the base. Before I got there I phoned my girlfriend Veronica Cruz to let her know I was okay and would come home as soon as possible. Of course she wasn't happy with me not coming home and let me have an ear full to prove it.

I got to my spot at the lake and sat under the same large Magnolia tree as usual. I'm not easily startled nor am I the one who like surprises. So when this Lieutenant Commander showed up at my spot while I was contemplating, I wasn't happy.

"A nice calm lake after a mission always made me feel better." Lieutenant Commander Lars Christopherson said.

Lars Christopherson is a man's man. Six feet three inches tall, with reddish-blonde hair trimmed high and tight, and about two hundred and ten pounds. This Swede arms probably took up most of his upper body weight along with his massive chest. Slow to anger but commanded respect with his baritone voice.

"I like it better alone." I responded with my eyes still closed.

When I opened my eyes to see who I was talking to, I noticed his bars on his lapel and then gave him my complete attention.

"My name is Lieutenant Commander Lars Christopherson…" the Commander extended his hand and then he continued as I got to my feet "…and this is Vance Beread of the CIA. If I'm not mistaken your Chief Petty Officer Emad Elijah McWhorter."

"Yes sir I am." I said as I took both men extended hands and then I continued "…how may I help you?"

"We have a mission for you to finish." Vance Beread added.

"A mission to finish and what do you mean by that?"

"While you were still in CIA training you took part in an op concerning a terrorist named Christian." Vance Beread said in an as-a-matter-of-fact voice.

"Yes I did."

"Well we need to finish the op Chief."

"As I remember Thomas and I captured one of his colleagues and turned him over to you guys…" I said pointing at Vance Beread and then I continued "…y'all didn't torture him enough for him to spill the beans on Christian's whereabouts."

"First of all we don't use those tactics anymore and secondly yes we don't know his whereabouts." Vance replied.

"We would like it if you two can give it a try again with the help of more men in your unit." Lieutenant Commander Lars Christopherson said.

"And who are these men?"

"You will know everything at the first meeting before deployment. You are to meet us fifteen klicks west of this location at sixteen hundred hours tomorrow. Do you understand?" Lars Christopherson commanded.

"Yes sir."

"See you then son." Vance Beread added.

Nineteen miles west of Corpus Christi

I tried to envision in my mind nineteen miles west from the base but I couldn't and I don't remember anyone in my unit ever talking about going there or this piece of land being owned by the US government. I even looked it up in an atlas and guess what, that's right nothing was there. So I went to the location Lieutenant Commander Lars Christopherson directed me to go blindly.

I guess I was about two miles outside of the fifteen mile spot when I came upon a security checkpoint.

The checkpoint was secured by three MPs (military police). One of the MPs manned a seated fifty cal machine gun mounted to the ground. Right behind the fifty cal was a security booth. One MP directly outside the door of the booth and the other one stayed inside.

Inside the booth was a latrine and the control panel to the electrical fence and gate. The fence with razor wire on the top and both sides of the bottom was the guardian of the perimeter along with its sidekick the video camera. They kept this secured government property safe from any nosy onlookers wishing to uncover any military secrets.

The MPs must've been briefed of my coming here because when I reached the gate the MP posted outside the door approached my car and bent over to the driver's side window and said "Go right on through Chief and follow the signs that read 'Hangar' ". After saying his peace he stood up straight and saluted me and in turn I returned the salutation. An alarm sounded and then the metal gate slowly opened.

I followed the signs as directed by the MP for two miles when I came upon a large building with metal siding. As far as I could see there was only one window per side of this building and only one door in the front. I parked my car alongside a Cadillac Escalade and exited my vehicle.

"Hey what's up?" I said extending my hand for a handshake.

"Nothing much, I guess we're back in the saddle again huh." Tristan replied shaking my hand.

"Yeah I guess so, how long have you been here?"

"Roughly twenty minutes..." Tristan said looking down at his watch and then he continued "...we got thirty minutes until sixteen hundred."

"Do you know who the other men the Commander said will be accompanying us on this mission?" I asked inquisitively.

"No I don't but I believe we're going to find out real soon who one of them is. Look!" Tristan answered pointing to the road behind me.

Coming to a screeching halt the car being driven by one of the unit's member kicked up a lot of dirt which caused a mini sandstorm.

"Whew I love this car!" Petty Officer Derrick Varnell said as he exited his Mazda.

"I should've known it was you." Emad exclaimed.

"This is going to be very interesting." Tristan added.

"Yea it's me the man of the hour, too sweet to be sour. Do y'all remember that?" Derrick jokily said.

"Man you stupid." Emad said with his hand extended for a handshake.

"Hey guys, I hear there's supposed to be a few more of us coming. Do any of you know who they are?" Derrick asked as he took Emad's hand.

"No, but I have a feeling who one of them might be." Tristan answered.

"Yeah me too." Emad added.

"And who might that be?"

In unison Tristan and I answered at the same time "Kata." Not a minute after Tristan and I said his name Kata appeared out from the hangar.

"Are you men going to just stand out there or join us inside?" Kata said.

Evidently Kata and the other two men beat us here and were inside with the Lieutenant Commander the whole time while we were waiting outside. So the three of us marched ourselves into the hangar.

The hangar for the most part was empty with exception of one area. There was an office that sat off to rear right side. There wasn't much light inside the hangar. In fact outside of the four windows that sat high which allowed minimal sunlight, there were three hanging lights that extended from the ceiling via a long pole and was covered by aluminum housing and plastic light cover.

I could see the office as I entered the hangar which was about a hundred yards away. As we got closer I could also see the Lieutenant sitting at a medium rectangle shaped table accompanied by three men. Aligned against the wall to his left was two computers, a fax and copier machines, and one large gray metal cabinet. On the wall directly behind him was pictures and names of people I couldn't quite make out just yet. But the way they were arranged on the wall I can tell they were related in some kind of way because there was lines extended from one to another like a family tree. Upon entering the room we all filed in and saluted the Lieutenant Commander.

"As you were men and have a seat. I am really happy to see all of you here." Lieutenant Commander Lars Christopherson said.

"Did we have a choice sir?" I responded.

"Yes you did and by you being here it tells me you all make the right decisions. First things first for all of you who don't know him this is Vance Beread from the CIA. The agency and United States Navy have been working together for some time now and I won't be getting into all of that today. But before we do get started why don't you guys go around the room and introduce yourself with rank."

"I am Petty Officer 3ʳᵈ Class Derrick Varnell sir."

"Petty Officer Tristan Thomas sir."

"Petty Officer Kata Jacob sir."

"And I'm Chief Petty Officer Emad McWhorter sir."

"I'm Petty Officer 3ʳᵈ Class Justice Wiggins sir."

"Last but not least I'm Petty Officer 3ʳᵈ Class Chester Fields but everybody call me Brick sir."

"From here on out this unit will be known as Alpha Squad. Is there any questions before we get started?" Lieutenant Commander Lars Christopherson said and then looked around the room and saw no one had his hand up so he continued "…There's some things I must make perfectly clear. This is a top secret mission and no one know of your involvement except our President, Secretary of Navy, Director of CIA, and everyone in this room. You're not allowed to share anything about this mission with your family or friends. If anything is leaked, you will be dealt with swiftly. Simply put, you will disappear. If you die or get captured by the enemy while on this mission. You will not get a medal and your family will be told a lie about your untimely death. A star will be place on the wall in memory of you. Are we clear?"

"Aye aye sir!" The men said in unison.

"Now let's get down to business. I have one name for you; Christian. The reason why we only have one name is because that's all we know."

"Pardon me sir but may I speak freely." Derrick asked.

"While we are in this hangar you all may speak freely."

"Okay then who the hell is Christian?"

"He is…"

"Excuse me sir but may I?" I asked.

"By all means."

"Like the Lieu said Christian is the only name we have on him and he is considered the worlds most wanted terrorist. He was involved in the hijacking and the destruction of the Delta 737 flight out of France back in 1982 that killed all 257 passengers, the bombing at the Ogilvie

Transportation Center in Chicago in 1983 which killed 103 people, and the use of bio hazardous chemicals in Japan's International Airport which led to the deaths of many Japanese citizens even after the chemical was contained. These are three of his terrorist acts as an international terrorist but we believe he has had his hands in many more..."

"We were close to getting him four years ago when we encountered one of his known associate Maxwell. But a man name Forrest O' Hagan was running the show." Tristan said.

"May I please finish?"

"Go right on ahead."

"Like Tristan said four years ago was the closest we got to him..." My eyes turned to Vance Beread and then I continued "...I also remember turning over one of his men to you guys. So I'm going to assume you guys must have got him to spill some beans and now y'all have a bead on either Forrest or Christian."

"Your assumptions is close Chief. We spotted Forrest O'Hagan girlfriend Xu Lan Xing in Genoa, Italy. Here's a picture of her now. And as you can see, she has changed her appearance considerably." Vance Beread said.

"What has she changed?" Justice Wiggins asked.

"For starters her hair was black and now its red and her eyes are green. She also had a nose job and a breast enhancement..." Vance said as he was pointing at a picture of her on the wall and then he continued "...and this is a picture of Forrest O'Hagan. You can see he has changed his appearance as well. If you look in front of you men on the table is a dossier with all these pictures on the wall inside and a brief description of the mission."

"Listen up men this mission is very vital to our nation's security and the reason why we assembled you six men together is because you're the best at what you do. Emad you will lead the unit out in the field. Tristan, you will work the computer and communication. Derrick you will handle the sniper position and Kata you're the demolition man and finally Wiggins and Fields you two will offer support in the form of your skill in weapons and tracking respectively..." Lars Christopherson paused to allow what he said to sank in and then he continued "...the mission is to kill the five heads of the terrorist organization Drapa. Which by the way means 'kill' in Swedish. And they are pictured here..." Lars pointed his right index finger at the wall and the top photo and then he continued "...starting from the top Christian and as you can see it's a blank photo, and then it filters down to Forrest O'Hagan and Xavier Knolls. Underneath them is Xu Lan Xing and Parker Bouvier. Inside the dossier is their complete bio as of what we know. Main thing I need from you men tonight is to study your enemy and be ready for the unexpected. Is there any question before you're dismissed...?" Lars Christopherson allowed time for anyone to ask any question but no one spoke up so he continued "...you're dismissed."

"Need I remind you that this is a highly classified mission and you are not to discuss this with no one, not even your mates? So go home and get some rest or do whatever it is you do to get your mind right and return here by oh four hundred hours tomorrow. Have a good night men." Vance Beread added.

With that being said the six of us saluted the Lieutenant Commander and went our separate ways.

CHAPTER TWENTY-NINE

I haven't been home from my last deployment for a whole week when I received my new orders. To make my situation worse with Veronica is I've been a little distant in the recent weeks prior to me going on my last deployment. I want to marry Veronica but I don't know how to ask. I don't want to just come out with it. She's really special and deserves to be asked in a romantic way. I was thinking about taking her to my special spot outside of the base near the lake. While we're lying together with Evan crawling around on the grass I'll have an airplane fly by with a banner that reads "Will You Marry Me Veronica" and when she look at me I'll have the ring out.

Well any way I have to tell her I'm leaving again and this time I don't know when I will return. Chasing Christian is a career growth move. It's what I was created to do.

"Hey baby" I said before kissing Veronica on her soft lips.

"Hey baby yourself." Veronica replied after she returned my kiss by poking her lips out.

"Where's Evan?"

"He's in his playpen playing."

"Vee, I got new orders today."

"How long do we have you before you leave?"

"About seven hours."

"Wow a whole seven hours huh."

"Baby you know what I do."

"Yes I do but..."

"But?"

"But nothing. I'm not going to spoil this night by nagging. Have you ate yet?"

"No I haven't. This is why I love you so much." As I said this I moved over to where Veronica was sitting and kissed her gently.

"Let me put Evan down and clean myself up a bit." Veronica said.

"I need a shower too. Would you like for me to join you?" I asked.

"That sounds nice. Give me fifteen minutes."

"Let me get him. You'll take too long."

Emad played with his son for a good half an hour before Veronica broke up their playtime. Emad saw the look in her eyes and then said "I'm going to eat you alive". They haven't made love to each other in over a month. They were well overdue. They will make the best of tonight and squeeze every second of their five hours together making each other moan.

While Veronica was lying Evan down, Emad rushed into the kitchen and retrieved a bottle of red wine and whip cream. Since they were out of strawberries the bananas on the countertop will have to do.

Next, he went into their bedroom and put on some soft music. Emad was acting like he had never had sex with Veronica before. When they were dating in the beginning he would get a hard on whenever they kissed. She still has that effect on him today. But sex was something else altogether. He gets nervous especially when he sees her naked. She's the most beautiful woman he knows and worships the ground she walks on. Veronica is up on a pedestal when it comes to Emad and she knows this fact.

Emad pulled the covers back on their king size bed and placed the bowl of bananas on the bed along with the whip cream. He walked over to the bathroom which was adjoined to their room. Turn the water on to the shower as hot as they both could take it. Veronica walked in the bathroom as soon as he was taking off his clothes and joined him. Emad stopped to watch her undressed and immediately got an erection.

"I guess someone is happy to see me." Veronica said with a wide grin on her face.

"Damn girl you are so beautiful." Emad replied with his hand extended out for her to take.

As they entered the shower they both cringed from the hot water. Emad pulled Veronica close to him and began kissing her. He thrust his tongue into her mouth and she welcomed it submissively. Veronica grabbed his penis and began to stroke it slowly. Emad went down to her neck and sucked hard while pinching her nipples. Veronica let out a sigh of enjoyment. Emad made his way down to her right nipple and bit down gently.

"Suck 'em harder." Veronica coached.

Emad did as he was told and so the left nipple wouldn't feel left out he did the same to it. He then turned her around and made her bend over so he could lick her asshole and vagina from the back. He grabbed her butt cheeks and spread them apart so he can go deep with his tongue. Emad licked between her vagina lips until Veronica was moaning loudly with pleasure and her vagina was dripping wet from inside. Emad lick her for a good five minutes until Veronica said "Stand up baby I want to taste your dick." Again Emad did as he was told.

Veronica took his long shaft and grabbed it with one hand and his balls with the other. Emad closed his eyes as his penis head enter her mouth. Veronica sucked slowly and then rapidly and then gave his balls some attention. Emad pulled Veronica up by her shoulders and then spun her around. His penis went into her without resistance and Veronica approved by moaning in acceptance. Emad grabbed her shoulders and his first stroke was long and hard. He held it there as he could feel the bottom of her vagina and then snatched his penis out quickly. He reinserted and began pumping. Veronica was gripping Emad's penis with her vagina muscles which made him moan and ejaculate after six minutes of sex.

"Let's wash up and go into the bedroom." Veronica advised.

"Sure baby. Damn girl I couldn't hold it any longer but we're not done by a long shot."

They washed each other caressingly and then they were at it again before they could rinse off. While they were kissing Veronica cut the water off and they stepped out. Emad loved drying her body off so he could get a close up look and smell of her vagina. Veronica had a birthmark of a rose on the left side of her vagina stamped on her inner thigh. Emad kissed it with approval.

They walked over to the bed and continued their night there. Playing with the whip cream and fruit. Emad needed to get some sleep so they stopped after three hours of love making.

"Baby you have drained me. My sack is completely dry." The both of them giggled and Veronica then said "So what my pussy is throbbing with pain but it's a good pain."

"Honey I'm sorry for being a little distant for the last few weeks."

"No apologies needed I know what you do. I'm happy we're together and I know you love me and won't hurt me."

"I'm glad you know that because it's true. Why you don't pressure me into marriage?"

"When you're ready you will ask me and I will accept and no moment sooner than that."

"See what I'm saying y'all she is the best. How did I get so lucky to be with you?" Emad shouted.

"First of all who are you talking to? And we both are lucky to have each other."

"I am talking to the world baby."

"Well keep it down before you wake up the baby."

"Now you want to worry about being loud. Just a few minutes ago you were so loud I know the neighbors are mad at us."

"It's all his fault." Veronica said as she grabbed Emad's penis.

"Whoa he's sore baby you have to be gentle."

"That's good for him for not being gentle with her."

"I love you baby." Emad said and then kissed Veronica on her cheek.

"I love you too baby. Would you care for a sandwich and some chips?"

"You read my mind."

"Okay I'll be back shortly and don't fall asleep we're not finished talking mister."

"I won't."

As soon as Veronica left the room, Emad started snoring.

CHAPTER THIRTY

I jumped out of bed when my alarm rang loudly. It's time to make the donuts I thought to myself. I took a quick hot shower after I shit and shave. Once I was dressed in my fatigues I ran into the kitchen for a bite to eat. Veronica had prepared the coffee machine for me last night, so I walked over to it and poured some water in the back and pushed the start button. I scrambled two eggs and made some toast. I sat quietly and ate my breakfast and drank my coffee while I read a magazine Veronica had subscribed too.

I looked up at the clock and noticed it was three oh five which meant it was time for me to grab my extra-large duffel bag and head towards my new work place only fifteen minutes away. Wiggins had asked me to pick him up so we could carpool to the base. It seem as though we were in a convoy because all my unit mates and myself made it to the gate at the same time. The guards were on point and check all our credentials.

Derrick gave me the eye as if he wanted to race to the hangar and I obliged him. I could see Fields in the car with Tristan. I guess Tristan and Kata must've got the hint because they were revving their engine. Derrick pressed the gas pedal to his car and it jumped ferociously and the rest of us followed suit. We tore up the road racing towards the hangar. Rocks and dirt ricocheted off my front windshield. As we were approaching the hangar Lieutenant Commander Lars Christopherson and Vance Beread were entering the hangar and if you're wondering who won the race. It was Kata.

Let me get back to the story. I was glad to get to the office so Kata can stop telling us how he won the race.

"Okay men have a seat and listen up…" Lieutenant Commander ordered and then he continued "…we are going to Genoa, Italy via the USS Klakring. There we have an office already set up so we can track and find Forrest O'Hagan and the rest of Drapa which will lead to Christian. So grab your gear and load up into the helo out back." The Lieutenant Commander said pointing with his thumb towards his back.

The six of us hit the floor with our feet and snatched up our gear and ran out back immediately. As we busted through the door the helicopter blades started to spin. Even though I have flown before I still get butterflies in my stomach whenever I fly. We loaded into the helicopter and sat quietly for about an hour into the ride to the Klakring, when Derrick began his tricks.

"Psst!"

"Psst!"

I opened one eye to see Derrick about to give Kata a wet wheelie. I shook my head no and Derrick paid me no mind.

"If you value your life you won't do that." Kata said with his eyes still closed and his knife in his hand.

"Man none of you guys can take a joke." Derrick replied.

"You should be resting your eyes because we don't know when we going to get any once we get there. It's just a suggestion." I added.

"Okay men we're about twenty minutes out from reaching the Klakring in the North Atlantic. Let's get ready to board."

The unit got into position to board the USS Klakring once it landed on the stern section of the deck. The Lieutenant Commander exited the helicopter first and was greeted by Admiral Howard Spingle. Soon all the men was standing on the deck and waiting for orders. They were led by a Petty Officer two decks below and four sections towards the bow. Once there they were settled in and began relaxing Derrick started doing his thing.

"Hey guys, the first one to bang his head on the overhead has to pay for lunch, once we get back to state side." Derrick joked.

"Since, you put it out there, lets up the ante?" Kata said smirking.

"And what's that?" Derrick asked.

"Not only do the person has to pay for lunch but he has to run butt naked down the port side, from bow to aft. Bet?"

"Bet. Eli are you down?" Tristan commented.

"I'm game if you are?" Emad replied.

"I'm liking this unit more and more. Well do we have to stay in this bunk all night or can we roam?" Derrick asked.

"Let's find out." Tristan added.

Tristan was the first to jump off his bunk and everyone else followed him. They explored the boat from bow to aft until they bumped into Seaman Nettles who had orders to find Emad and escort him to the Admiral's quarters and tell the rest of the unit to return to their quarters.

When Seaman Nettles and Emad got to the Admiral's quarters, the Seaman knocked twice and was told to enter. Once Emad enter the quarters the Seaman was excused and did an about face and closed the door behind Emad.

Emad was standing at attention until Lieutenant Commander told him to have a seat.

"I need you to take lead with the men. Set an example for them to follow. This mission is very dangerous as you already know. When we get to the safe house in Genoa, I need all of you on point. So it starts now. If we are to save some lives I need serious thinking men not children. Are we on the same page Chief?"

"Yes sir!"

"Alright you're excused."

Sunday, April 18th, 1:05am; Bordeaux, France

The USS Klakring pulled into dock at Bordeaux and the Navy Seals team dressed in civilians disembark. Once they were on the ground they loaded into two cars waiting for them to take them to Aeroport de Bordeaux where they will board a flight commercially to Cristoforo Colombo Airport. After traveling almost twenty-four hours Emad and his unit needed some sleep. Lieutenant Commander Lars Christopherson understands in order to get the best out of his men they need rest and ordered everyone to take a four hour catnap.

While they were resting Lars and Vance set up their makeshift office. Tristan was the first to awake and walked over to the kitchen for a bite to eat. One by one the men were all awake and eating.

"Ok men listen up, once you're done eating I need you to get the computer up and running…" Vance said pointing at Tristan and then he continued "…the rest of you finish unpacking your gear and get ready to move once we have a location to where Xu Lan Xing and Parker Bouvier is living. They were last seen together walking around the mall here. Wiggins and Derrick why don't you two go hang out over there for the rest of the day and just survey the area once you're done. Here's some money don't spend it to fast in one spot."

"We need to find what they have plan or maybe we can start a game they're willing to play." Emad suggested.

"What type of game do you suggest?" Lars asked.

"Well it seems to me that terrorists are always looking to infiltrate or kill an agent of justice. So why don't we give them what they want." Emad explained.

"And how do we do that?" Derrick asked.

"Let's say there's a few men who have expelled themselves from the agency. They vowed revenge and have formed their own group but need some money so they can get it up and running…"

"You know that may just work." Lars interjected.

"Ok we have another safe house on the other side of town by the mall. This is what we're going to do. Tristan put it out on the wire that a group of ex- CIA agents have started their own terrorist group hell bent on getting back at the agency. Also put out that they are selling some secrets to bank roll their revenge. They're set up in Genoa and will be leaving the area in a week. Make it seems as though we don't know where exactly they are held up but we have an ideal that it's near the mall across from the caruggi with the man that sleeps there. Kata get ready to become a bum. Tristan don't post it until we get Kata ready and in place. Copy." Vance said.

"I copy sir." Tristan replied.

"Emad here's the address…" Vance paused while he was writing the address on a note "…to the apartment in that alleyway." Vance handed the note to Emad.

"I'm on it." Emad said as he took the note.

"Wait Fields go with him." Lars commanded.

"Aye aye sir."

"Vance and I will remain here and the rest of you will go to the safe house in the alleyway. Am I clear?"

"Yes sir!" Alpha Squad said in harmony.

"Well then pack your gear up and high tail it over there."

Lars commanded.

The safe house in the alleyway was well equip with things Alpha Squad needed. In the main room on the wall was a map of the entire town of Genoa and surrounding towns as well. One black metallic file cabinet filled with information on every important figure that run the town of Genoa. Costumes of different types of employment in Genoa. There was even a suit of a beggar in the closet. Two large bedrooms, each with two beds. One bathroom equip with one bath tub and two showers. A medium size kitchen with all the trimmings.

Most of Alpha Squad was at the safe house except Derrick and Justice. While they were busying themselves with the orders they were given someone was knocking on the door.

Knock.

Knock.

"Let me get it…" Emad said and then he answered the door "… who is it?"

"Jehovah's Witnesses."

"Sorry but we're not interested." Emad said as he snatched open the door.

"That's ok maybe we can come back at another time?" The lady in a floral dress said.

"No that won't be necessary."

"May I leave this with you?"

"Sure." Emad replied and took the pamphlet after which he closed the door.

"Why you take it Eli? Tristan asked.

"Why not? Anyway, everybody get back to what you're doing."

CHAPTER THIRTY-ONE

April 20th, 8:05 pm, Genoa, Italy

This morning was uneventful just as yesterday. Waiting for Christian to take the bait is exhausting. He is clever but I bet the chance of getting his hands on some very serious CIA secrets is too much for him not to peek. And that's all we want him to do is peek his head out so we can cut it off. If the opportunity doesn't present itself soon we're going to have to think outside of the box.

Nighttime has shown its face and some activity sparked up not far away from Kata. It was two men arguing over a parking space. Soon as the pushing and shoving started a crowd began to gather to spectate. The police arrived and broke up the crowd first. Then they turned their attention on the two men arguing. Kata moved his position farther down the alley so the cops wouldn't bother him. Kata wasn't fast enough because as soon as the cops solve the issue between the men, they directed their attention on him.

Kata Jacob is a towering man standing at 6'5" and weighing 236lbs. He's able to blend in with natives of Genoa because of his olive complexion. Kata loves a real fight but handles his temper with meditation. A trick his sensei taught him while learning the art of Wado Ryu. Once while on vacation in the Caribbean with his family during spring break when he was twelve. Kata was attacked by three boys wanting his wallet and any other valuables he may have had on his person. They were able to overpower him and took all of his money (ten dollars). That's when the thirst of fighting began. After that Kata began fighting in school and his father's brother suggested martial arts as a way to teach him discipline. At first it just made him a better fighter. It wasn't until his sensei vowed to stop teaching him that Kata changed his ways. But the thirst was always there, lurking and wanting to come out.

If these policemen threaten to interfere with this op he will take them out without any second thought.

Kata was in full swing of putting on his façade. As the officers got closer it appeared to them as if he was mumbling to himself and staggering around. But what he was really doing was explaining the situation to Emad into his hidden microphone which was being transmitted to the safe house speaker system.

"Emad the cops are approaching me. Please advise." Kata said into his mic attached to his sleeve.
"Please standby and stall them." Emad advised.

Emad snapped into action and directed Tristan to get dressed into a costume of the local police force.

"Take them out." Emad said into the receiver.
"Hey buddy you can't be here like this. Show me your ID?" One of the officers asked Kata.

Kata's reply was a spinning back fist with his right hand to the officer's face and followed by a crescent kick with his left leg to the head which rendered the officer unconscious. The other officer looked shocked and went for his sidearm. Kata reached down and grabbed his hand which was on his gun and elbowed the officer to his chin. His body went limp and Kata double punched him in his midsection and all the wind left the officer's body. When the officer's body hit the ground, Kata leaped into the air and came down on the officer's chest. Both lied there unconscious but alive. Kata grabbed both men by their shirts and dragged them closer to the outer wall of the house diagonally across from the safe house.

"It's done."
"We're on our way."

The plan is for Emad and Tristan to take the place of the officers but first they have to get rid of the bodies and then the car. So Tristan went out on the road and retrieved the patrol car and drove it down the caruggi to where the bodies were lying. Emad and Kata loaded the bodies into the trunk of the car and Kata got into the car with his hands behind. Brick exit the house via through the drainage system. He exit the drainage system through a drain cover and enter an all -black van which was parked on top. As Tristan drove pass, Brick followed them down to the edge of town, which is on the Mediterranean Sea. When they got there they burned the car along with their police costume. While Brick was driving Emad and Tristan got dressed into their street clothes. Finally, after waking up the cops from their slumber, they dropped them off naked in an alley behind a bar with a message "If you mention this to anyone we will find you and kill you and your families". Emad had no intentions of killing a cop or a cop's family but if he had to in order to protect America, he'll kill a generation.

"Emad you better get back here asap. We have some activity in the alley." Derrick advised.
"What type of activity?"
"The kind we been waiting for."
"On my way."
"Emad we're going to be cutting it really close without them seeing us? Kata asked.
"I don't see how when we'll be entering from underneath." Tristan replied.

Which meant they would have to go through the drain system to enter the safe house the same way Brick exited the house. Tristan pushed hard down on the gas pedal and the van reacted with a burst of speed as the engine roared. After about five minutes they pulled over about a street block away from the house next to a drain cover. Fields slid a black metal cover back which revealed a hole in the floor of the van. Wiggins gave Fields a crowbar so he could remove the drain cover. One by one they went down the ladder into the drain system. Once all of them were safely down in the drain system Tristan found the hidden door and they trek down the walkway about 100 yards until they reached the end and a metal door. Attached to the door was an electronic door keypad.

Tristan tapped the keys on the keypad and after an alarm sounded the door swung open.

Once inside Tristan met Emad in a separate room to listen in on the conversation. They couldn't be seen just in case Forrest O'Hagan was the one walking up the caruggi. Kata, Derrick, Brick, and Justice will run the op under the direct direction of Emad.

Knock
Knock
Knock

"How can I help you?" Derrick said into the intercom.
"I would like to speak to Mr. Smith."
"Who may I ask is asking for him?"
"A friend who has business with him."
"What's your name friend?"
"Parker Bouvier."

Parker Bouvier is a Frenchmen around 5' 10" and slim as a bean. He didn't grow up in France because his father worked for a military contractor based in North China. He spoke three languages fluently with Mandarin being his favorite. Never married but had one child who was the jewel of his eye. He keeps his daughter Lijuan Mei and longtime companion Jia who is a talented artist hidden away from his business. They know not who he is involve with nor do they know what he do.

"Mr. Bouvier, I'll be there to let you in."
Derrick hurried to the door to let Parker and his companion in.
"Mr. Bouvier, I am Derrick Varnell, Mr. Smith partner. Please come in and step over here..." Derrick said and motioned with his right hand for Parker Bouvier and his companion to move over to the wall inside the foyer and then he continued "...Mr. Bouvier if you and your companion will assume the position and then we can get down to business."
"Are you serious?"
"As a heart attack."
"Huh."

"It's a saying we say back home. Never mind all that. If you want to meet Mr. Smith I need to pat you down for weapons and wires."

When Derrick went to pat Parker down, Parker swung around and grabbed Derrick by his arm and threw him against the wall and put his forearm up against his throat.

"Stop with all the cloak and dagger shit and take me to Mr. Smith or I'll kill you now."

"Release Derrick now or I'll put two into your friends head." Chester Fields said pointing a gun.

Parker let up and Derrick disarmed him and his companion.

"Ok now we're getting somewhere…" Parker said looking at Chester Fields and then he said to his companion "…put down your gun."

Chester waved his gun for Parker to enter into a side room and then he said "You came here for what?"

"The bidding on the plans to build a Falcon X-15 is to begin tomorrow am I correct?"

"And I say again, you came here for what?"

"Ok my boss don't want that bidding to happen and will pay a handsome amount for that bidding not to occur."

"How handsome?"

"Ten million."

Derrick looked around and said "I don't see money."

"If you allow my colleague to retrieve the money from the car, we will have a deal."

"Brick."

Brick escorted Parker colleague to the car and returned with the money.

"May I ask how did you come across these plans?"

"Well I was a computer analysis with the agency and my job was to set up firewalls to prevent hackers from hacking into the database. What I did was leave a hidden door for me to go through at a later time to take a peek at things while not on the clock." Derrick said as per Tristan advice.

"And why would you do that?"

"Just being curious and what I found out was that our handlers were planning on having us killed out in the field."

"Us, where is the rest of your team? You're the muscle…" Parker said pointing at Brick and then he continued "…and you're too smart…" he said looking at Derrick and then he finished by saying "…so where is your team leader?"

"He's here. He's a little shy." Derrick said slyly.

"Before we go any further I'm going to have to meet him."

"Why should we show you our whole hand and evidently the guy behind you isn't your leader and you're not the leader of whatever group you represent? So what we can do is you show me yours and we'll show you ours." Derrick said in an as a matter of fact tone.

"Let's stop the bull, you know who I am. If you want to meet the man, have your man contact him at this number to set up a meeting. Now may we please have our weapons back?" Parker said while handing a card to Derrick.

"Sir I don't have a clue who you are or who your boss is. Will you please enlighten me?" Derrick said without taking the card.

"My boss is a Mr. Christian. I assume you know who Mr. Christian is?"

"Yes I do."

Derrick took the card and gave Parker and his companion their weapons back.

"Hope to hear from you soon. Have a nice day gentlemen." Parker said before walking through the door.

CHAPTER THIRTY-TWO

April 22nd, 11:22am, Genoa, Italy

When Kata called the number Parker Bouvier gave Derrick yesterday, the answer machine had a message for him:
You have reached Christian if you're serious
about doing business with me please be at the
corner of Via Trento and Scalinata at 12 noon.
Wear a red hat and a blue tourist shirt from
Mama's Gift Shop on that corner. Tell your friends
don't follow us, you will be going on a ride.
See you soon.

We carefully prepared for what most likely will be a kidnapping by placing a tracer in Kata's right ear lobe. We won't be able to follow him via satellite and watch him on our computer because he has to activate it first. He won't do that until he's wand for body bugs during their search.

"Time to go Kata." I shouted.
"I'm ready Chief." He responded.

The taxicab driver was waiting outside and blowing his horn impatiently. Kata needed to be on time or we'll miss our chance of getting close to Christian and maybe even capturing him. We were only ten minutes away from the meeting spot and it was twenty minutes to twelve. Kata darted out the door and hop into the cab. After a twelve minute ride Kata pulled up to the corner for which he is to meet Christian's men.

Twelve o'clock on the dot a green sedan with curtains covering the rear windows pulled over to the corner where Kata was standing. The front passenger window came down and Parker Bouvier asked Kata to get into the rear right passenger seat. The same man that was with Parker when he came to the safe house was sitting in the back. He asked Kata to get on his knees so he could frisk him. After Kata was frisk the bodyguard took out a wand and went over Kata's body with it searching for any bugs or trackers Kata may have on his body or clothing. Parker directed Kata to have a seat and then handed him a blindfold.

"What's this?" Kata asked.

"Your ticket to revenge." Parker replied.

"I thought we were going to be doing business." Kata said calmly.

"You didn't think we were going to show you where we're taking you now did you?" Parker responded.

"I thought maybe we could build a relationship of trust."

"If Christian doesn't like what you're going to say, you won't be around for a relationship for us to build a trust on."

With that being said the driver pushed down on the gas pedal and the sedan sped off. Just in case they had a tracker blocker in the car Kata started to count. And whenever they made a turn he would stop his count and start a new count. Kata would be able to get back to where he is going if he make it back to the safe house alive.

They drove around for fifteen minutes and then they came to a sudden stop.

"Thirty-two." Kata said to himself.

"You may remove the blindfold." Parker said.

"Is Christian here?" Kata asked while he was removing his blindfold and trying to adjust his eyes to the sunlight.

"You will see. Come they awaits us."

Kata followed Parker closely with the other two men right behind him closely. They enter the house through a large arched doorway. Kata looked down as they got to the foyer and could see the chandelier's lights reflecting off the marbled floor which made him look up.

"Please come this way." Parker said as he pulled on Kata arm lightly.

They walked over to the room to their left and Parker opened a double door to an enormous room. The walls were painted bright white which clashed with the wall to wall burgundy carpeting. All the windows were covered with thick curtains hanging from ceiling to floor. Only a single long rectangle table with chairs surrounding it, stood in the center of the room. Sitting at the table was a man and a lady standing next to him.

"Mr. Kata come in and have a seat." The lady said.

"You know my name, now may I ask you what's yours?" Kata said walking towards the lady and the man.

"My name is Xu Lan Xing and this is Forrest O'Hagan…"

"Glad you can join us this afternoon…" Forrest interjected with his hand out for Kata to take and then he continued "…please sit here…" Forrest added while pointing at a chair next to his and then he spoke once more "…I expect your ride over went without a hitch?" Forrest asked.

"Not too bad except for the blindfold."

"Well we have to protect our anonymity. Anyway, let's get down to business. You have something I want and I have something you need. Now all we need to do is trade. Mr. Kata, what's an even trade in your eyes?"

"Ten million dollars."

"Wow, that's a bit steep after we already gave you ten. The only way this is going to work is if you give us something we can verify."

"I figured you would want something…" Kata paused while he reached into his inner jacket pocket.

"Wait!" O'Hagan said to Kata and then he looked at the man standing to Kata's left and said something to him in German. The man moved towards Kata and reached into his jacket.

"…Whoa it's only the information you just asked for." Kata said in an as a matter of fact tone.

The man gave the note he retrieve from Kata's jacket pocket to Xu Lan Xing and she gave it to Forrest O'Hagan.

"What's this?" O'Hagan asked after opening the note.

"The propulsion formula to the Falcon X-15. Your scientist can verify the formula. You do have scientist Mr. O'Hagan?" Kata asked.

"Yes we do…" O'Hagan answered and then he looked over to the man that was standing at the door and said "…Luther, take this over to the lab and tell Crenshaw to diagnose this ASAP…" O'Hagan handed the note to him and then he looked at Kata and continued talking "… If it checks out we have a deal."

"And you get all the plans to build a Falcon X-15."

"Sounds good but how soon can we do the exchange?" Xu Lan Xing asked.

"It's based on how long it will take for you to put the money together." Kata said looking at Forrest and he never looked in Xing direction.

"It will take a few hours to put the money together so let's say six o'clock tonight. Is that sufficient for you?" Forrest asked.

"Yes I'll be waiting for your call to meet your men back at the corner."

"Very well, my associates will show you out and take you back to the corner. Until tonight then." Forrest said and stood up to shake Kata's hand.

"See you then." Kata replied and took his hand.

Kata knew something was amiss because the meet went too smoothly. *"Why would Forrest come out like that? Why didn't they hold me and make my teammates bring the plans?"* He asked himself. *"Think outside the box."* He was telling himself. *"Bingo! They plan on either coming to the house and killing us or killing me at the next meeting while at the same time taking over the house. Shit we need to get into gear when I get back."*

<u>*Safe house*</u>

Everyone was assembled in the safe house largest room to have a briefing on the ops next mission.

"Office are you there?" Emad asked into the speaker phone.

"Yes we are, go ahead Alpha Squad." Lieutenant Commander Lars Christopherson answered.

"Well we ran the op with Kata as the leader. It'll be better if he take the lead on the briefing and we all listen to what he has to say. Do you agree?"

"Petty Officer Jacobs the floor is yours."

"I will be quick and short because we have a limited time if you get my meaning sir." Kata suggested.

"I do, go ahead Petty Officer."

"Well I met with Forrest O'Hagan, Parker Bouvier, and Xu Lan Xing. They took the bait but they took it too easily. I think they're planning an attack on the safe house or killing me at the next meet while simultaneously taking out this safe house. My suggestion is to get into counterattack mode and still run the op sir."

"Emad, what's your suggestion?"

"If Jacobs is still willing to run the op even though the threat is high. I say let's go ahead with the op sir."

"Ok men get it done and if you can bring in Forrest alive that'll be even better. Godspeed men. Office out."

"Thanks sir. Alpha Squad out."

The safe house was quiet except the voice of Emad giving orders and the noise from footsteps of Alpha Squad prepping for a counterattack. If needed more agents could be called in for support but for the most part Alpha Squad was on their own.

<u>*5:31pm*</u>

"All boobies are set and ready for fire sir!" Justice shouted.

"Very good, now we need to get ready for the next meet. Tristan is the cd ready?"

"This isn't something you can just rush, it'll take some time but I'm close. Five more minutes."

"You have four."

"Do my best."

"Copy that."

"Weapons and ammo check Derrick?" Emad yelled.

"All weapons is loaded and on the ready sir."

Tristan finished the disc fully equipped with a tracking program. Once the authentication is completed, the disc will send off a signal of its location.

"Ten minutes until Kata leave for the meet." Emad barked.

It was time to see if all the planning they done will work. Christian and his band of terrorist need to be brought to justice. Alpha Squad justice.

CHAPTER THIRTY-THREE

This time Kata will drive himself to the meet. Emad and the rest of Alpha Squad will remain at the safe house to safe guard all the Intel they have on Drapa. Anyway Kata can take care of himself.

"Remember once they search and run the wand over you, you're safe to wipe your left eyebrow to activate the tracker in your ear lobe. We will be able to hear everything 20 feet of your diameter. Plus it will trigger the beacon I put in your inner thigh that will allow us to know where you're located." Tristan reminded Kata.

"You do know I just went through this right."

"Let's go it's time Kata!" Emad shouted.

Kata ran out the door and jump into the car and started making his way to the meet. Kata drove ten minutes until he pulled up to the same corner he met Parker this afternoon. Just as he was shifting the gear into the park position, a man was at his driver's side window tapping. It's really hard to startle Kata and this time was no different. Kata acted as though he knew the man was there and very smoothly lowered his window to talk.

"Exit the vehicle and come with me. Mr. O'Hagan awaits you."

"Do you mind if I get my shades out the glove compartment?" Kata asked.

"Leave them and no more questions." The man said with a German accent.

As he assumed, Kata went through the same thing as before. He was searched and wand for weapons and bugs, after which he was blindfolded. The only difference is that they drove to the house a different way.

So Kata rode in the back seat completely emerged in darkness because of the shroud he was wearing over his head. Kata could tell the driver had driven almost in a complete circle. He figured they did this to see if they were being followed. This action made Kata smile under his shroud. There was one thing they didn't take into an account and that was his ears. While we were prepping the safe house to counterattack any attack, I had Brick to do a 3 mile radius recon of the pick-up location. This along with Kata's photographic memory, it will be impossible for him not to be able to get back to wherever they were taking him.

Kata was very comfortable in the darkness. In fact he could see more clearly in the dark then most could see in the light. The ride was a little longer than before so he allowed his mind to drift back to his CIA training.

CIA Training, On an island in the Pacific, 1984

"Lights off…" Instructor Henry Calvin yelled out and then paused for five seconds and then continued "…Lights on…" When the lights came back on there were seven people in the room. Henry Calvin paused again and then he added "…turn them off. Now Kata while the lights are off describe the people that are in this room. Tell me their gender, race, complexion, eye and hair color, height, weight, and clothing they're wearing. Go!"

"Three women and four men. The lady sitting down is Italian but tanned. She's a brunette with brown eyes, 5'2" and about 110lbs, and she's wearing a red blouse, blue jeans, and white tennis shoes. The woman standing six feet away from her to her right is German and pale complexion. Blue eyes, blonde hair, 5'10", 154lbs, and she is wearing a midnight blue skirt suit with a pink blouse. Her 3" heels make her seem taller than. The Korean man standing next to her isn't tanned. He has brown eyes, black hair, 5'8", 150lbs, and he's wearing a dark grey suit, a solid blue tie with a white shirt with blue pinstripes, and black dress shoes…"

Kata went on to describe all seven people exactly as they were.

Back to today

Once the car stopped they removed Kata from the car and walked him inside the building with his head still covered. When they got inside someone grab his hands and tied them behind his back. A chair was shoved under him.

"Have a seat Mr. Long." A lady said with a Swedish accent.

"Thanks, now can someone please remove this thing from my head?"

"Are you sure you want this Mr. Long?"

"Quite sure thank you."

The woman motioned for one of her men to remove the shroud. The room was dimly lit but I still had to adjust my eyes. Once my eyes could focus there was a tall slim lady sitting with her legs crossed in front of me.

"Do you know you're the only man outside of my colleagues who have seen my face?"

"And who face am I looking at?" Kata asked.

"Christian, now let's get down to business. You have the information for me yes?"

"They found this on him when he was searched." Forrest O'Hagan said.

"What's this Mr. Long?" Christian asked.

"Well as you can see it's a mini safe with a digital combination. How it works is this. Once you type in one number of the combination you have five minutes to finish the sequence. If the sequence isn't finished within the time allowed whatever is inside will be destroyed. So if you want the information I need my hands. Trust me you know the agency I use to work for so torture or truth serum won't work on me. Let's be civil about this and free my hands. It's the only way you will get the combination. Plus where's the money?"

Christian snapped her fingers and four men rolling in suitcases appeared. She ordered them to open them and revealed the money. She had my hands untied also.

"Are you happy? Now please for the last time unlock the safe so we can retrieve the blueprints."

I finally had time to activate the chip and send a signal to the team so they know my location.

Back at the safe house

A loud feedback noise ring into Tristan's ears.

"Chief, Kata activated the chip and from the looks of it he isn't in the same place as before. As you can see here…" Tristan stopped and pointed at the screen on his computer and then he continued "…I say he's about 3 kilometers west of the first location they took him to."

"Okay men let's gear up and move out. Tristan can you hear what's going on? Emad asked.

"Yes, Kata is about to open the safe. We have 20 minutes."

"We go as we are. Forget the extra gear. Tristan print out the location."

"Already on it Chief."

Christian's secret location

Christian didn't spend any money to renovate the outside or the inside of this location. Dirt and sand surrounded the structure. The building outer shell were made of metal sidings, which has started to rust in over 75% of the building. Only two lights worked inside the abandon warehouse and they were using one of them. Most of the windows were broken out. The warehouse was dark and cold with a stench of blood and mildew in the air. This is where Drapa tortured and killed their victims.

"Do anyone have a black light bulb?" Kata asked looking at Christian.

"A black light. Why?" Alice replied.

"So I can see the numbers on my arm. Before you think about killing me, not only do you have to know the combination but also the sequence to put them in."

Christian looked to the left at the big blonde haired man and said "Fetch a black light bulb and make it quick…" and then looked at Kata and said "…you're trying my patience. If there's any more delays, I will have you killed and forget about the Falcon X-15 altogether. Do we have an understanding Mr. Long?"

"Loud and clear Ms. Christian."

My name was Alexandra Gorski. I was born in 1939 to a Polish-Jewish couple who were tortured and killed when I was 4 years old. This happened during Hitler's reign of Eastern Europe. My maternal grandmother hid me along with my five siblings whom I am the youngest in an underground bunker she and my grandfather built before his death. Nana saved our lives from the SS.

When I graduated from high school I ran away to Hungry and I changed my name to Alice Christian. There I met my husband whose sir name was also Christian by no coincidence. I double majored at the university and graduated with a bachelors in math and chemistry. About a year after I graduated college I blew up my first building in 1958. Two months later I killed my husband and fled to Germany for that crime.

In Germany is where I would get my payback for the murder of my parents. I tracked down and killed as many of the men, who took part in the killings by the SS during 1943. The thirst for never ended, I started to kill for fun. 1962 through 1965 the world witness some of the worst terroristic catastrophes up to those years. They believed a man by the name of Christian was responsible for most if not all of them. After 1965 the world was given a break and the terrorist known only by Christian laid in dormant until he came back on the scene in the mid to late 70's.

"Here's the black light bulb you asked for." The blonde haired man said to Christian.

"Give it to him." Christian ordered.

"Kata if you can't stall any longer say 'alright now'." Tristan said.

"Alright now." Kata replied.

"Yes get on with it."

"We are 5 minutes away." Tristan relayed.

"In order for the black light to work all other lights must be off." Kata explained.

"Shut them off!" Christian yelled and then said "I grow tired of this Mr. Long."

"Here we go see the numbers on my arm? Okay press eight two five two seven three and that should do it."

"Before I let you go my scientist need to check the formula."

"Yea I kind of figured that. Is he here?"

"Of course not. You will wait here for my return."

"She's not coming back. Kata get on with it, we're here now." Emad ordered.

Kata charged at the big blonde haired man and spin kicked him in his abdomen. The man bent over in agony and Kata grabbed his gun before he could reach for it. Kata then dove to the floor while at the same time chambering a bullet by sliding the slide back on the gun. He shot the man twice in the chest and then pointed the gun at Christian. Forrest grab Christian and pushed her out the way as Kata shot twice her way. Forrest returned fire but Kata was already on his feet moving for shelter behind a beam.

The three men standing guard outside the warehouse heard the gun shots. As they made their move towards the door, one of them collapsed to the ground with blood spewing out his head. The other two froze and then turned around to see who it was shooting at them and their heads exploded as well.

"Emad they going for the door." Kata informed.

Christian was pulled away from the door by Forrest and down to the ground behind some empty black metal barrels just in time as three bullets came crashing through the door center mass. Three of Christian's henchmen ran to their aid. A worried look flowed over Forrest's face. Christian was stoic as usual. She looked at Forrest and her eyes said let's get out of here. Forrest changed his expression immediately and nodded his head with agreement. Now there was another problem. Kata was holding position and firing sporadically to keep them off guard.

"Emad there's a door to your left as your approaching. Can you see it?" Kata asked.

"Yes." Emad responded.

"I'm going to give them hope of that door. Tell Derrick to set his sights on that door and to hold it there until they come through."

"Roger that."

"Give us cover fire so we can head out that door…" Forrest ordered the two men standing to his right looking to his left and to the man standing to his left he said "…shoot that damn gun or I'll kill you myself…" while pointing to his left and then he continued "…on the count of three we're going to make a run for it. One, two, three go."

All at once the men opened fire on Kata's position. Bullets ricocheted off the ground near him. Kata balled up into a fetus position to protect his body. Christian and Forrest made it to the door unscathed.

"Let me go out first." Forrest insisted.

Forrest opened the door quickly and nothing happened. When he went to exit the warehouse. A bullet exploded through his forehead. Forrest collapsed to the ground and Christian screamed loudly "Nooooo!!!"

Knowing now there was no escape and she found herself at a cross road. Her only escape from prison was death. Christian didn't want any part of going to prison and she wasn't ready to die either. She was a survivor. "How can I get out of here with my life intact?" She said to herself.
Christian ordered her men to put down their guns and then she spoke loudly so everyone could hear.

"I will surrender if you will sacrifice my life as well as my men lives."
"We have no problem with that deal. Throw your weapons out the door and come out with your hands held high." Emad replied.

Christian did exactly as Emad said and once they were all out in the open, Emad ordered Derrick to shoot her men. One by one they fell to the ground with holes in their heads.

"Ahhhhh. You bastard. You lied to me!"
Emad and his team were walking towards Christian when he pulled his sidearm out from it's holster and shot Christian twice in the face.

THE END

Thank you for reading Darkghost Assignments. Be on the lookout for more installments on the life of Emad McWhorter.

Printed in the United States
By Bookmasters